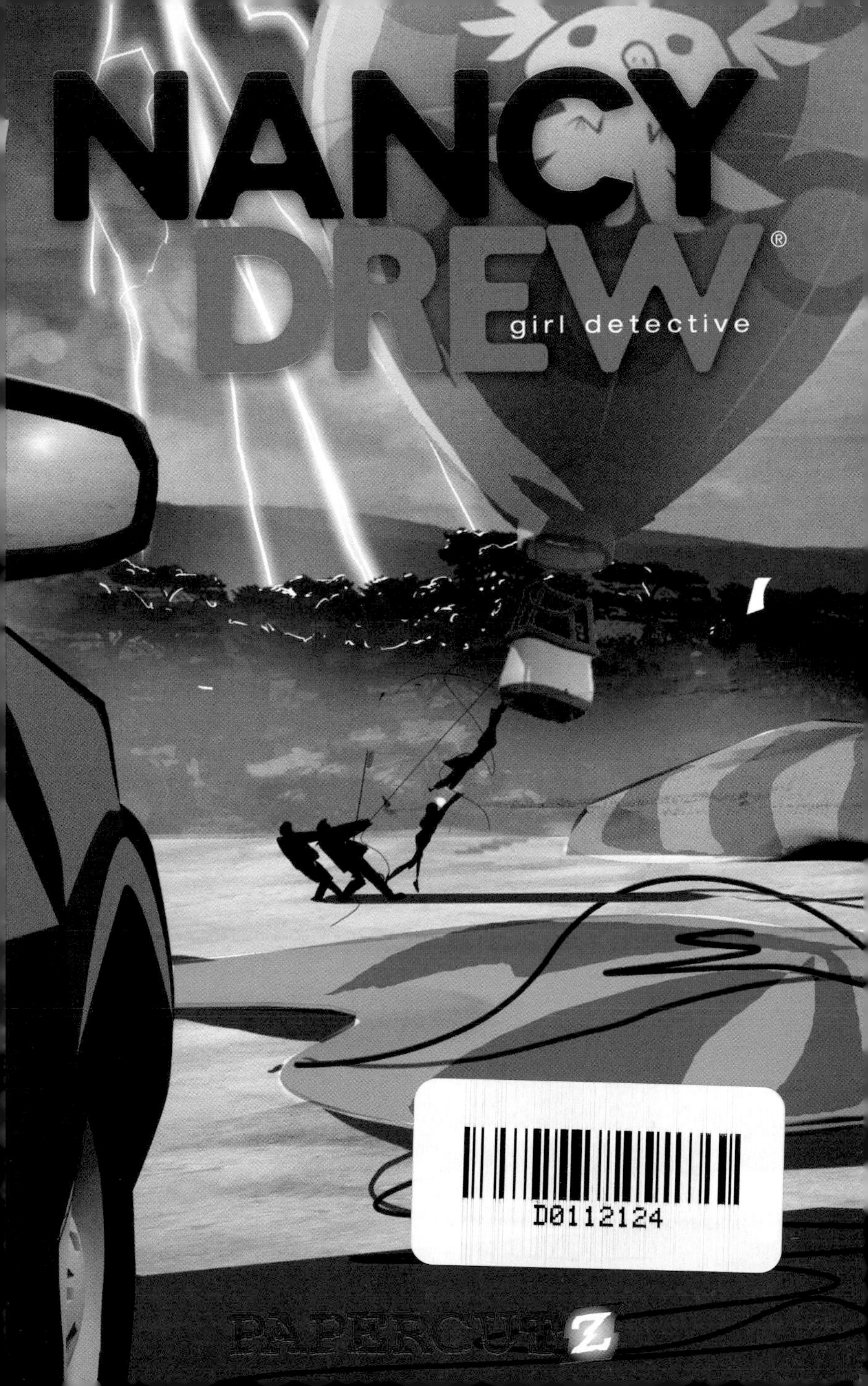
NANCY DREW®
girl detective
PAPERCUTZ

NANCY DREW GRAPHIC NOVELS AVAILABLE FROM PAPERCUTZ

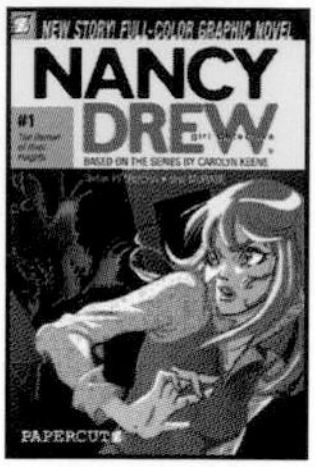
NEW STORY! FULL-COLOR GRAPHIC NOVEL
NANCY DREW
PAPERCUTZ
#1 "The Demon of River Heights"

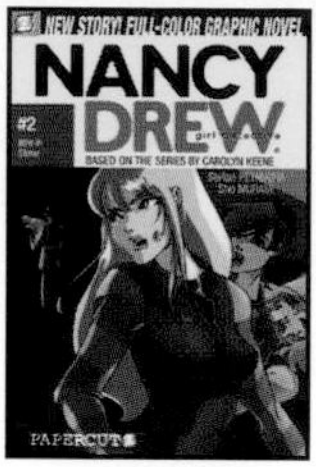
NEW STORY! FULL-COLOR GRAPHIC NOVEL
NANCY DREW
PAPERCUTZ
#2 "Writ In Stone"

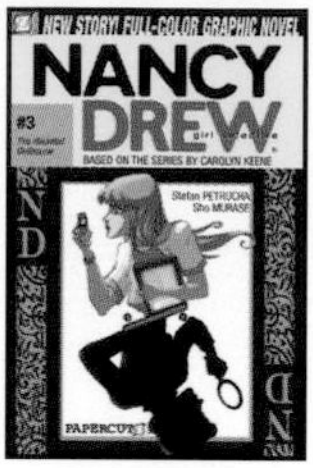
NEW STORY! FULL-COLOR GRAPHIC NOVEL
NANCY DREW
BASED ON THE SERIES BY CAROLYN KEENE
PAPERCUTZ
#3 "The Haunted Dollhouse"

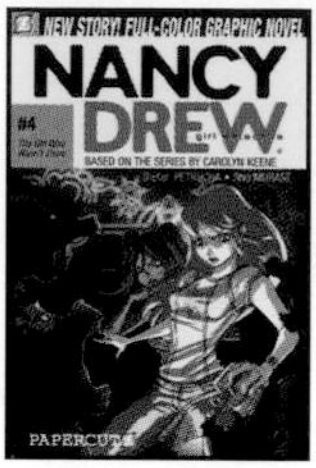
NEW STORY! FULL-COLOR GRAPHIC NOVEL
NANCY DREW
PAPERCUTZ
#4 "The Girl Who Wasn't There"

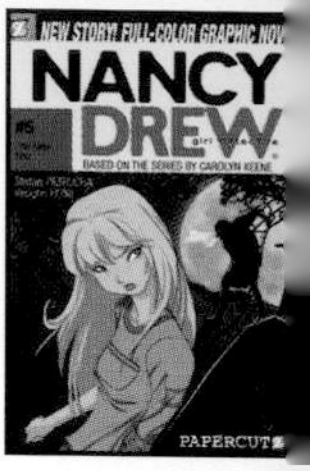
NANCY DREW
PAPERCUTZ
#5 "The Fake Heir"

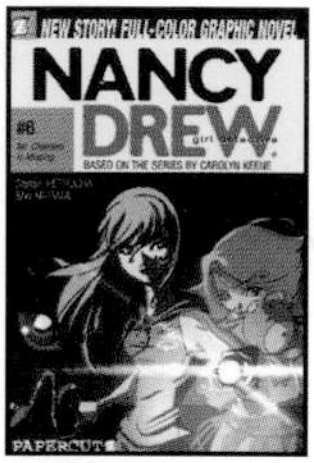
NEW STORY! FULL-COLOR GRAPHIC NOVEL
NANCY DREW
PAPERCUTZ
#6 "Mr. Cheeters Is Missing"

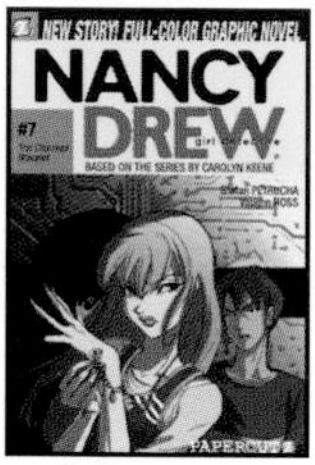
NEW STORY! FULL-COLOR GRAPHIC NOVEL
NANCY DREW
PAPERCUTZ
#7 "The Charmed Bracelet"

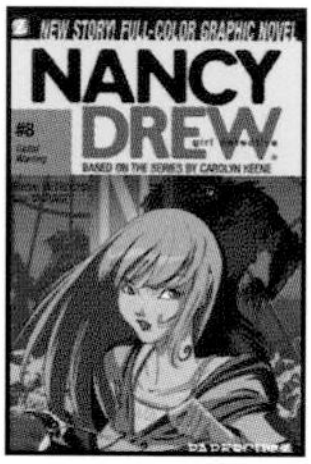
NEW STORY! FULL-COLOR GRAPHIC NOVEL
NANCY DREW
#8 "Global Warning"

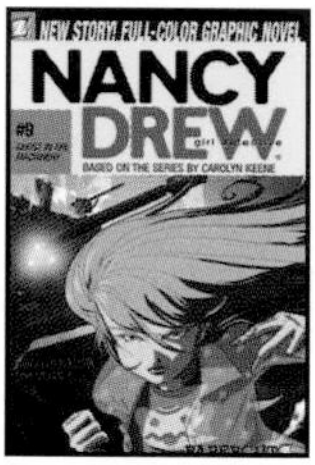
NEW STORY! FULL-COLOR GRAPHIC NOVEL
NANCY DREW
#9 "Ghost In The Machinery"

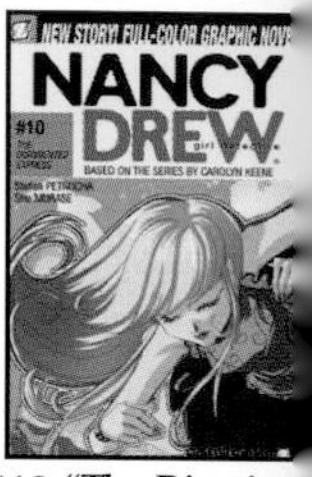
NANCY DREW
#10 "The Disorien ed Express"

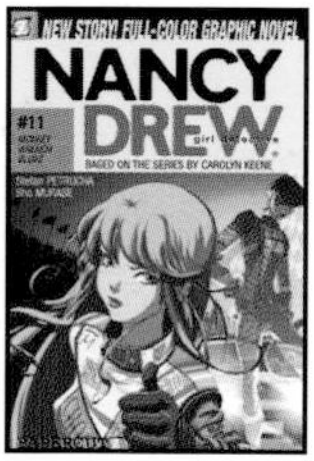
NEW STORY! FULL-COLOR GRAPHIC NOVEL
NANCY DREW
#11 "Monkey Wrench Blues"

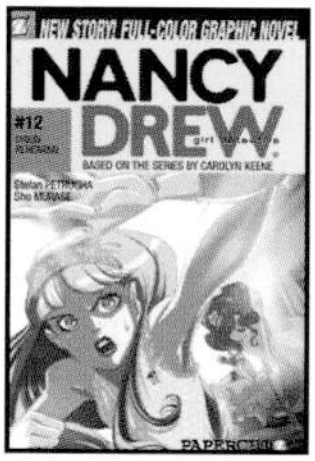
NEW STORY! FULL-COLOR GRAPHIC NOVEL
NANCY DREW
#12 "Dress Reversal"

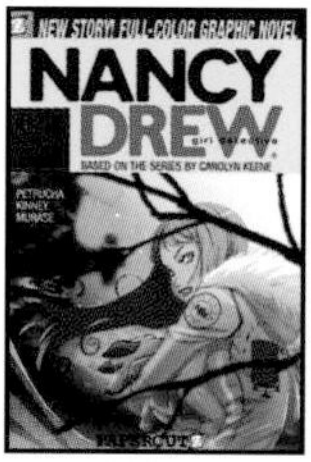
NEW STORY! FULL-COLOR GRAPHIC NOVEL
NANCY DREW
#13 "Doggone Town"

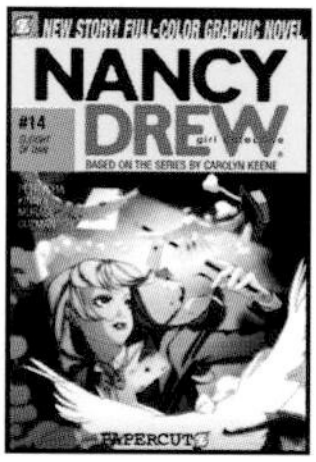
NEW STORY! FULL-COLOR GRAPHIC NOVEL
NANCY DREW
PAPERCUTZ
#14 "Sleight of Dan"

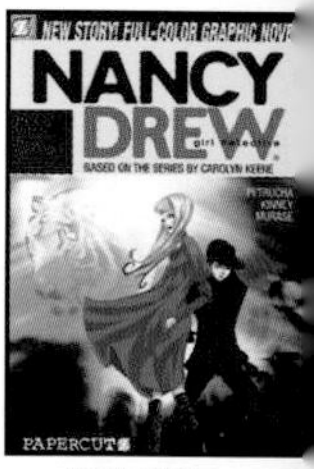
NANCY DREW
PAPERCUTZ
#15 "Tiger Counter"

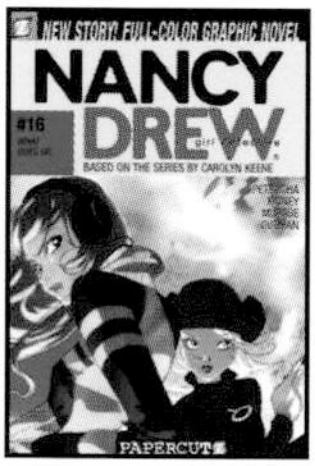
NEW STORY! FULL-COLOR GRAPHIC NOVEL
NANCY DREW
BASED ON THE SERIES BY CAROLYN KEENE
PAPERCUTZ
#16 "What Goes Up..."

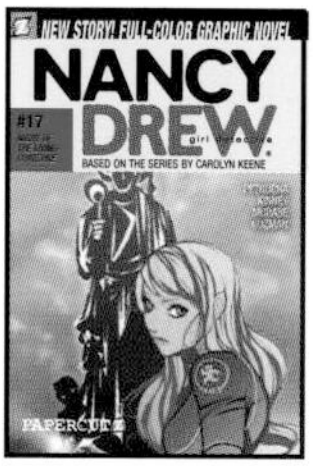
NEW STORY! FULL-COLOR GRAPHIC NOVEL
NANCY DREW
BASED ON THE SERIES BY CAROLYN KEENE
PAPERCUTZ
Coming March '09
#17 "Night of the Living Chatchke"

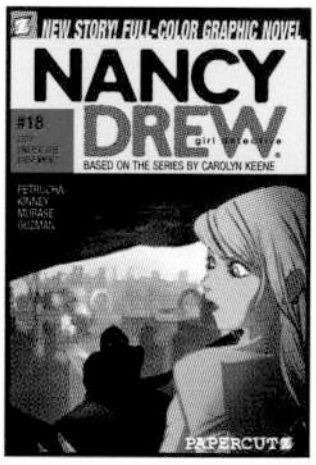
NEW STORY! FULL-COLOR GRAPHIC NOVEL
NANCY DREW
BASED ON THE SERIES BY CAROLYN KEENE
PAPERCUTZ
Coming July '09
#18 "City Under the Basement"

$7.95 each in paperback, $12.95 each in hardcover. Please add $4.00 for postage and handling for the first book, add $1.00 for each additional book. Please make check payable to NBM Publishing. Send to:

Papercutz, 40 Exchange Place, Suite 1308 New York, NY 10005, 1-800-886-1223

www.papercutz.com

NANCY
DREW

#16 **girl detective** ®

What Goes Up...

STEFAN PETRUCHA & SARAH KINNEY • Writers
SHO MURASE • Artist
with 3D CG elements and color by CARLOS JOSE GUZMAN
Based on the series by
CAROLYN KEENE

New York

What Goes Up...
STEFAN PETRUCHA & SARAH KINNEY – Writers
SHO MURASE – Artist
with 3D CG elements and color by CARLOS JOSE GUZMAN
BRYAN SENKA – Letterer
MIKHAELA REID and MASHEKA WOOD – Production
MICHAEL PETRANEK - Editorial Assistant
JIM SALICRUP
Editor-in-Chief

ISBN 10: 1-59707-134-X paperback edition
ISBN 13: 978-1-59707-134-5 paperback edition
ISBN 10: 1-59707-135-8 hardcover edition
ISBN 13: 978-1-59707-135-2 hardcover edition

Printed in China.
Distributed by Macmillan.

10   9   8   7   6   5   4   3   2   1

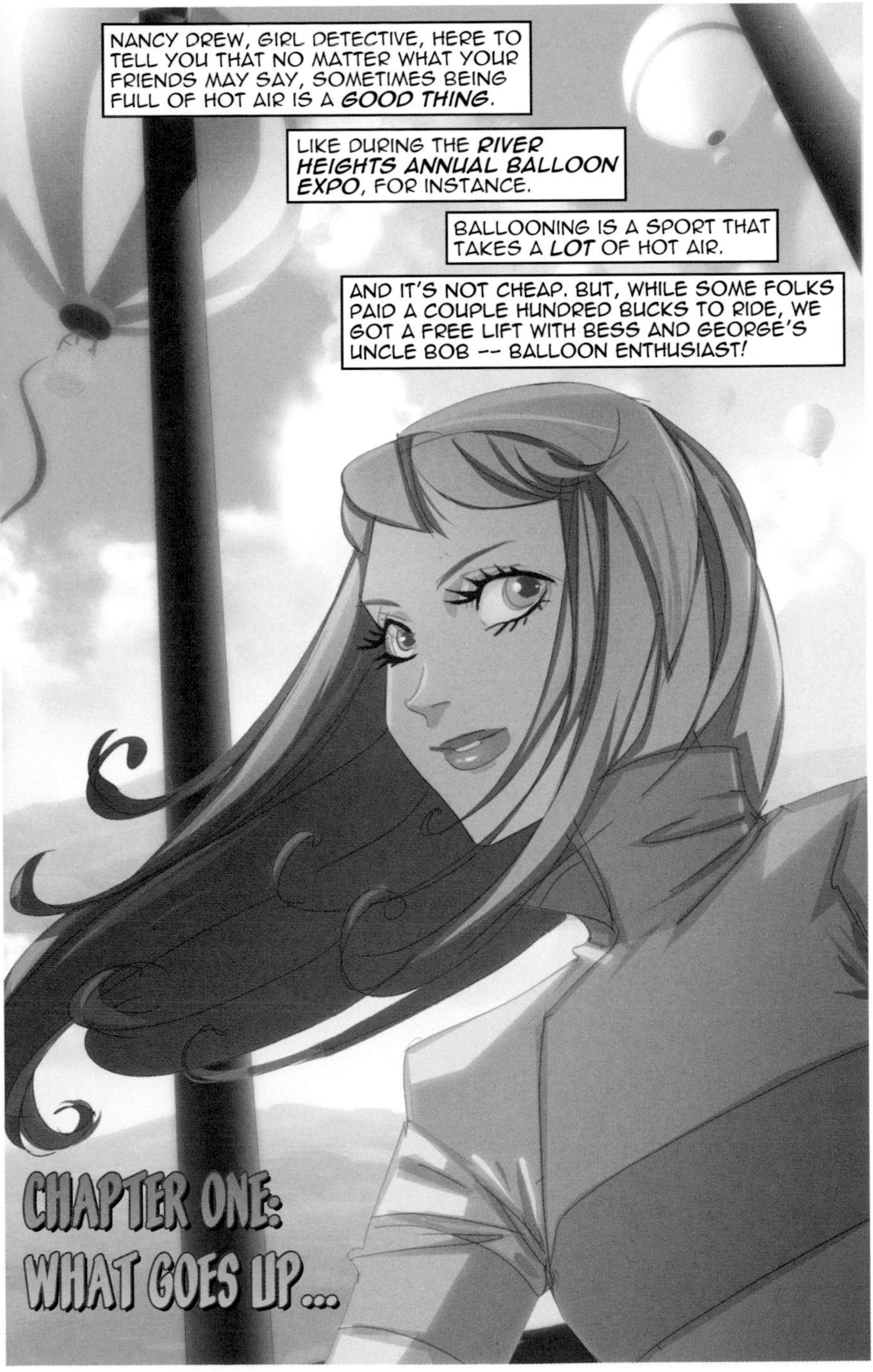
NANCY DREW, GIRL DETECTIVE, HERE TO TELL YOU THAT NO MATTER WHAT YOUR FRIENDS MAY SAY, SOMETIMES BEING FULL OF HOT AIR IS A *GOOD THING*.
LIKE DURING THE *RIVER HEIGHTS ANNUAL BALLOON EXPO*, FOR INSTANCE.
BALLOONING IS A SPORT THAT TAKES A *LOT* OF HOT AIR.
AND IT'S NOT CHEAP. BUT, WHILE SOME FOLKS PAID A COUPLE HUNDRED BUCKS TO RIDE, WE GOT A FREE LIFT WITH BESS AND GEORGE'S UNCLE BOB -- BALLOON ENTHUSIAST!
CHAPTER ONE: WHAT GOES UP...

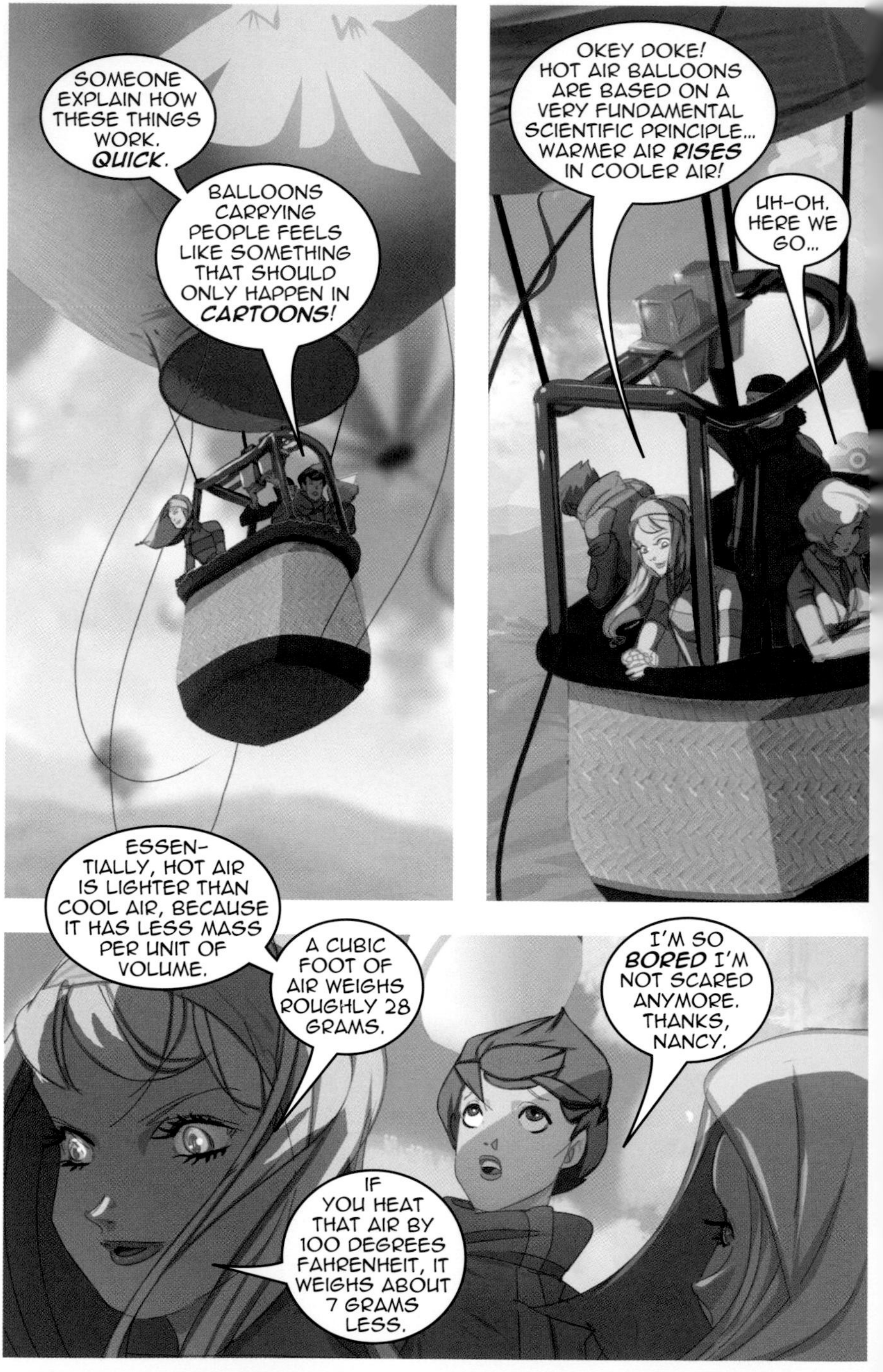
SOMEONE EXPLAIN HOW THESE THINGS WORK. *QUICK*.
BALLOONS CARRYING PEOPLE FEELS LIKE SOMETHING THAT SHOULD ONLY HAPPEN IN *CARTOONS*!
OKEY DOKE! HOT AIR BALLOONS ARE BASED ON A VERY FUNDAMENTAL SCIENTIFIC PRINCIPLE... WARMER AIR *RISES* IN COOLER AIR!
UH-OH. HERE WE GO...
ESSEN-TIALLY, HOT AIR IS LIGHTER THAN COOL AIR, BECAUSE IT HAS LESS MASS PER UNIT OF VOLUME.
A CUBIC FOOT OF AIR WEIGHS ROUGHLY 28 GRAMS.
I'M SO *BORED* I'M NOT SCARED ANYMORE. THANKS, NANCY.
IF YOU HEAT THAT AIR BY 100 DEGREES FAHRENHEIT, IT WEIGHS ABOUT 7 GRAMS LESS.

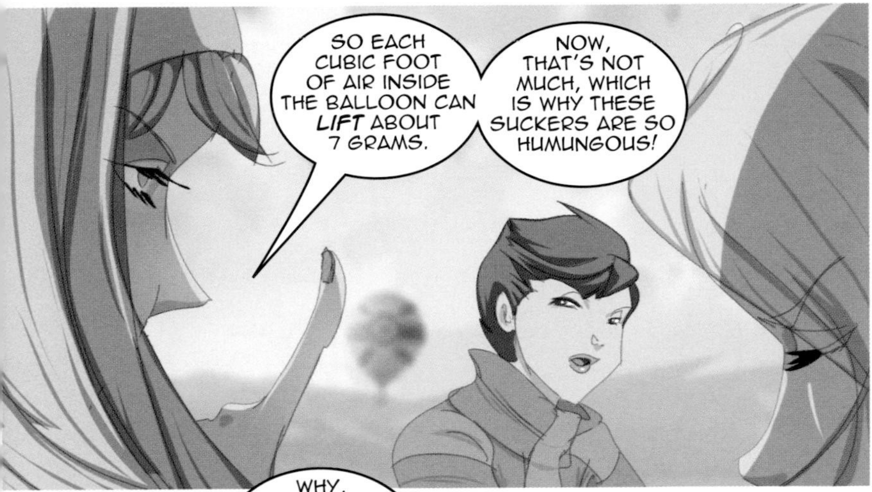
SO EACH CUBIC FOOT OF AIR INSIDE THE BALLOON CAN ***LIFT*** ABOUT 7 GRAMS.
NOW, THAT'S NOT MUCH, WHICH IS WHY THESE SUCKERS ARE SO HUMUNGOUS!

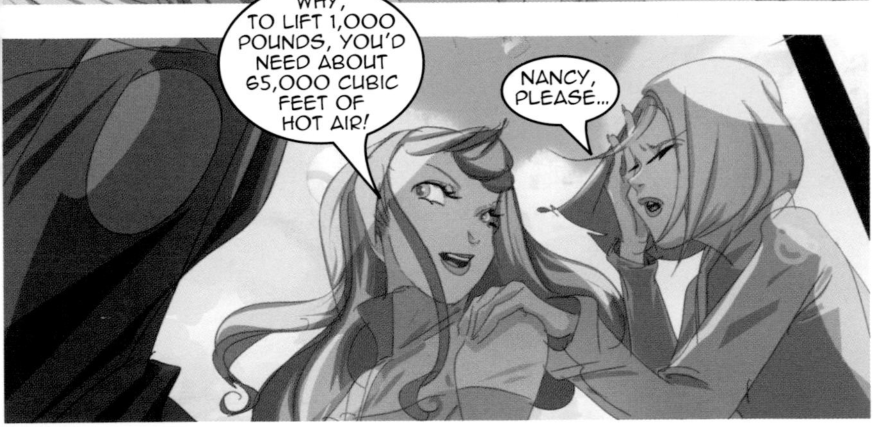
WHY, TO LIFT 1,000 POUNDS, YOU'D NEED ABOUT 65,000 CUBIC FEET OF HOT AIR!
NANCY, PLEASE...

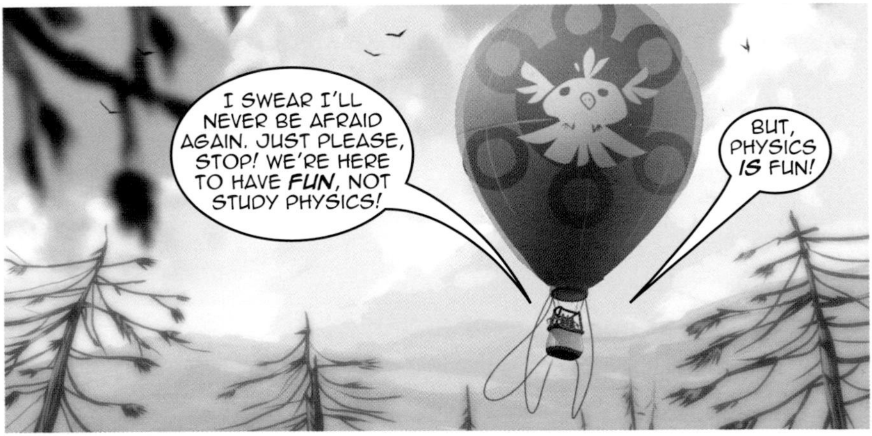
I SWEAR I'LL NEVER BE AFRAID AGAIN. JUST PLEASE, STOP! WE'RE HERE TO HAVE ***FUN***, NOT STUDY PHYSICS!
BUT, PHYSICS ***IS*** FUN!

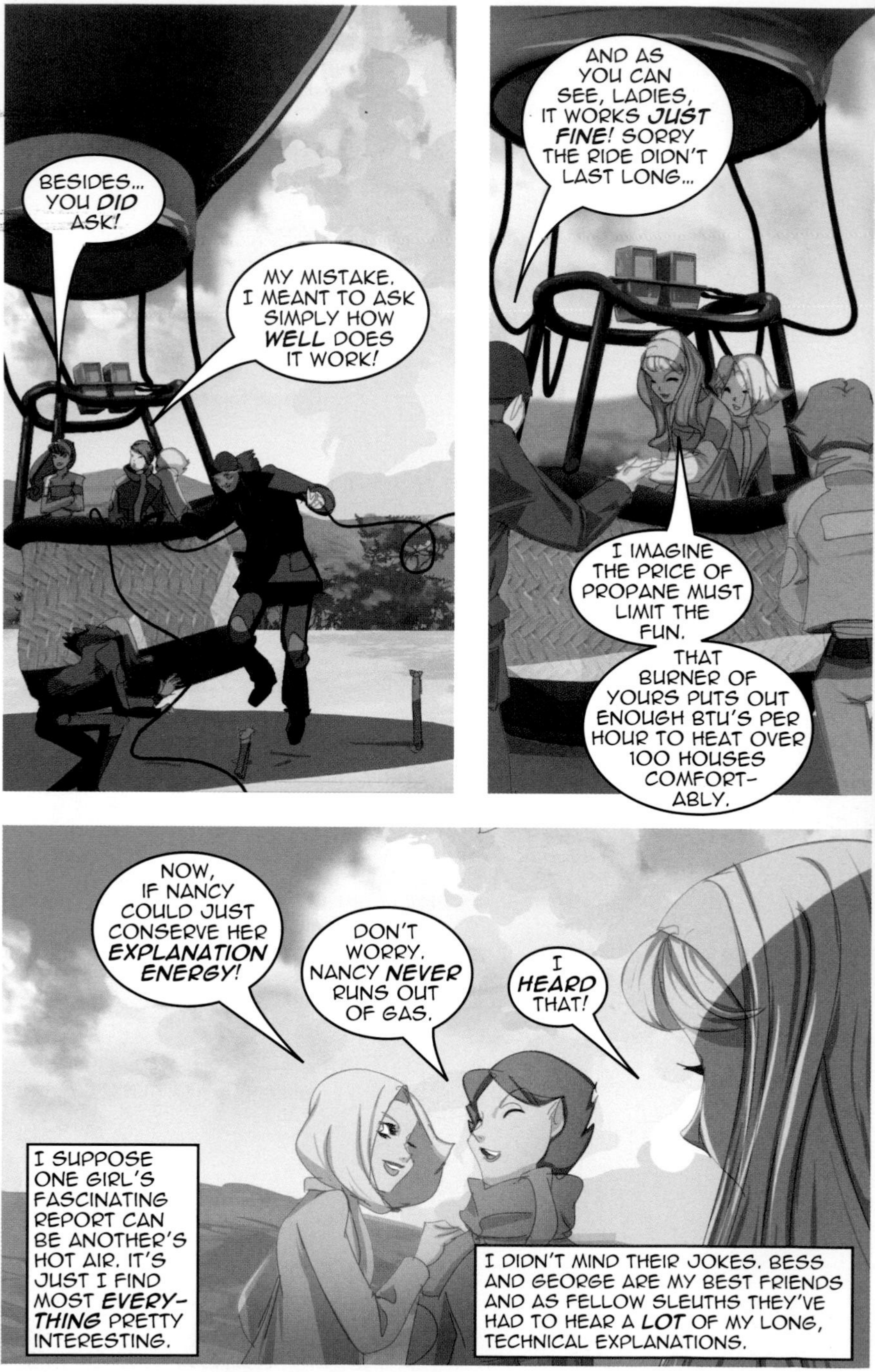
BESIDES... YOU *DID* ASK!
MY MISTAKE. I MEANT TO ASK SIMPLY HOW *WELL* DOES IT WORK!
AND AS YOU CAN SEE, LADIES, IT WORKS *JUST FINE*! SORRY THE RIDE DIDN'T LAST LONG...
I IMAGINE THE PRICE OF PROPANE MUST LIMIT THE FUN.
THAT BURNER OF YOURS PUTS OUT ENOUGH BTU'S PER HOUR TO HEAT OVER 100 HOUSES COMFORT-ABLY.
NOW, IF NANCY COULD JUST CONSERVE HER *EXPLANATION ENERGY*!
DON'T WORRY. NANCY *NEVER* RUNS OUT OF GAS.
I *HEARD* THAT!
I SUPPOSE ONE GIRL'S FASCINATING REPORT CAN BE ANOTHER'S HOT AIR. IT'S JUST I FIND MOST *EVERY-THING* PRETTY INTERESTING.
I DIDN'T MIND THEIR JOKES. BESS AND GEORGE ARE MY BEST FRIENDS AND AS FELLOW SLEUTHS THEY'VE HAD TO HEAR A *LOT* OF MY LONG, TECHNICAL EXPLANATIONS.

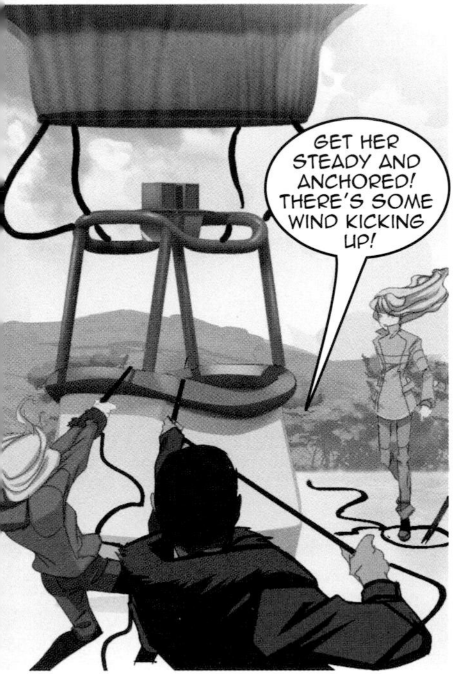
GET HER STEADY AND ANCHORED! THERE'S SOME WIND KICKING UP!

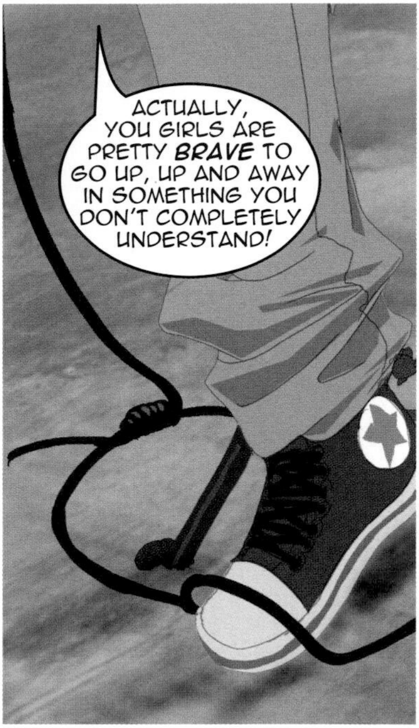
ACTUALLY, YOU GIRLS ARE PRETTY **BRAVE** TO GO UP, UP AND AWAY IN SOMETHING YOU DON'T COMPLETELY UNDERSTAND!

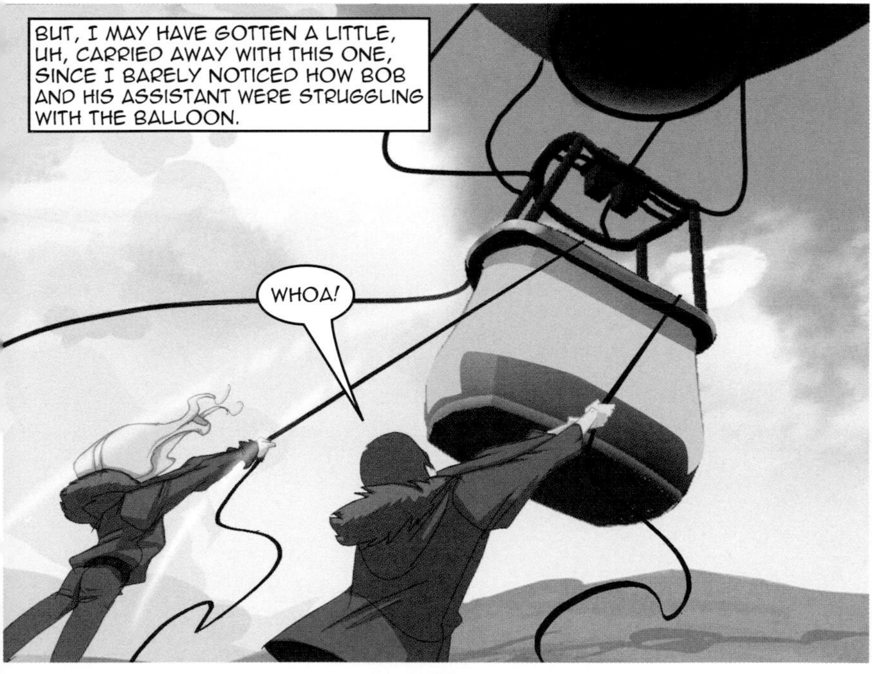
BUT, I MAY HAVE GOTTEN A LITTLE, UH, CARRIED AWAY WITH THIS ONE, SINCE I BARELY NOTICED HOW BOB AND HIS ASSISTANT WERE STRUGGLING WITH THE BALLOON.
WHOA!

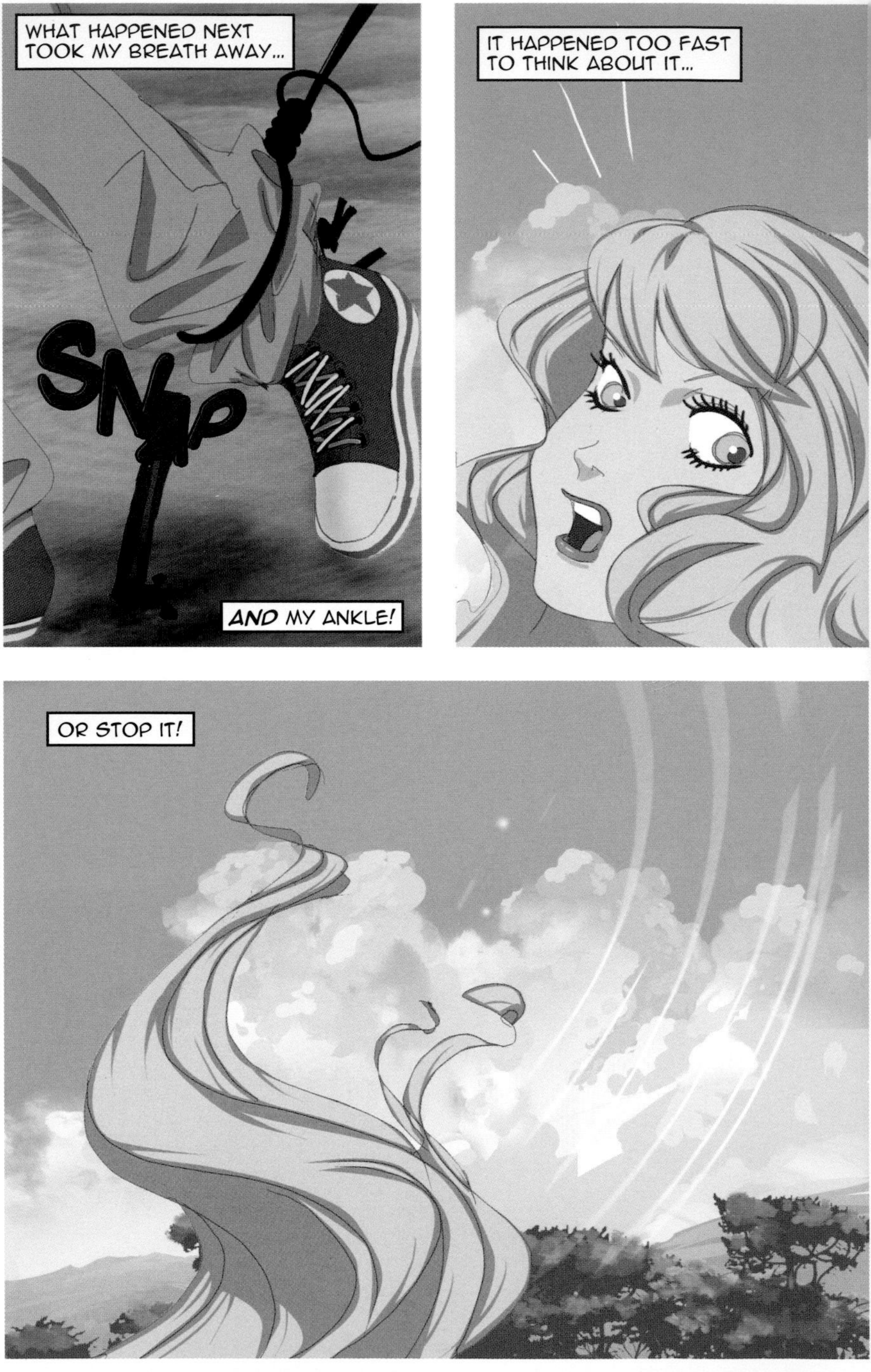
WHAT HAPPENED NEXT TOOK MY BREATH AWAY...
SNAP
AND MY ANKLE!
IT HAPPENED TOO FAST TO THINK ABOUT IT...
OR STOP IT!

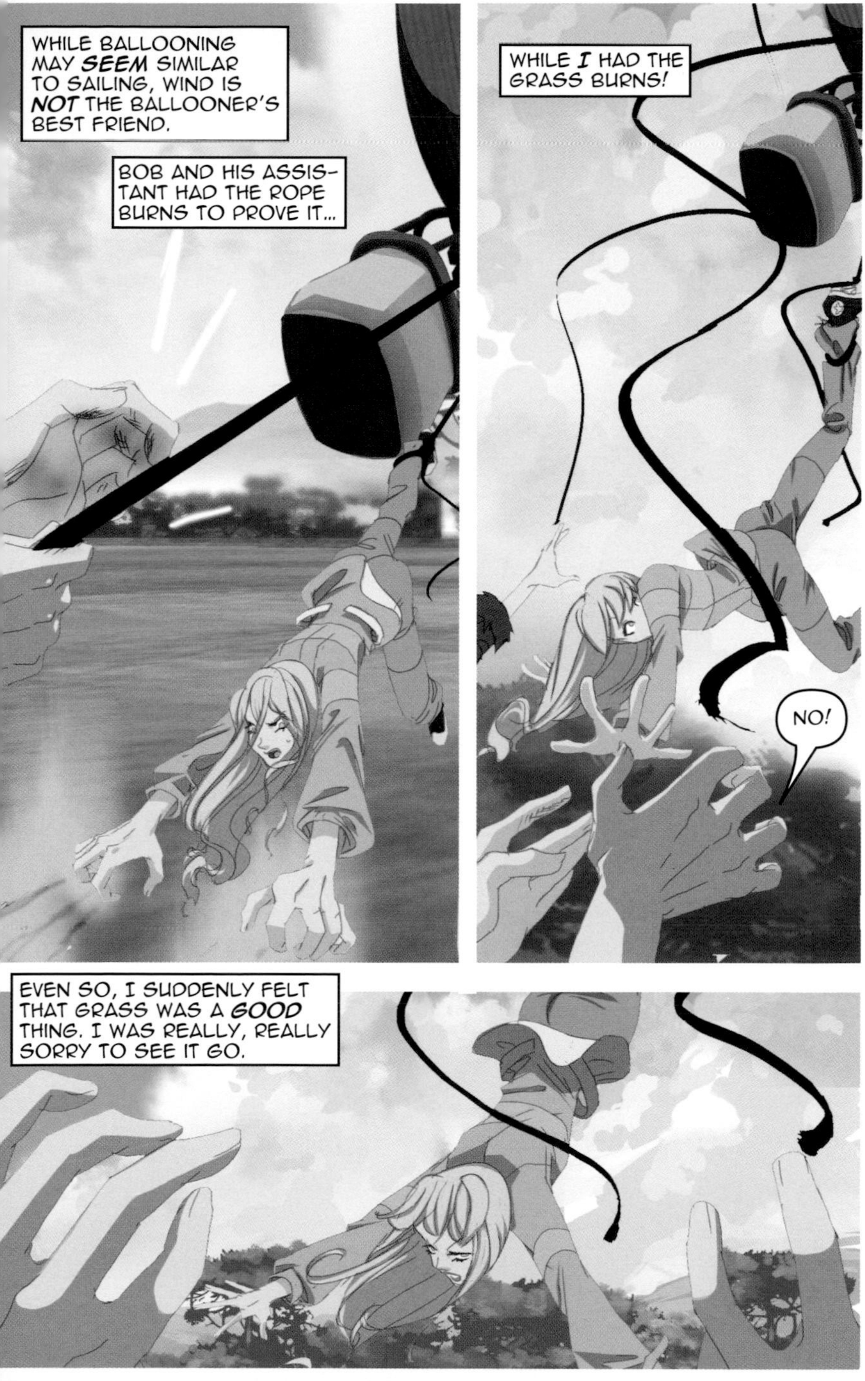
WHILE BALLOONING MAY SEEM SIMILAR TO SAILING, WIND IS NOT THE BALLOONER'S BEST FRIEND.
BOB AND HIS ASSISTANT HAD THE ROPE BURNS TO PROVE IT...
WHILE I HAD THE GRASS BURNS!
NO!
EVEN SO, I SUDDENLY FELT THAT GRASS WAS A GOOD THING. I WAS REALLY, REALLY SORRY TO SEE IT GO.

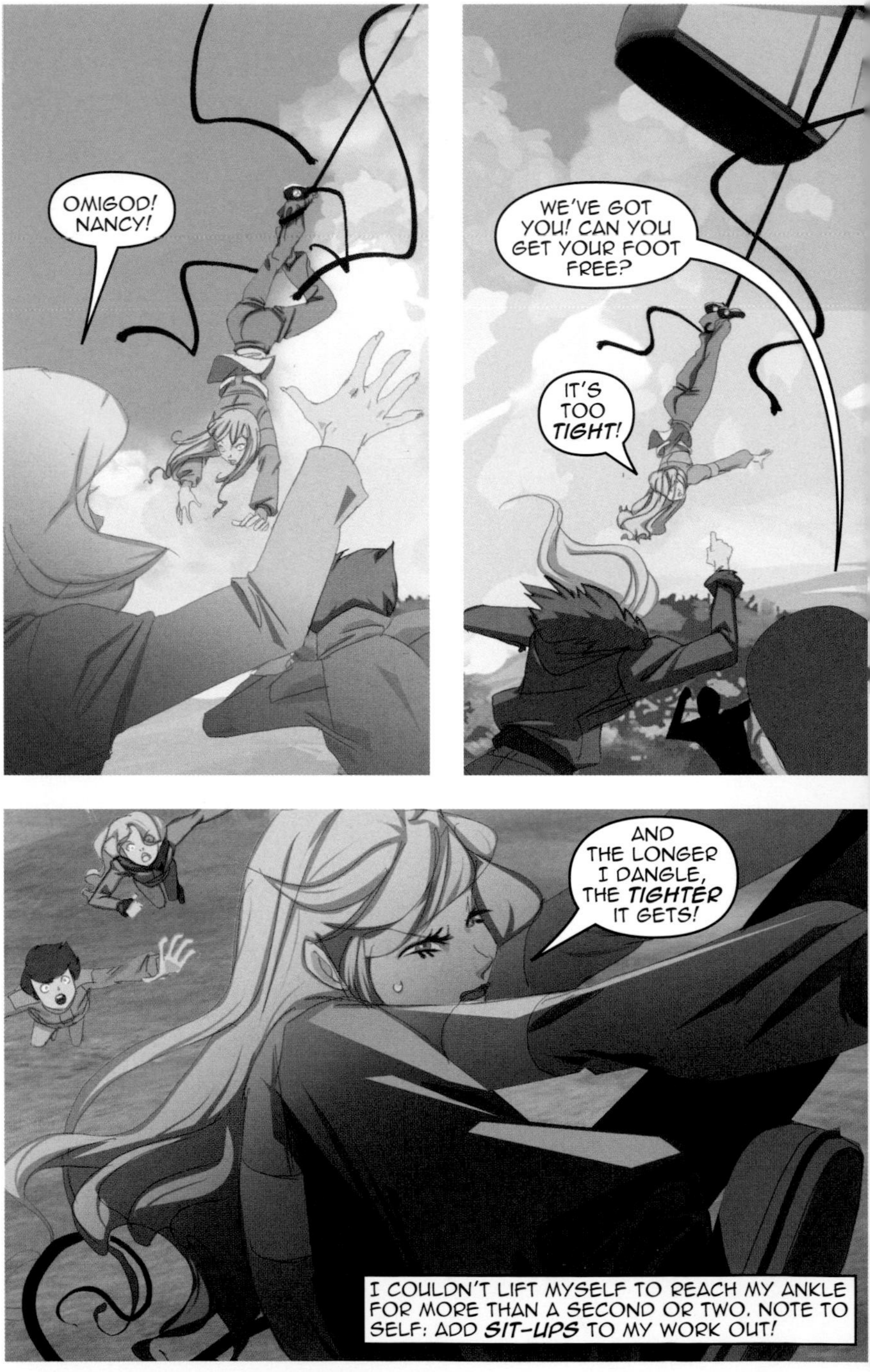
OMIGOD! NANCY!
WE'VE GOT YOU! CAN YOU GET YOUR FOOT FREE?
IT'S TOO TIGHT!
AND THE LONGER I DANGLE, THE TIGHTER IT GETS!
I COULDN'T LIFT MYSELF TO REACH MY ANKLE FOR MORE THAN A SECOND OR TWO. NOTE TO SELF: ADD SIT-UPS TO MY WORK OUT!

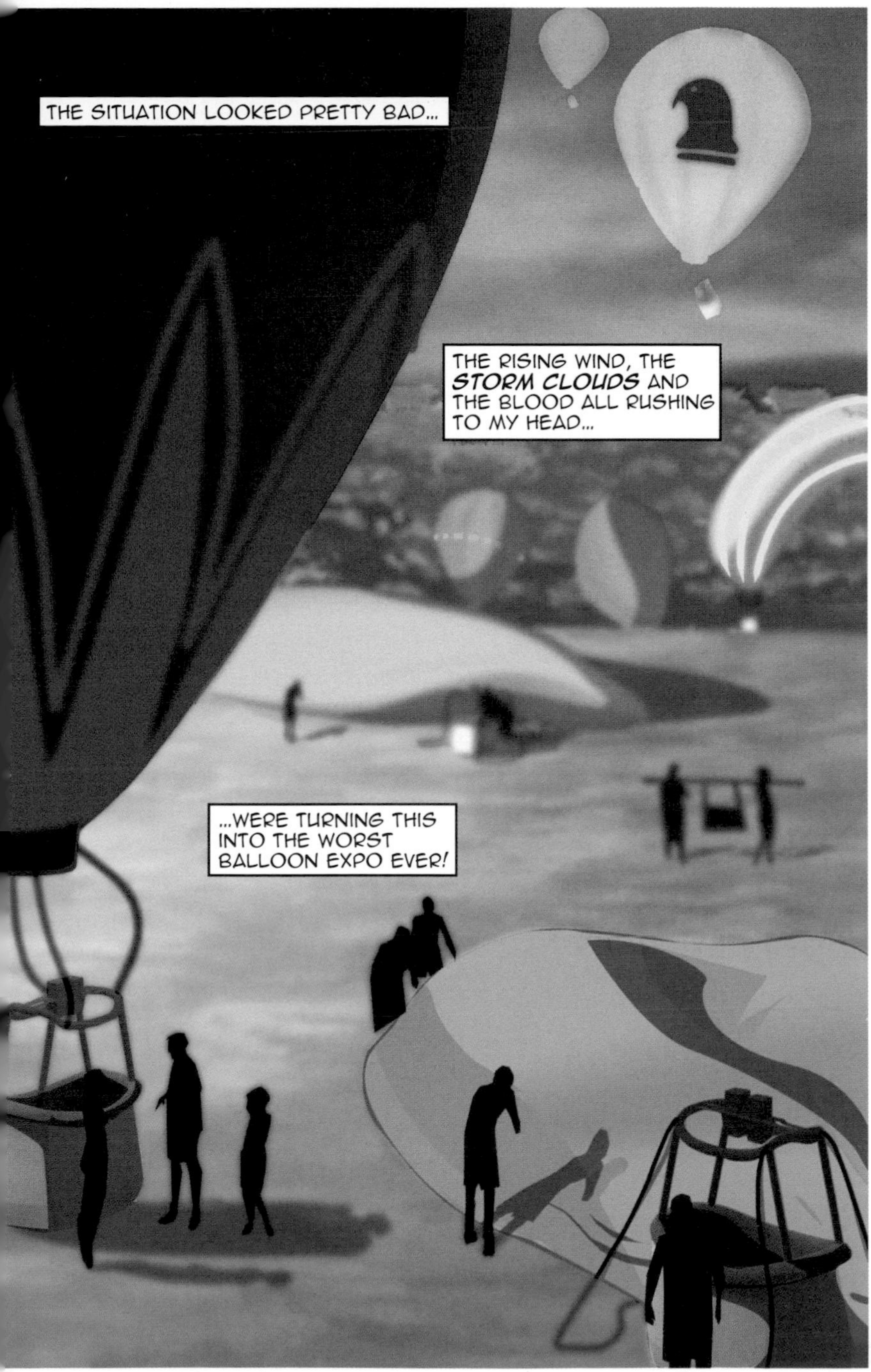
THE SITUATION LOOKED PRETTY BAD...
THE RISING WIND, THE *STORM CLOUDS* AND THE BLOOD ALL RUSHING TO MY HEAD...
...WERE TURNING THIS INTO THE WORST BALLOON EXPO EVER!

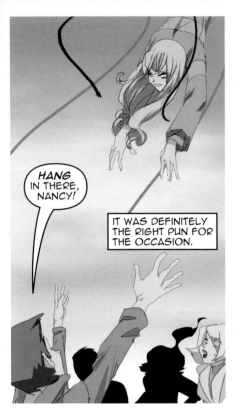

HANG IN THERE, NANCY!

IT WAS DEFINITELY THE RIGHT PUN FOR THE OCCASION.

I TRIED TO SMILE BUT AS THE *DISTANCE* BETWEEN MY HEAD AND THE GROUND GREW, I GREW MORE AFRAID.

GOT IT!

UNGH!

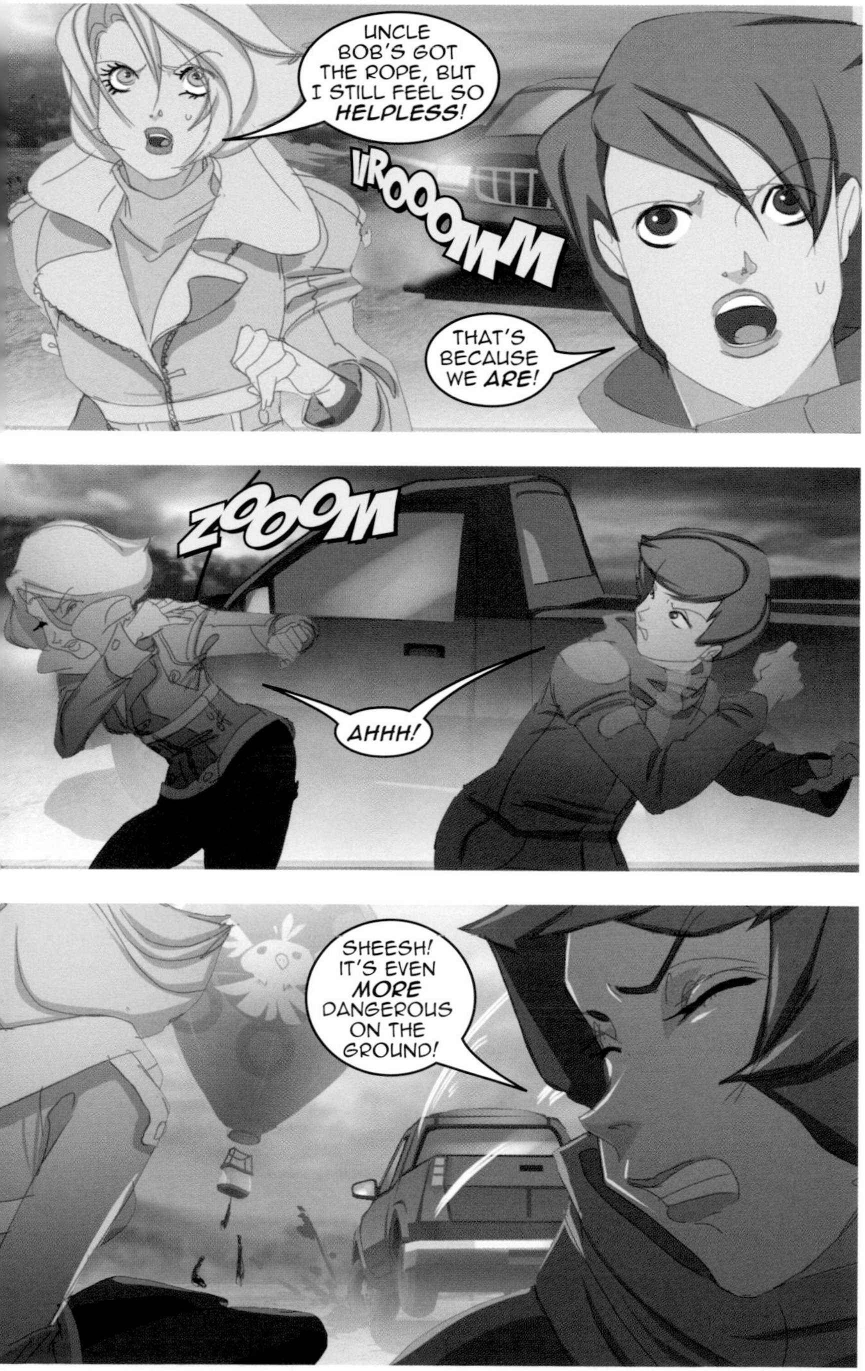
UNCLE BOB'S GOT THE ROPE, BUT I STILL FEEL SO HELPLESS!
VROOOOMMM
THAT'S BECAUSE WE ARE!
ZOOOM
AHHH!
SHEESH! IT'S EVEN MORE DANGEROUS ON THE GROUND!

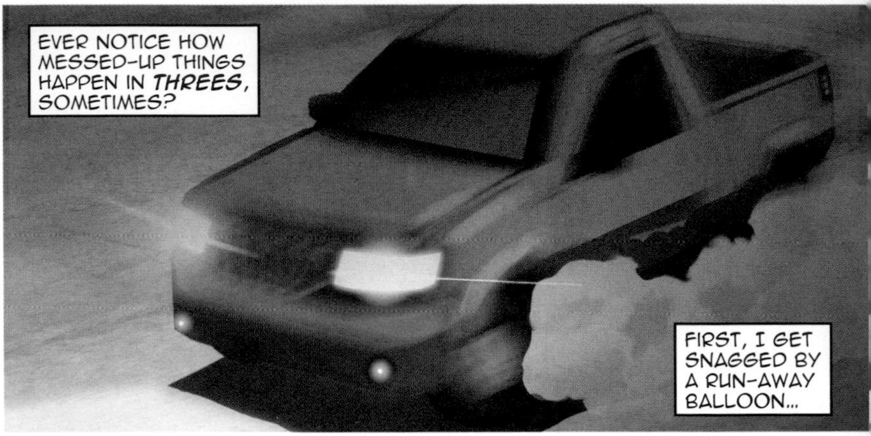
EVER NOTICE HOW MESSED-UP THINGS HAPPEN IN *THREES*, SOMETIMES?
FIRST, I GET SNAGGED BY A RUN-AWAY BALLOON...

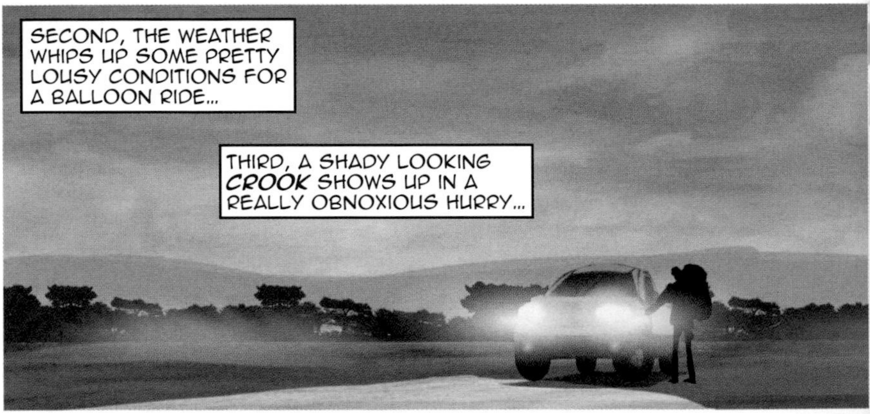
SECOND, THE WEATHER WHIPS UP SOME PRETTY LOUSY CONDITIONS FOR A BALLOON RIDE...
THIRD, A SHADY LOOKING *CROOK* SHOWS UP IN A REALLY OBNOXIOUS HURRY...

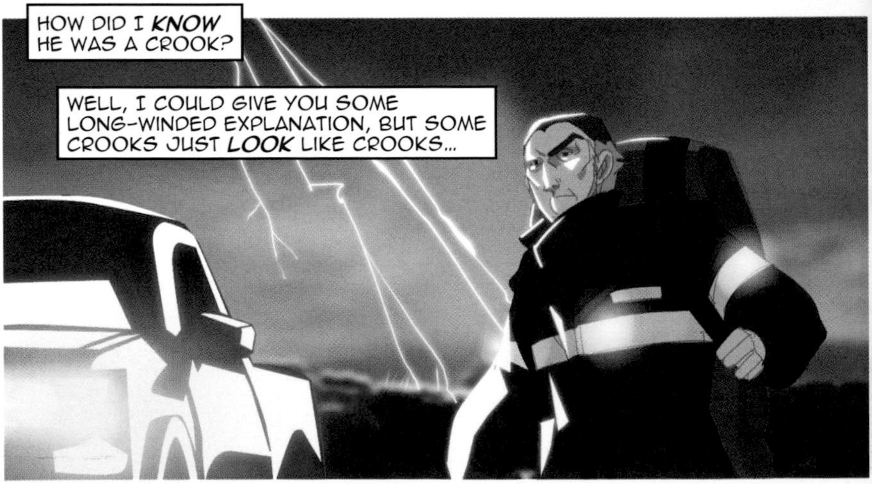
HOW DID I *KNOW* HE WAS A CROOK?
WELL, I COULD GIVE YOU SOME LONG-WINDED EXPLANATION, BUT SOME CROOKS JUST *LOOK* LIKE CROOKS...

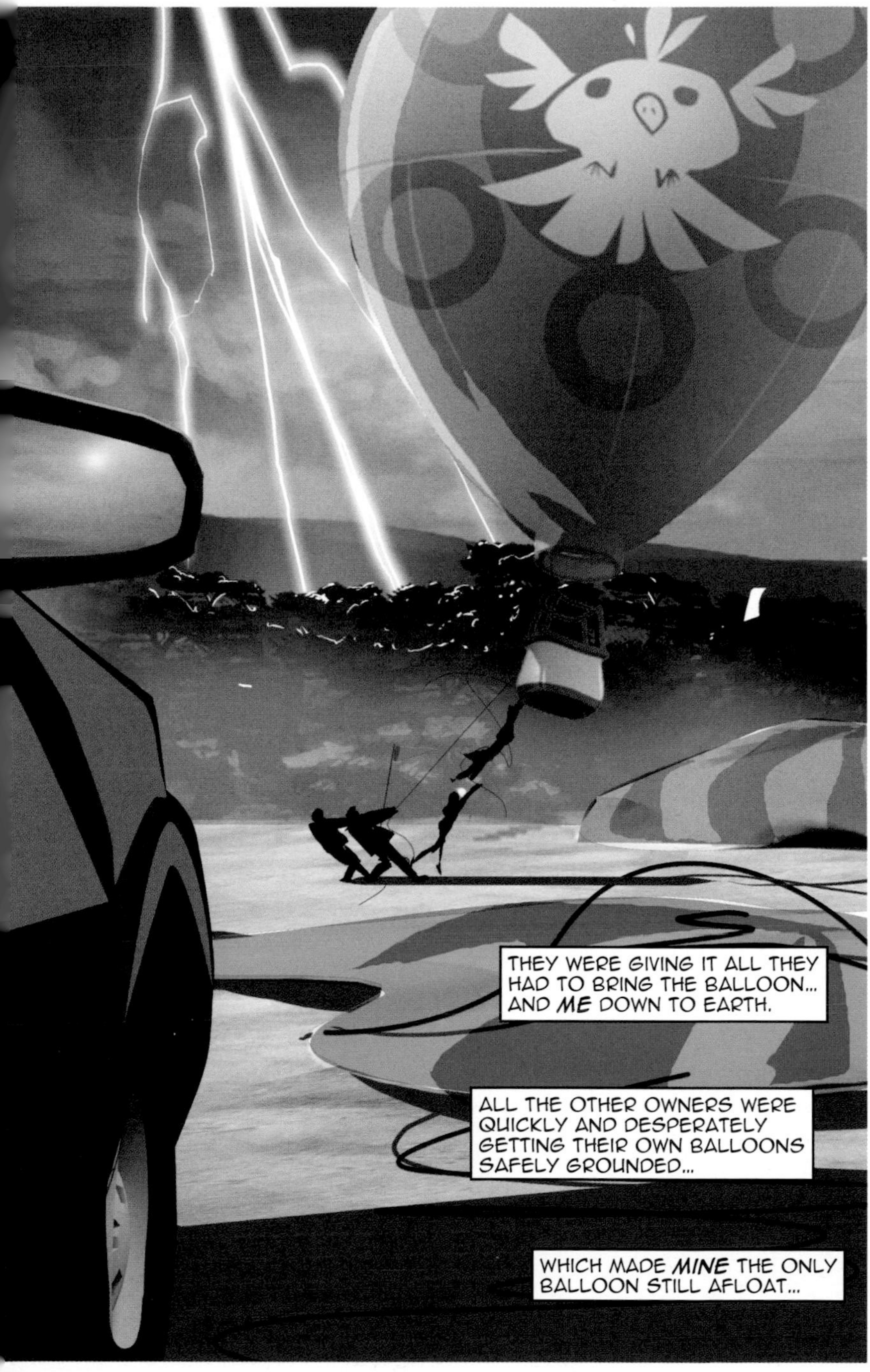
THEY WERE GIVING IT ALL THEY HAD TO BRING THE BALLOON... AND *ME* DOWN TO EARTH.
ALL THE OTHER OWNERS WERE QUICKLY AND DESPERATELY GETTING THEIR OWN BALLOONS SAFELY GROUNDED...
WHICH MADE *MINE* THE ONLY BALLOON STILL AFLOAT...

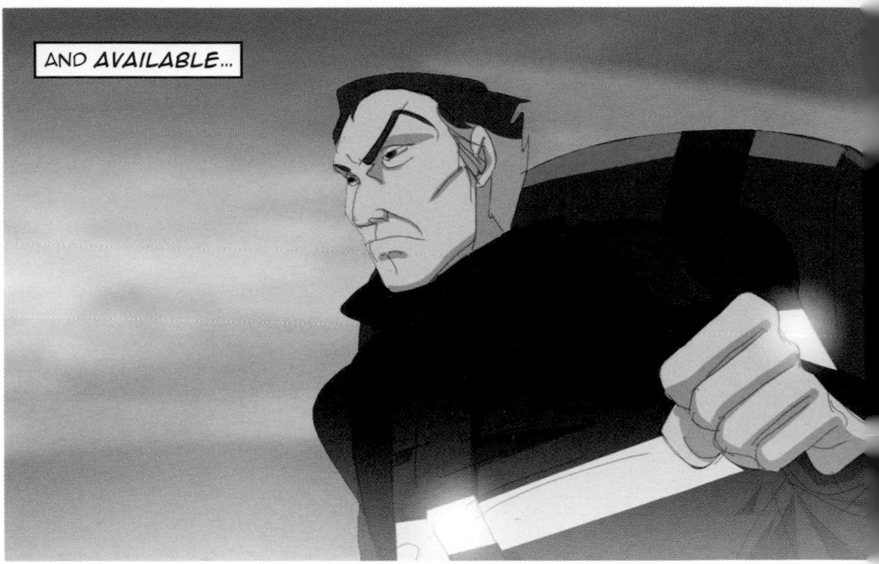
AND AVAILABLE...

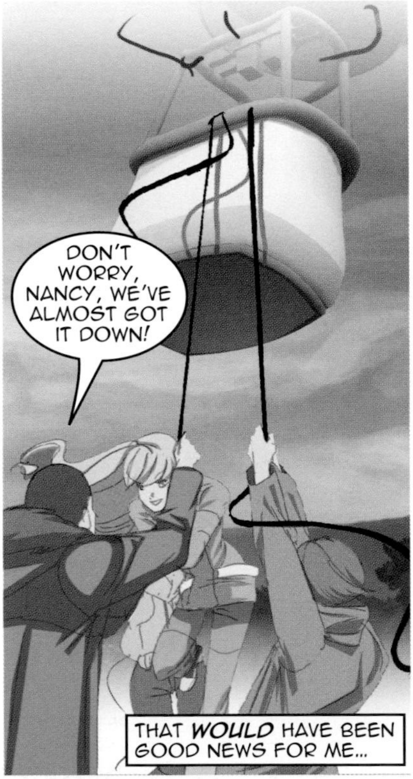
DON'T WORRY, NANCY, WE'VE ALMOST GOT IT DOWN!
THAT WOULD HAVE BEEN GOOD NEWS FOR ME...

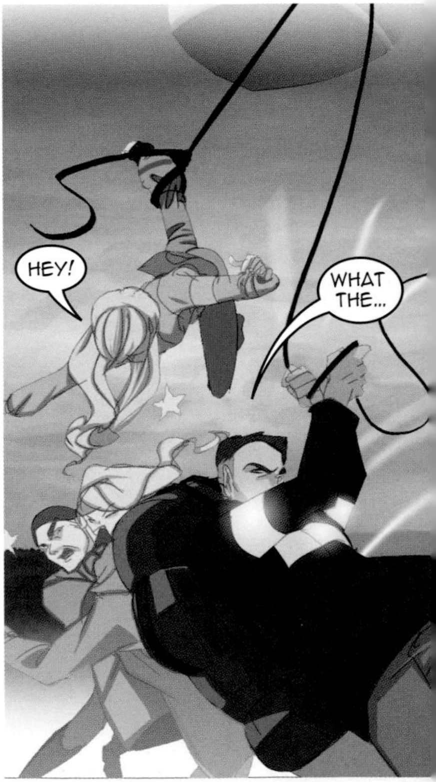
HEY!
WHAT THE...

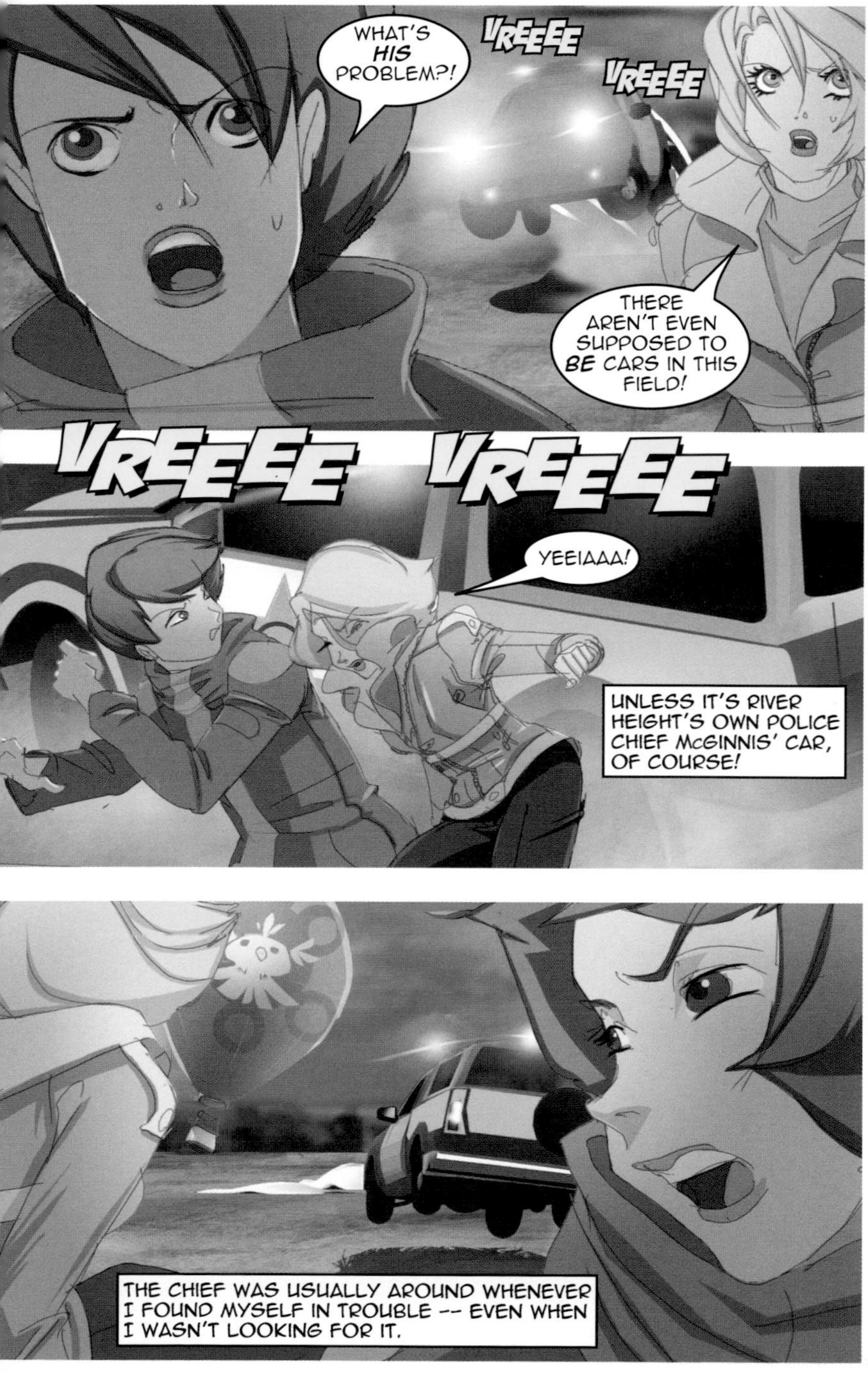
WHAT'S HIS PROBLEM?!
VREEEE
VREEEE
THERE AREN'T EVEN SUPPOSED TO BE CARS IN THIS FIELD!
VREEEE VREEEE
YEEIAAA!
UNLESS IT'S RIVER HEIGHT'S OWN POLICE CHIEF McGINNIS' CAR, OF COURSE!
THE CHIEF WAS USUALLY AROUND WHENEVER I FOUND MYSELF IN TROUBLE -- EVEN WHEN I WASN'T LOOKING FOR IT.

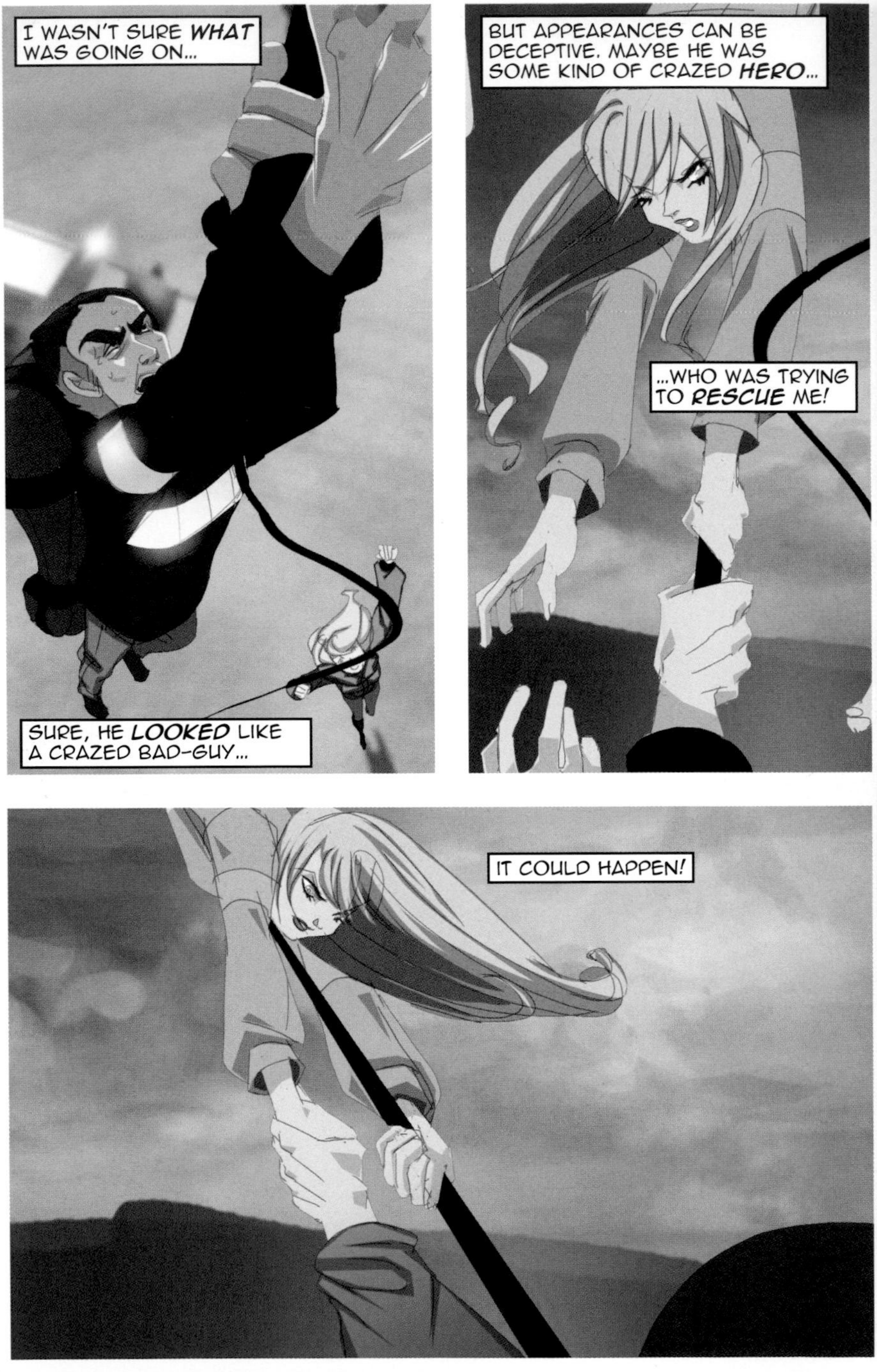
I WASN'T SURE *WHAT* WAS GOING ON...
SURE, HE *LOOKED* LIKE A CRAZED BAD-GUY...
BUT APPEARANCES CAN BE DECEPTIVE. MAYBE HE WAS SOME KIND OF CRAZED *HERO*...
...WHO WAS TRYING TO *RESCUE* ME!
IT COULD HAPPEN!

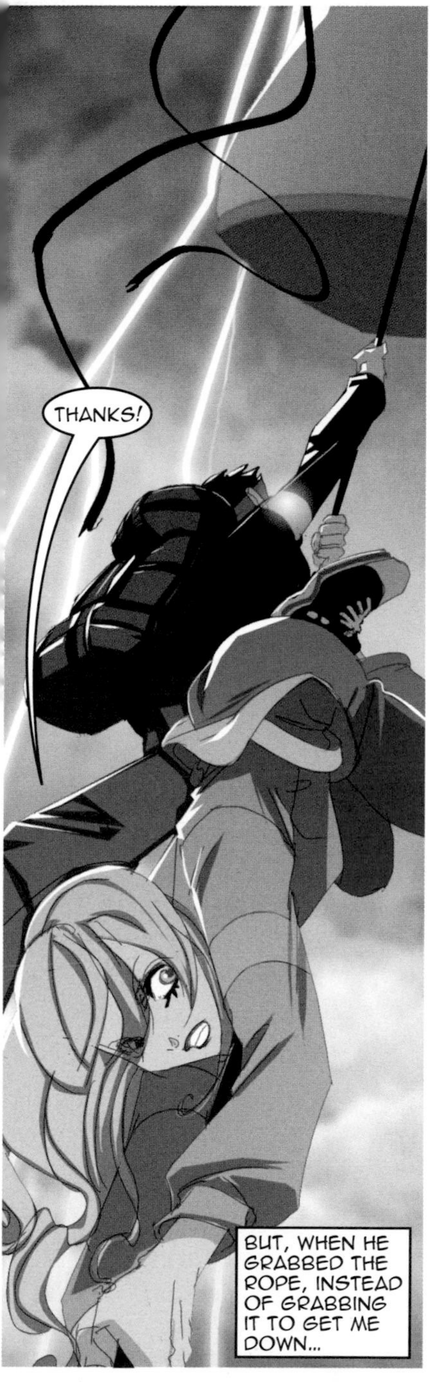
THANKS!
BUT, WHEN HE GRABBED THE ROPE, INSTEAD OF GRABBING IT TO GET ME DOWN...

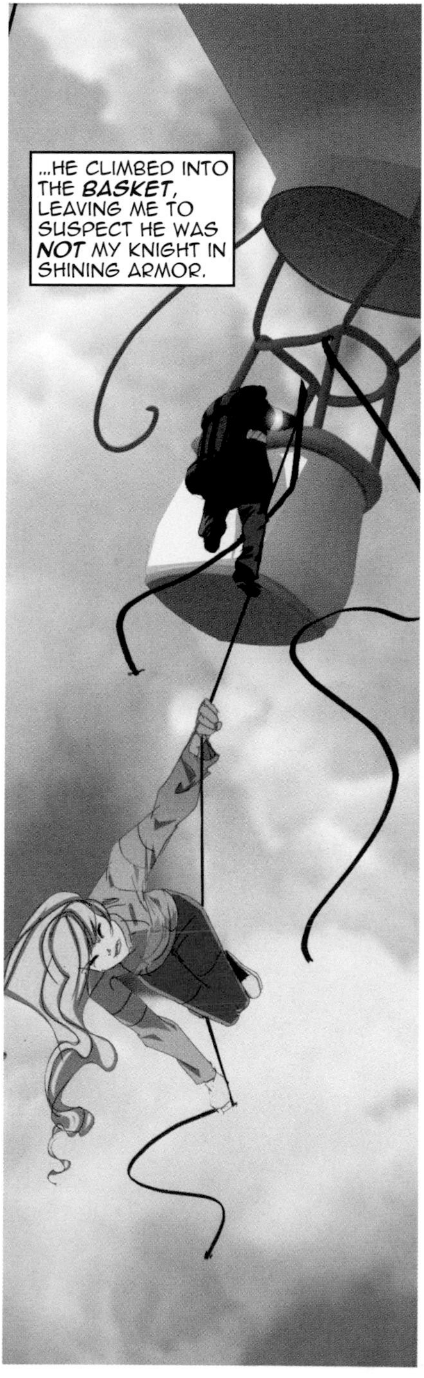
...HE CLIMBED INTO THE BASKET, LEAVING ME TO SUSPECT HE WAS NOT MY KNIGHT IN SHINING ARMOR.

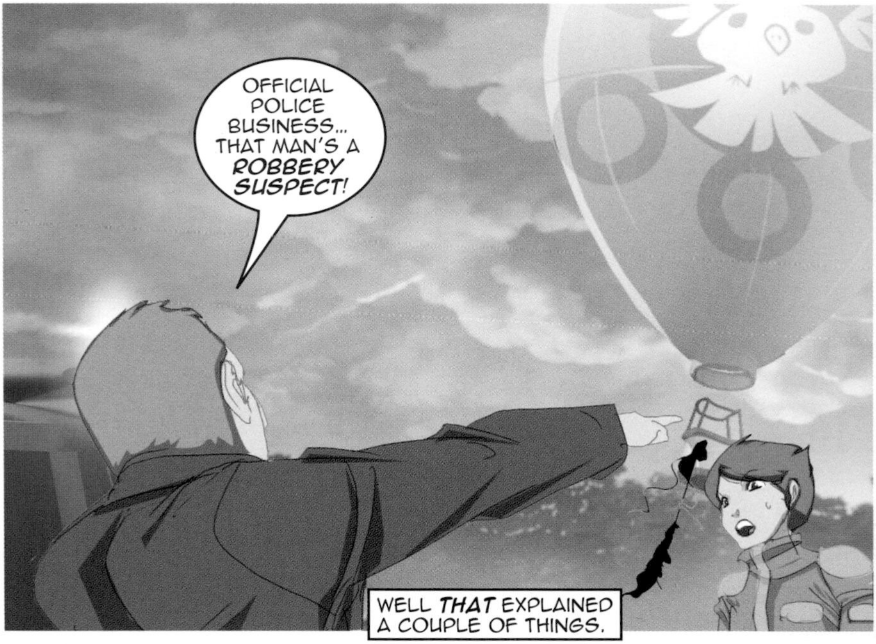
OFFICIAL POLICE BUSINESS... THAT MAN'S A ROBBERY SUSPECT!
WELL THAT EXPLAINED A COUPLE OF THINGS.

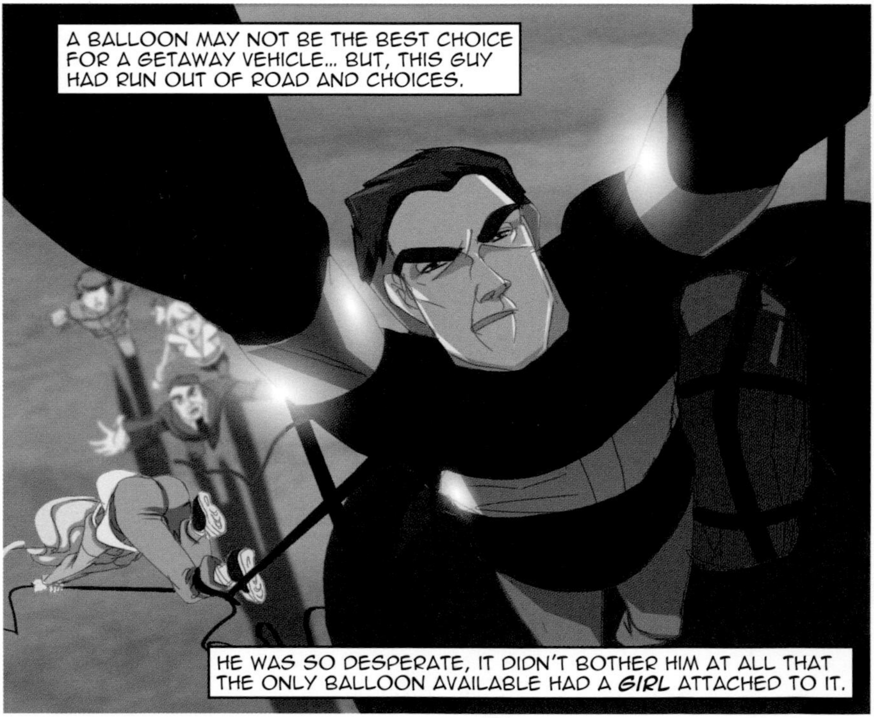
A BALLOON MAY NOT BE THE BEST CHOICE FOR A GETAWAY VEHICLE... BUT, THIS GUY HAD RUN OUT OF ROAD AND CHOICES.
HE WAS SO DESPERATE, IT DIDN'T BOTHER HIM AT ALL THAT THE ONLY BALLOON AVAILABLE HAD A GIRL ATTACHED TO IT.

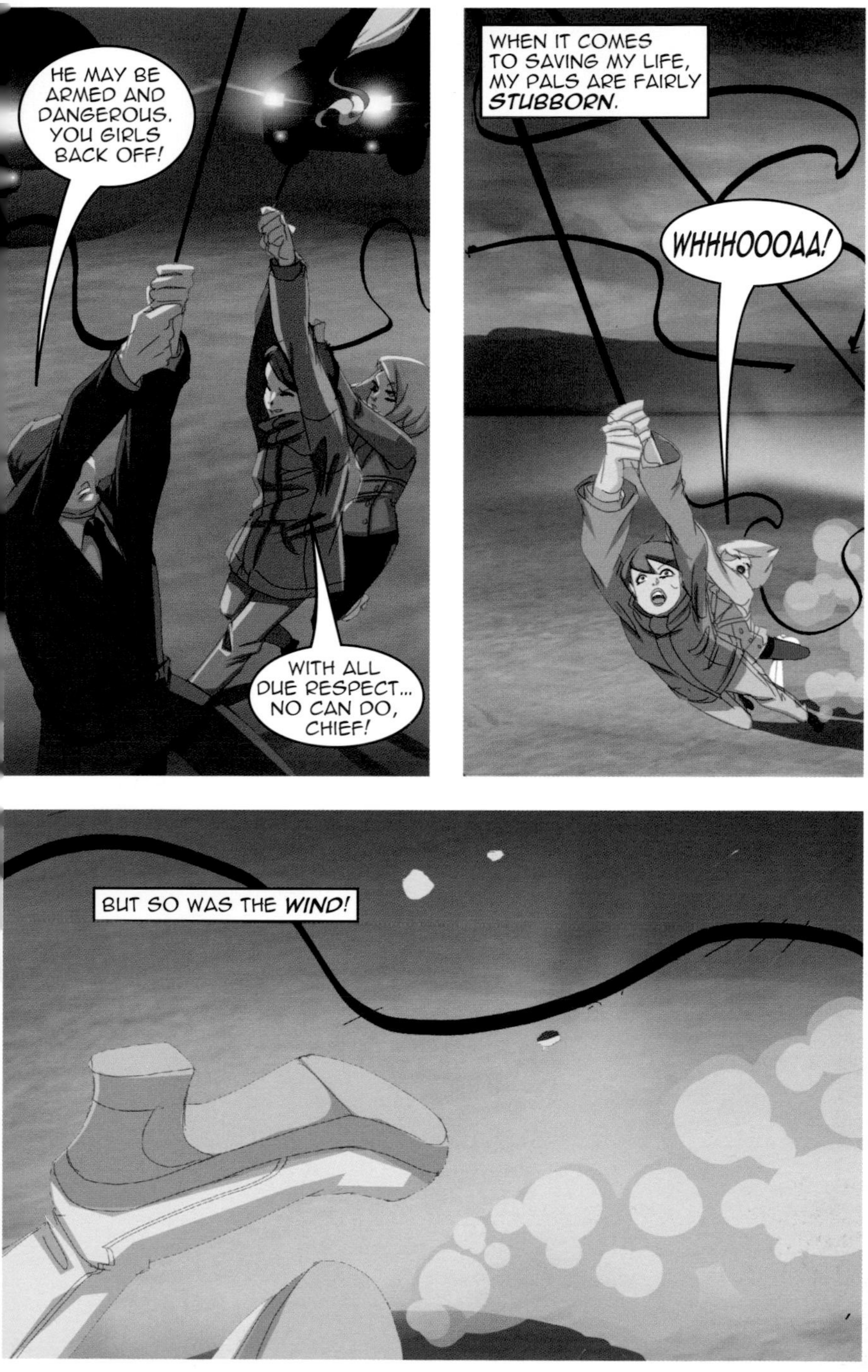
HE MAY BE ARMED AND DANGEROUS. YOU GIRLS BACK OFF!
WITH ALL DUE RESPECT... NO CAN DO, CHIEF!
WHEN IT COMES TO SAVING MY LIFE, MY PALS ARE FAIRLY STUBBORN.
WHHHOOOAA!
BUT SO WAS THE WIND!

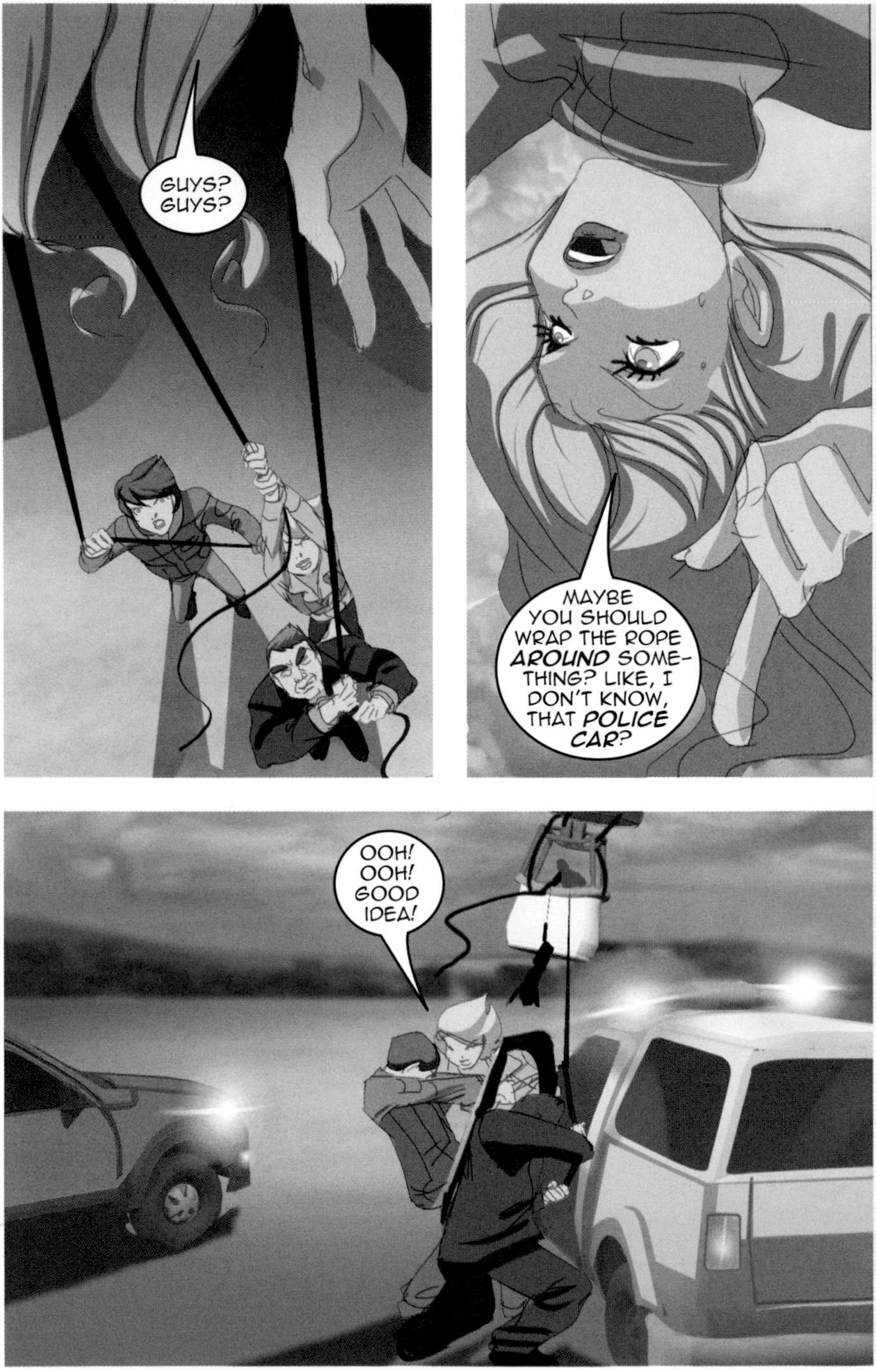
GUYS? GUYS?
MAYBE YOU SHOULD WRAP THE ROPE AROUND SOME-THING? LIKE, I DON'T KNOW, THAT POLICE CAR?
OOH! OOH! GOOD IDEA!

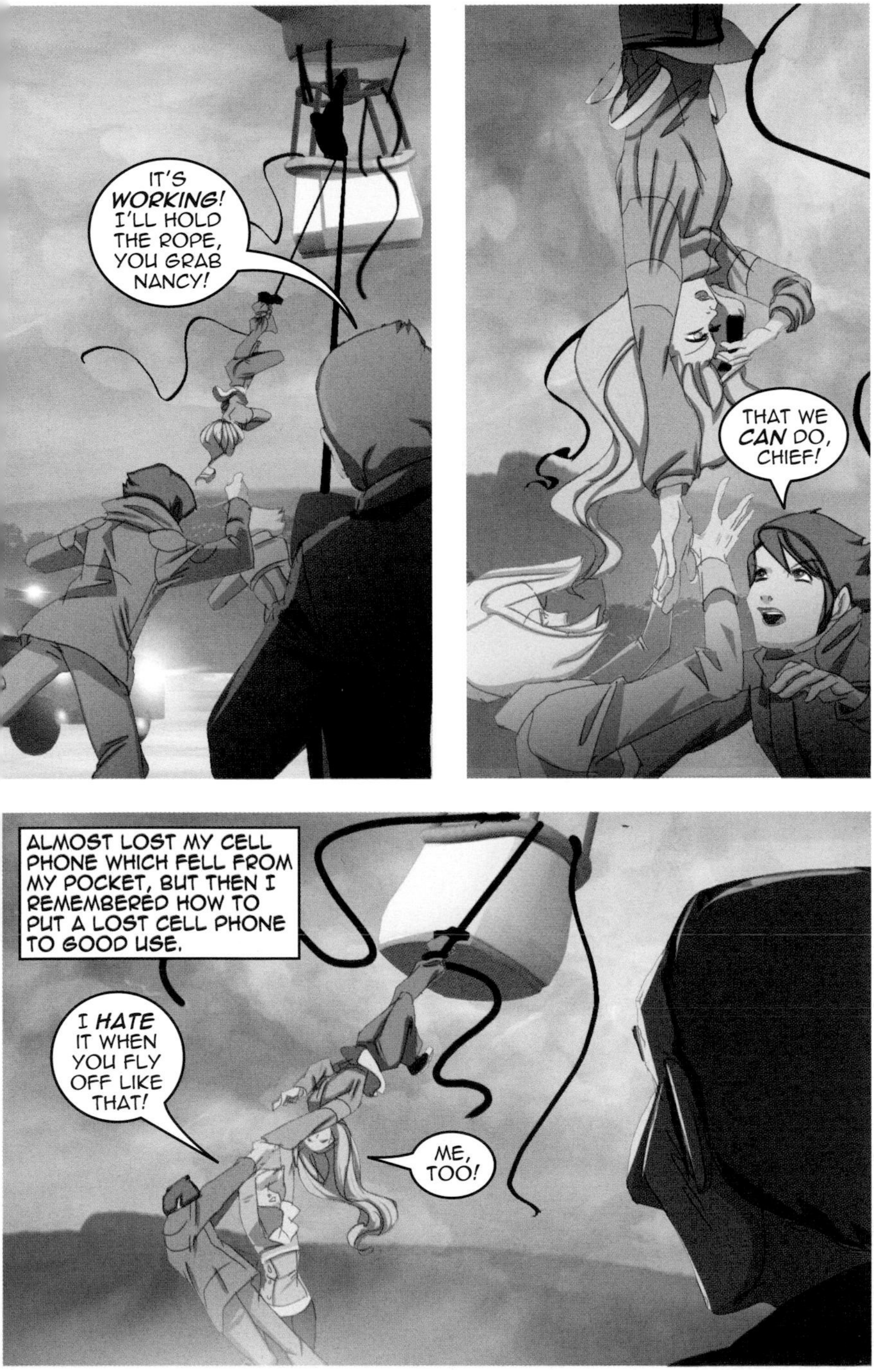
IT'S *WORKING!* I'LL HOLD THE ROPE, YOU GRAB NANCY!
THAT WE *CAN* DO, CHIEF!
ALMOST LOST MY CELL PHONE WHICH FELL FROM MY POCKET, BUT THEN I REMEMBERED HOW TO PUT A LOST CELL PHONE TO GOOD USE.
I *HATE* IT WHEN YOU FLY OFF LIKE THAT!
ME, TOO!

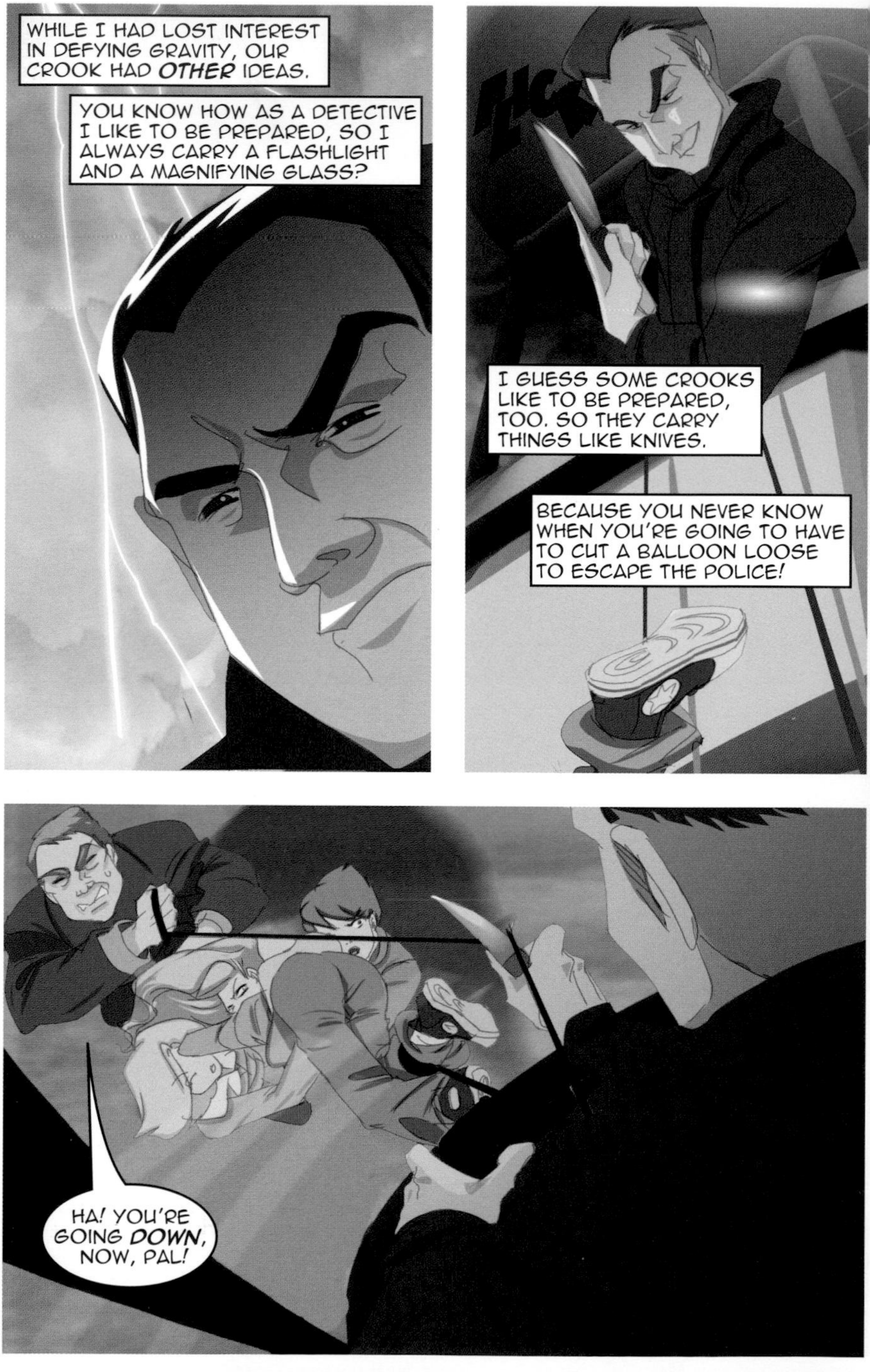

WHILE I HAD LOST INTEREST IN DEFYING GRAVITY, OUR CROOK HAD *OTHER* IDEAS.
YOU KNOW HOW AS A DETECTIVE I LIKE TO BE PREPARED, SO I ALWAYS CARRY A FLASHLIGHT AND A MAGNIFYING GLASS?
I GUESS SOME CROOKS LIKE TO BE PREPARED, TOO. SO THEY CARRY THINGS LIKE KNIVES.
BECAUSE YOU NEVER KNOW WHEN YOU'RE GOING TO HAVE TO CUT A BALLOON LOOSE TO ESCAPE THE POLICE!
HA! YOU'RE GOING *DOWN*, NOW, PAL!

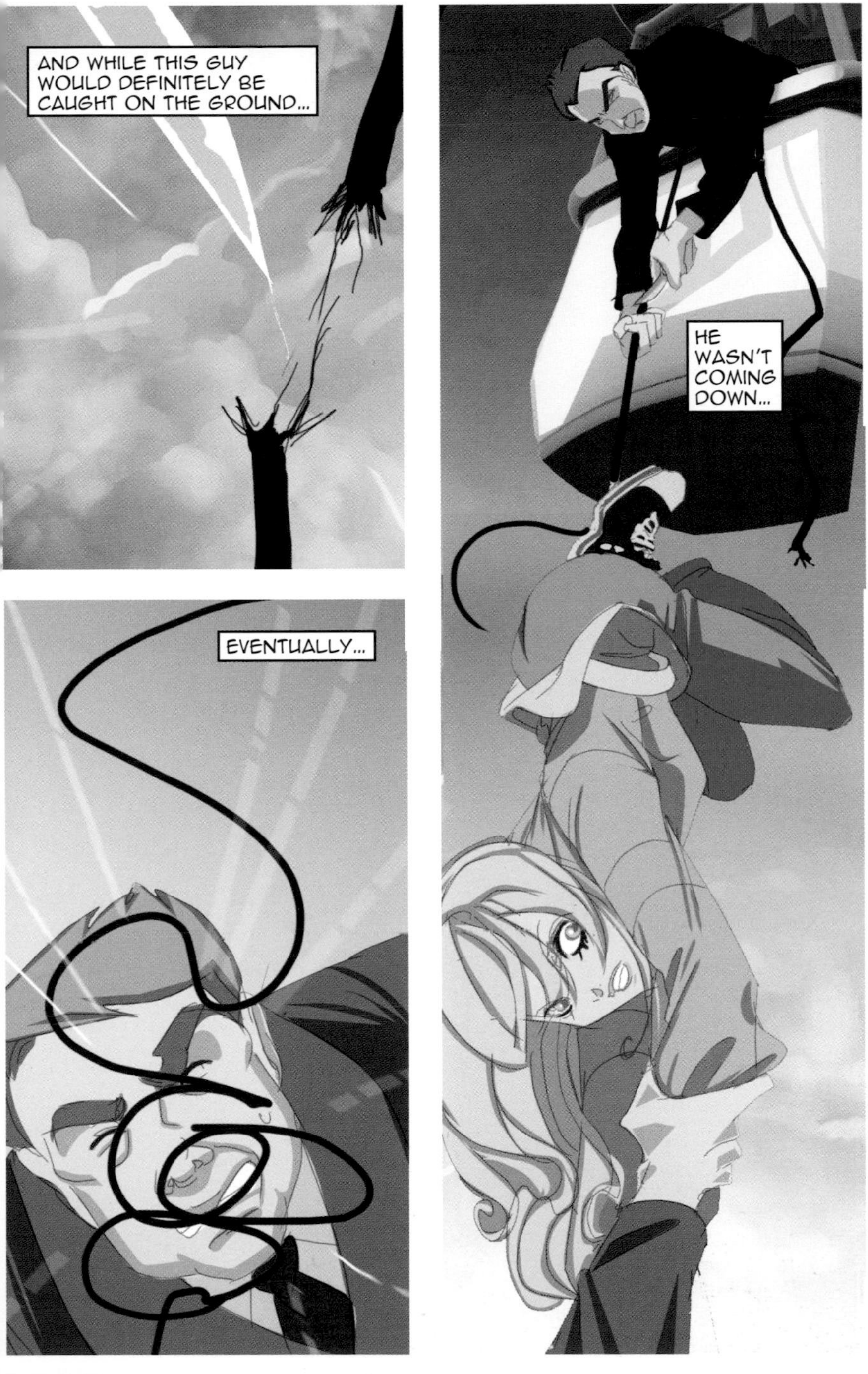
AND WHILE THIS GUY WOULD DEFINITELY BE CAUGHT ON THE GROUND...
EVENTUALLY...
HE WASN'T COMING DOWN...

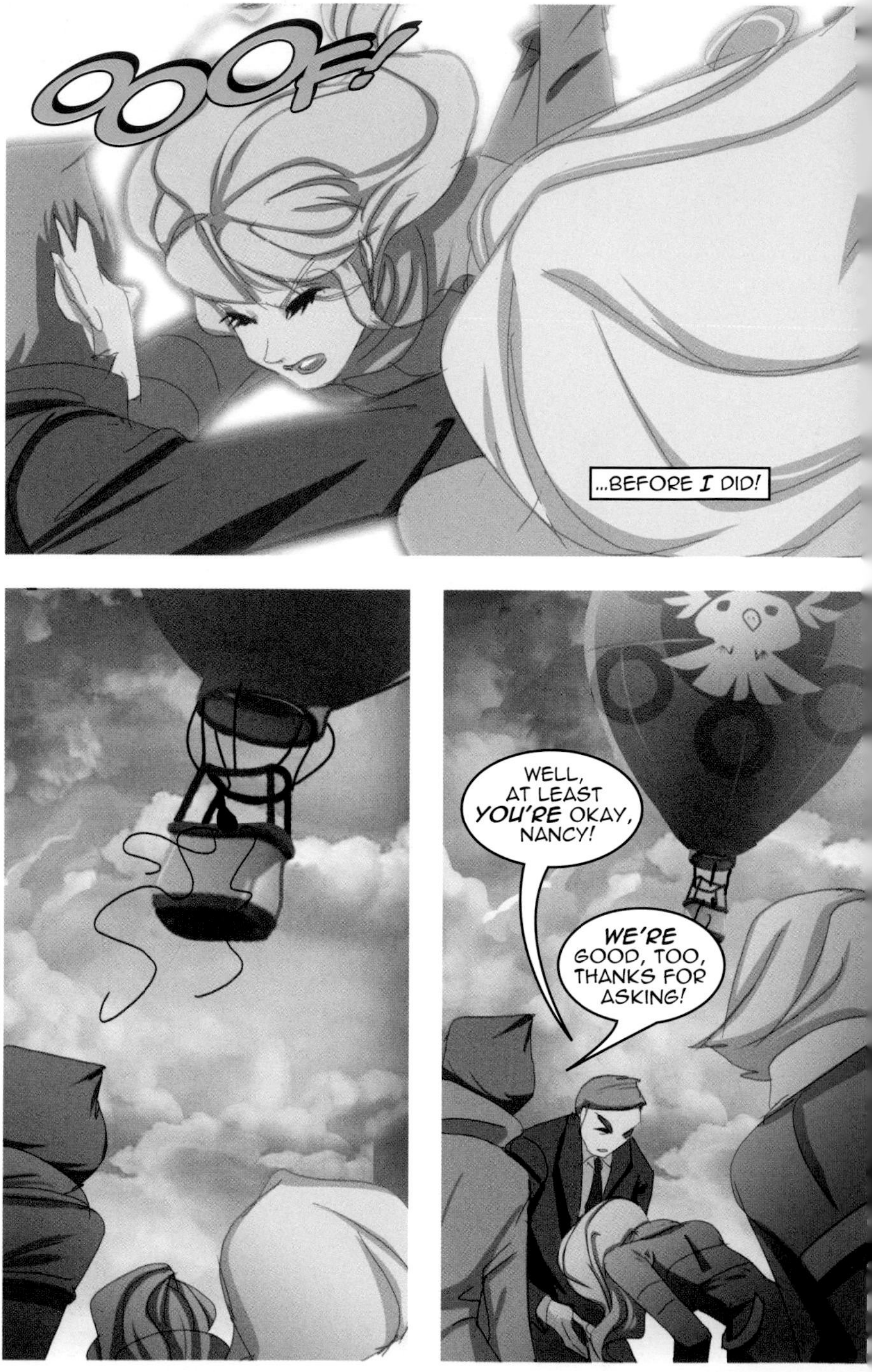
OOOF!
...BEFORE I DID!
WELL, AT LEAST YOU'RE OKAY, NANCY!
WE'RE GOOD, TOO, THANKS FOR ASKING!

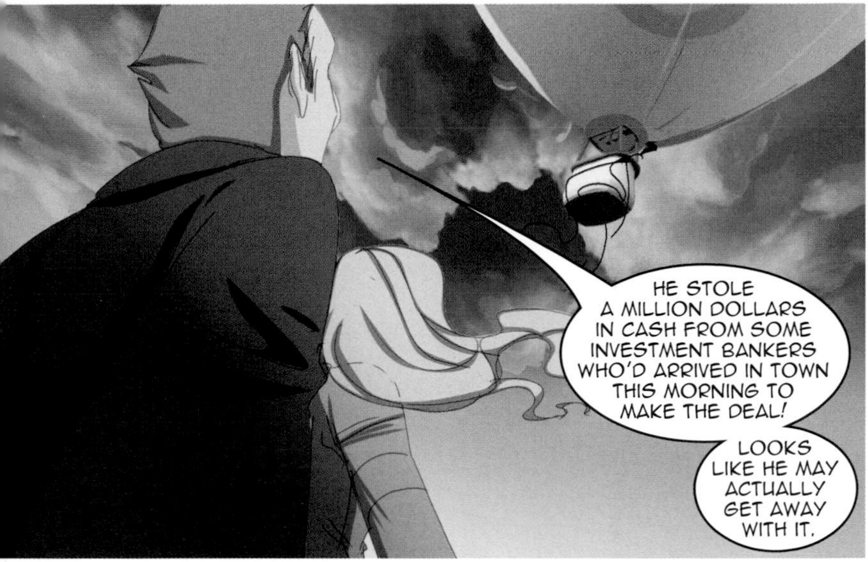
HE STOLE A MILLION DOLLARS IN CASH FROM SOME INVESTMENT BANKERS WHO'D ARRIVED IN TOWN THIS MORNING TO MAKE THE DEAL!
LOOKS LIKE HE MAY ACTUALLY GET AWAY WITH IT.

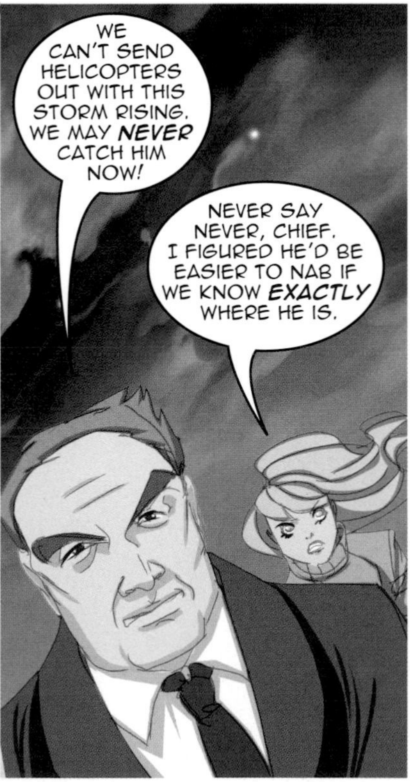
WE CAN'T SEND HELICOPTERS OUT WITH THIS STORM RISING. WE MAY ***NEVER*** CATCH HIM NOW!
NEVER SAY NEVER, CHIEF. I FIGURED HE'D BE EASIER TO NAB IF WE KNOW ***EXACTLY*** WHERE HE IS.

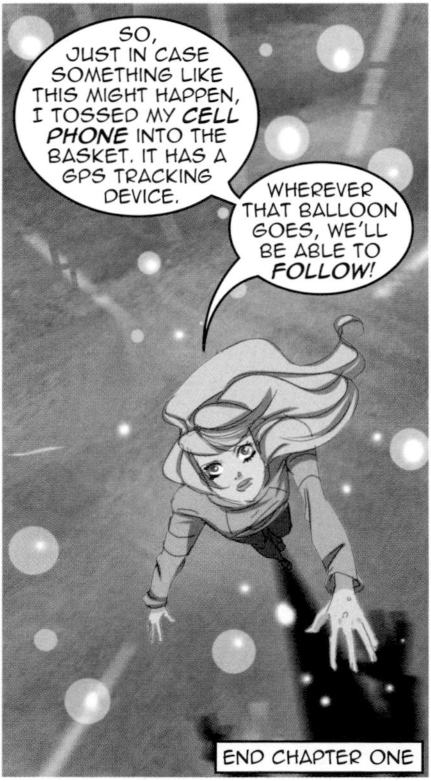
SO, JUST IN CASE SOMETHING LIKE THIS MIGHT HAPPEN, I TOSSED MY ***CELL PHONE*** INTO THE BASKET. IT HAS A GPS TRACKING DEVICE.
WHEREVER THAT BALLOON GOES, WE'LL BE ABLE TO ***FOLLOW!***
END CHAPTER ONE

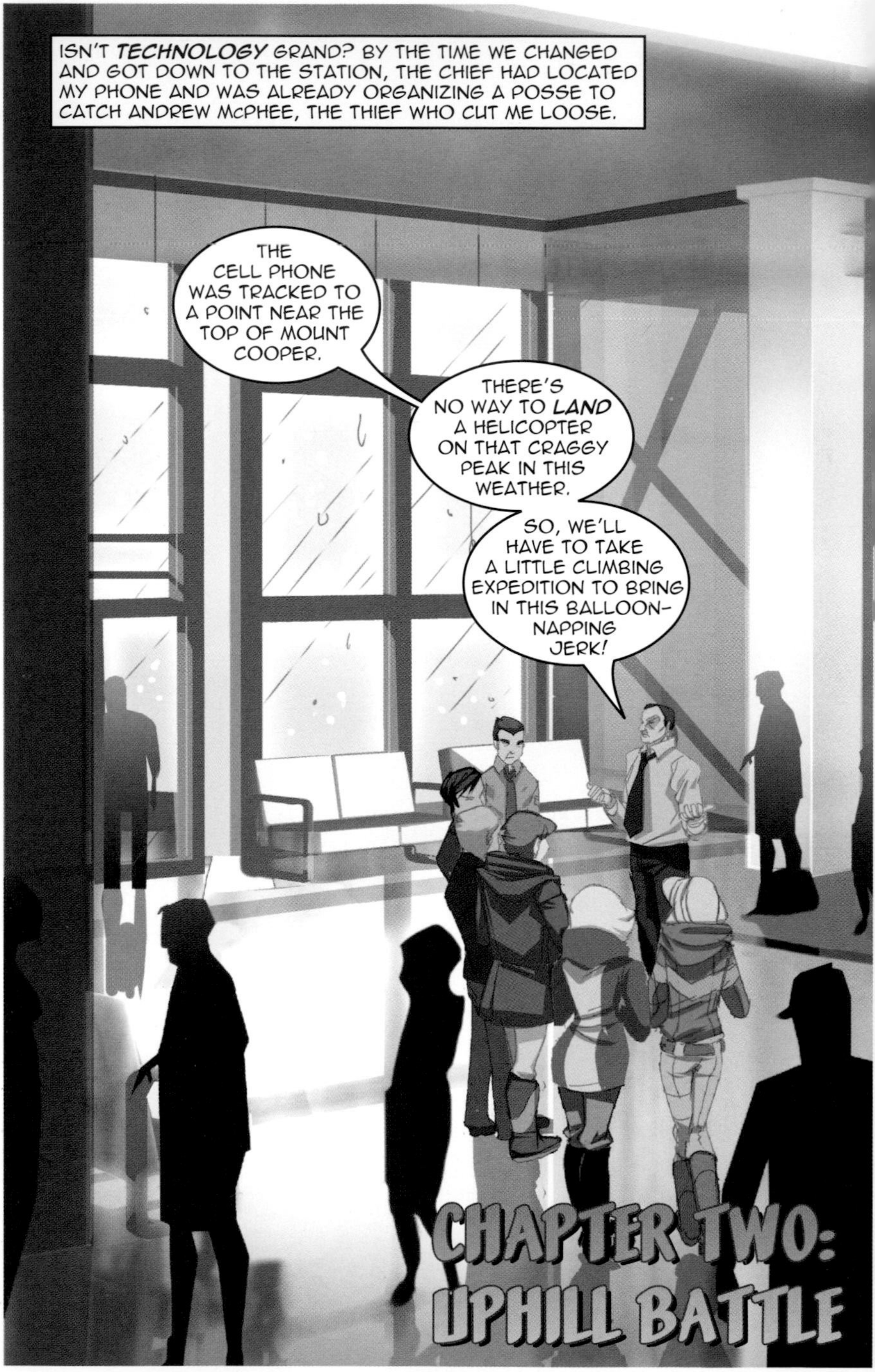
ISN'T TECHNOLOGY GRAND? BY THE TIME WE CHANGED AND GOT DOWN TO THE STATION, THE CHIEF HAD LOCATED MY PHONE AND WAS ALREADY ORGANIZING A POSSE TO CATCH ANDREW McPHEE, THE THIEF WHO CUT ME LOOSE.
THE CELL PHONE WAS TRACKED TO A POINT NEAR THE TOP OF MOUNT COOPER.
THERE'S NO WAY TO LAND A HELICOPTER ON THAT CRAGGY PEAK IN THIS WEATHER.
SO, WE'LL HAVE TO TAKE A LITTLE CLIMBING EXPEDITION TO BRING IN THIS BALLOON-NAPPING JERK!
CHAPTER TWO: UPHILL BATTLE

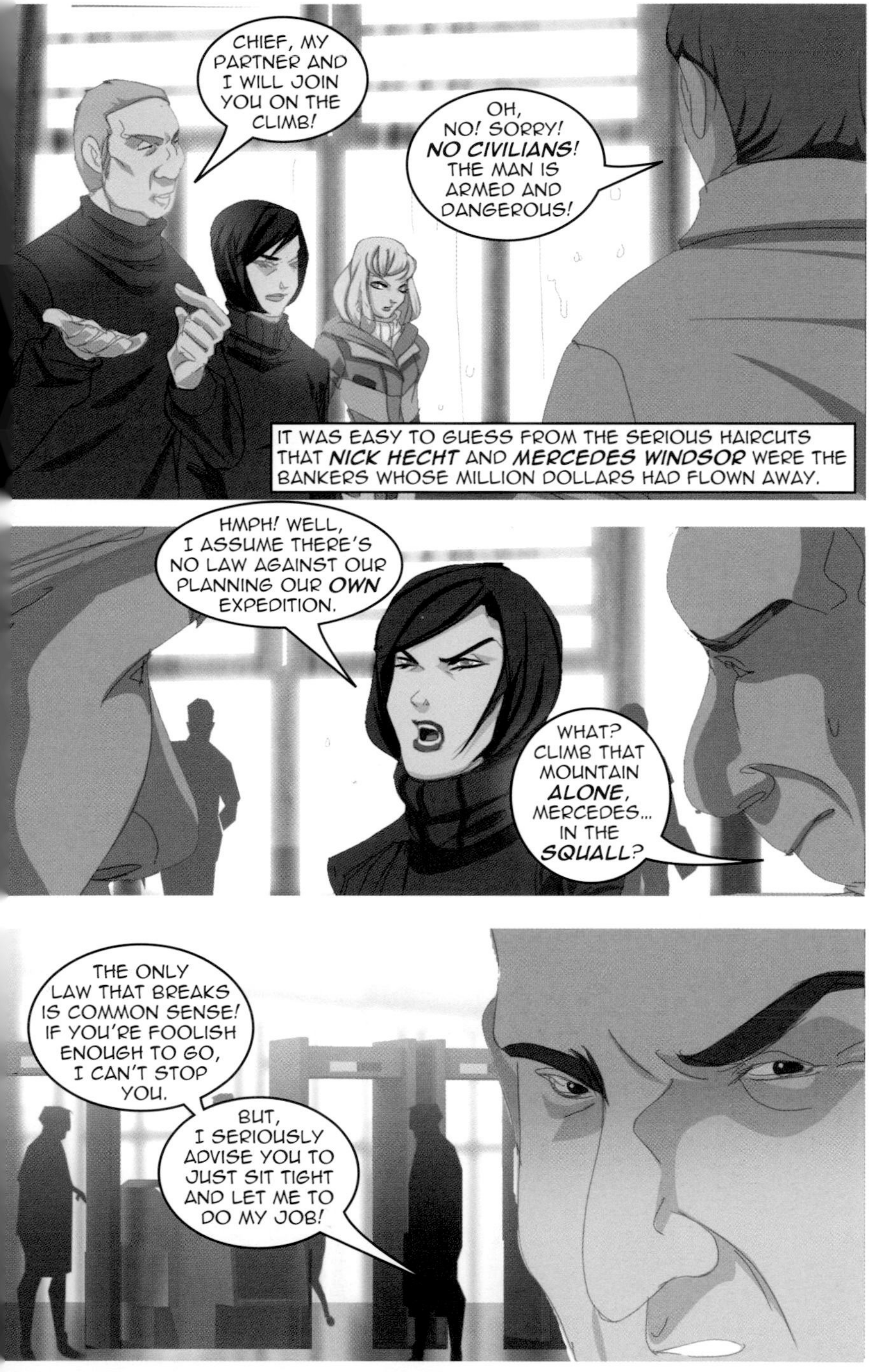
CHIEF, MY PARTNER AND I WILL JOIN YOU ON THE CLIMB!
OH, NO! SORRY! NO CIVILIANS! THE MAN IS ARMED AND DANGEROUS!
IT WAS EASY TO GUESS FROM THE SERIOUS HAIRCUTS THAT NICK HECHT AND MERCEDES WINDSOR WERE THE BANKERS WHOSE MILLION DOLLARS HAD FLOWN AWAY.
HMPH! WELL, I ASSUME THERE'S NO LAW AGAINST OUR PLANNING OUR OWN EXPEDITION.
WHAT? CLIMB THAT MOUNTAIN ALONE, MERCEDES... IN THE SQUALL?
THE ONLY LAW THAT BREAKS IS COMMON SENSE! IF YOU'RE FOOLISH ENOUGH TO GO, I CAN'T STOP YOU.
BUT, I SERIOUSLY ADVISE YOU TO JUST SIT TIGHT AND LET ME TO DO MY JOB!

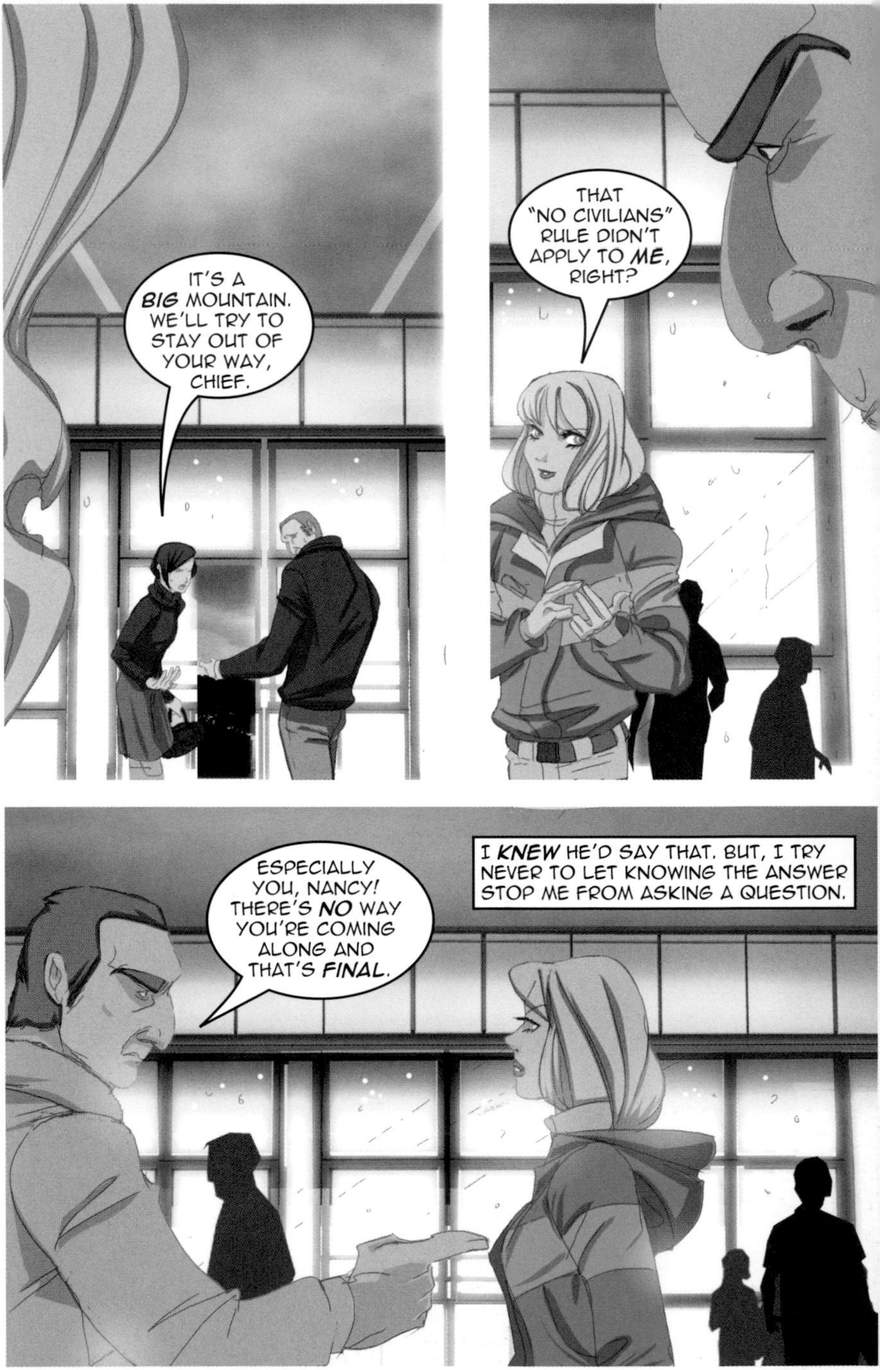
IT'S A BIG MOUNTAIN. WE'LL TRY TO STAY OUT OF YOUR WAY, CHIEF.
THAT "NO CIVILIANS" RULE DIDN'T APPLY TO ME, RIGHT?
ESPECIALLY YOU, NANCY! THERE'S NO WAY YOU'RE COMING ALONG AND THAT'S FINAL.
I KNEW HE'D SAY THAT. BUT, I TRY NEVER TO LET KNOWING THE ANSWER STOP ME FROM ASKING A QUESTION.

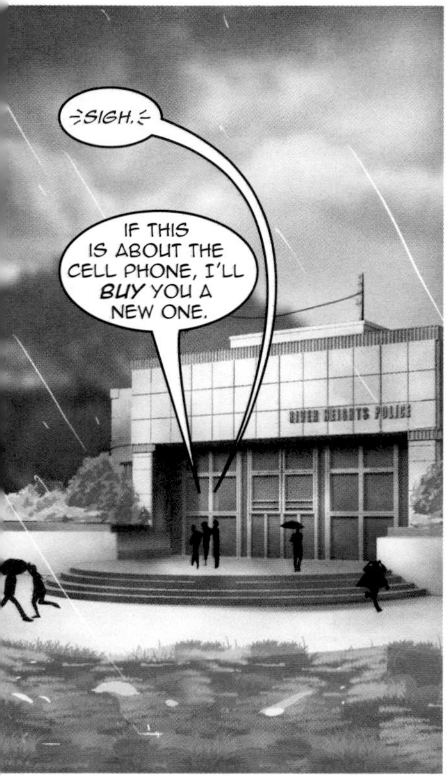
SIGH.
IF THIS IS ABOUT THE CELL PHONE, I'LL BUY YOU A NEW ONE.
RIVER HEIGHTS POLICE

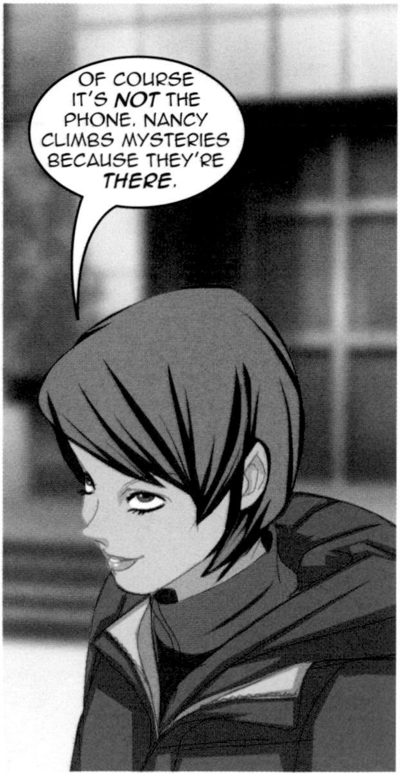
OF COURSE IT'S NOT THE PHONE. NANCY CLIMBS MYSTERIES BECAUSE THEY'RE THERE.

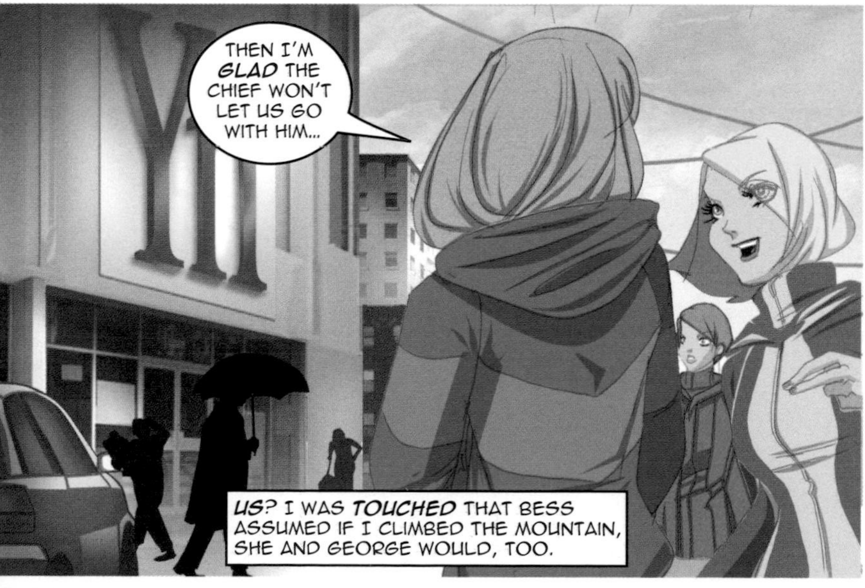
THEN I'M GLAD THE CHIEF WON'T LET US GO WITH HIM...
US? I WAS TOUCHED THAT BESS ASSUMED IF I CLIMBED THE MOUNTAIN, SHE AND GEORGE WOULD, TOO.

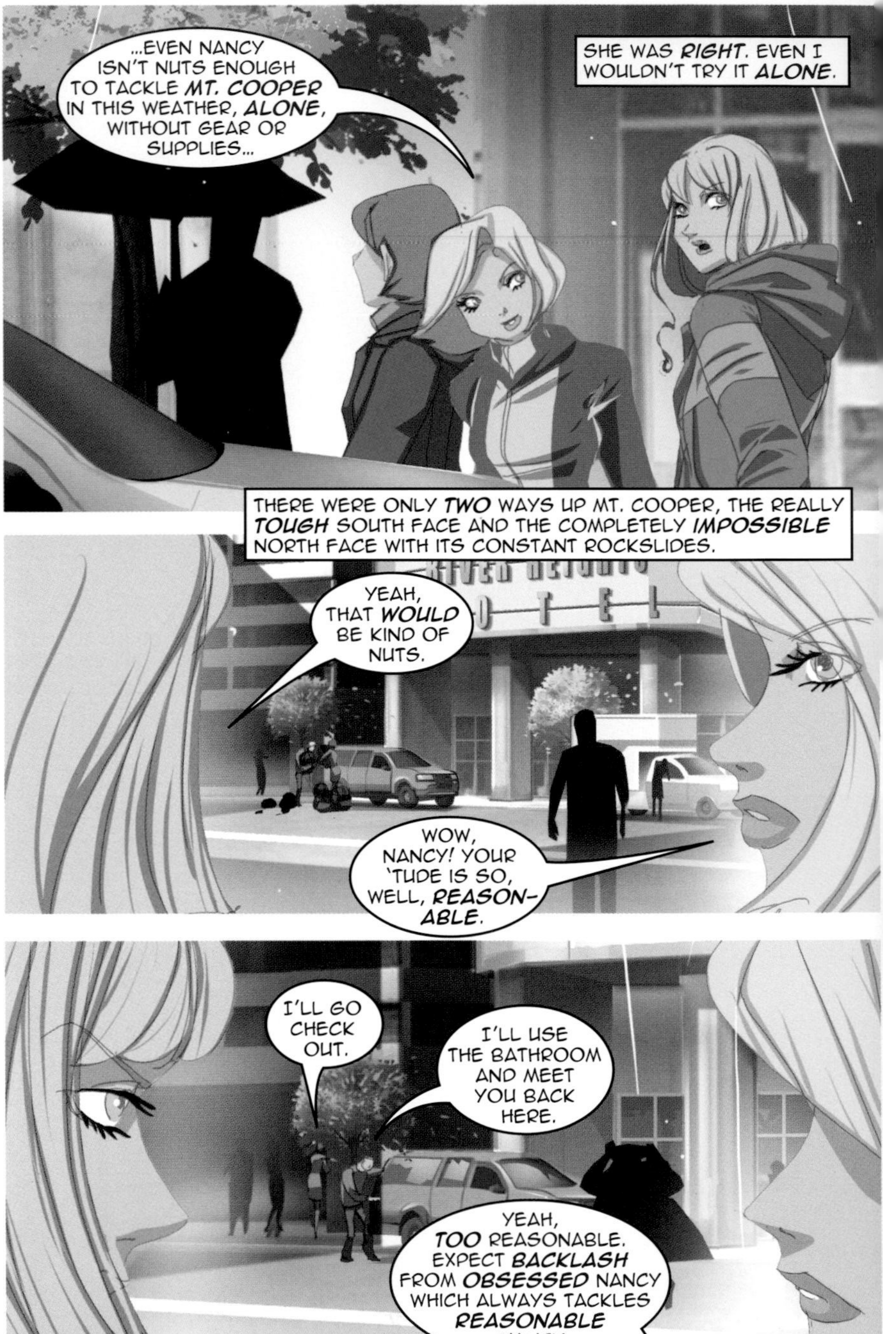
...EVEN NANCY ISN'T NUTS ENOUGH TO TACKLE MT. COOPER IN THIS WEATHER, ALONE, WITHOUT GEAR OR SUPPLIES...
SHE WAS RIGHT. EVEN I WOULDN'T TRY IT ALONE.
THERE WERE ONLY TWO WAYS UP MT. COOPER, THE REALLY TOUGH SOUTH FACE AND THE COMPLETELY IMPOSSIBLE NORTH FACE WITH ITS CONSTANT ROCKSLIDES.
YEAH, THAT WOULD BE KIND OF NUTS.
WOW, NANCY! YOUR 'TUDE IS SO, WELL, REASON-ABLE.
I'LL GO CHECK OUT.
I'LL USE THE BATHROOM AND MEET YOU BACK HERE.
YEAH, TOO REASONABLE. EXPECT BACKLASH FROM OBSESSED NANCY WHICH ALWAYS TACKLES REASONABLE NANCY.

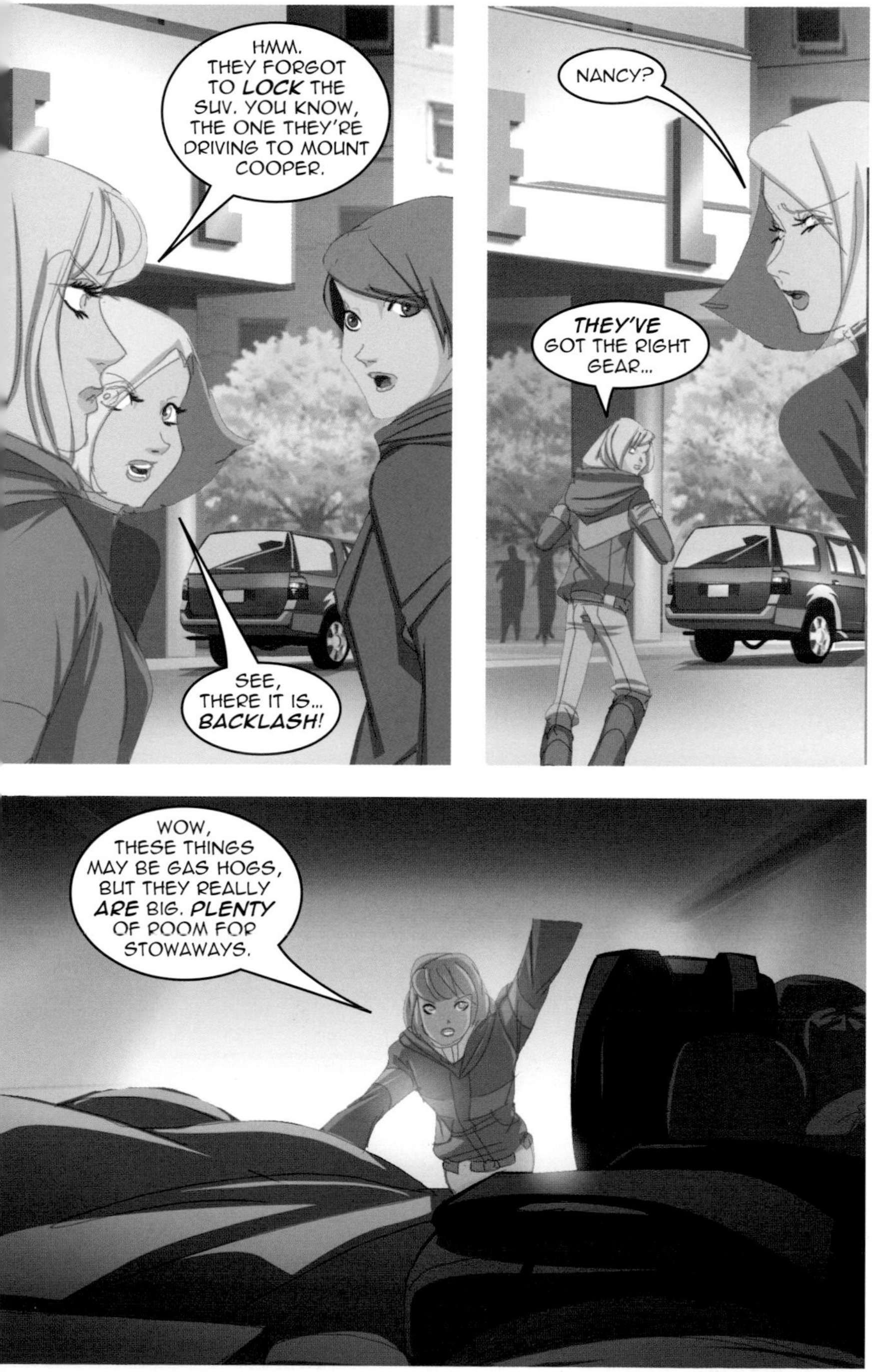
HMM. THEY FORGOT TO **LOCK** THE SUV. YOU KNOW, THE ONE THEY'RE DRIVING TO MOUNT COOPER.
SEE, THERE IT IS... **BACKLASH**!
NANCY?
THEY'VE GOT THE RIGHT GEAR...
WOW, THESE THINGS MAY BE GAS HOGS, BUT THEY REALLY **ARE** BIG. **PLENTY** OF ROOM FOR STOWAWAYS.

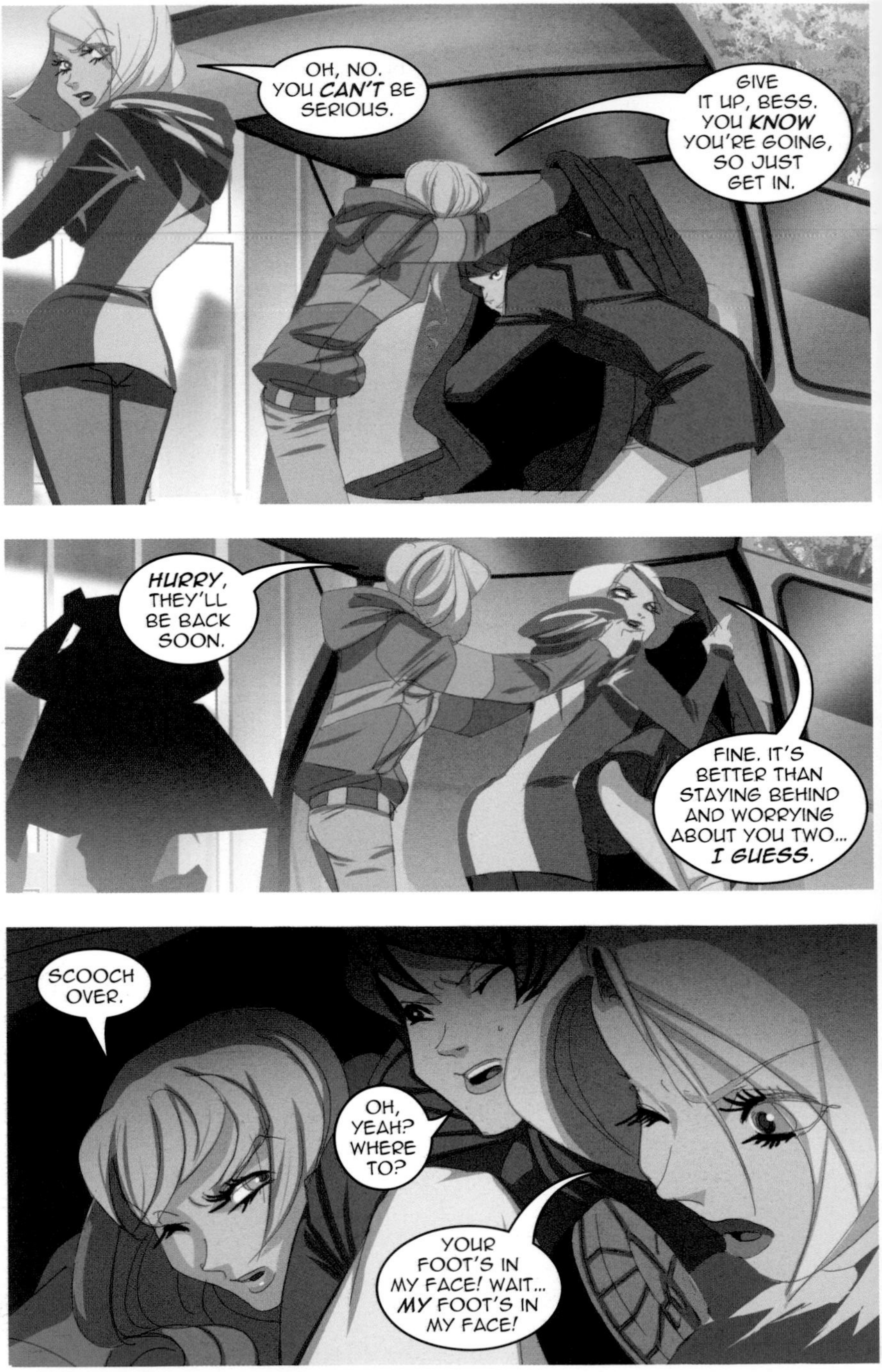
OH, NO. YOU CAN'T BE SERIOUS.
GIVE IT UP, BESS. YOU KNOW YOU'RE GOING, SO JUST GET IN.
HURRY, THEY'LL BE BACK SOON.
FINE. IT'S BETTER THAN STAYING BEHIND AND WORRYING ABOUT YOU TWO... I GUESS.
SCOOCH OVER.
OH, YEAH? WHERE TO?
YOUR FOOT'S IN MY FACE! WAIT... MY FOOT'S IN MY FACE!

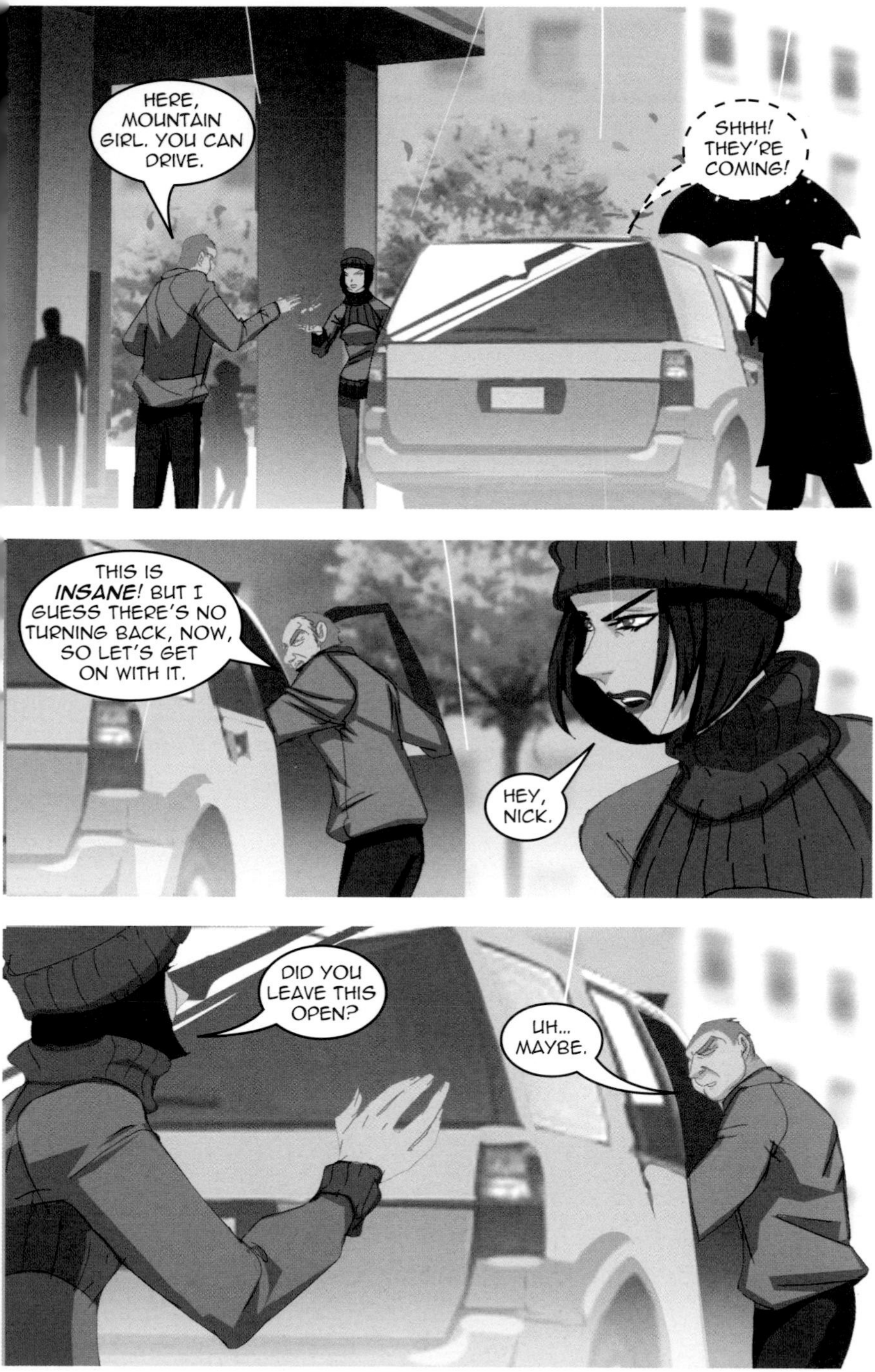
HERE, MOUNTAIN GIRL. YOU CAN DRIVE.
SHHH! THEY'RE COMING!
THIS IS *INSANE*! BUT I GUESS THERE'S NO TURNING BACK, NOW, SO LET'S GET ON WITH IT.
HEY, NICK.
DID YOU LEAVE THIS OPEN?
UH... MAYBE.

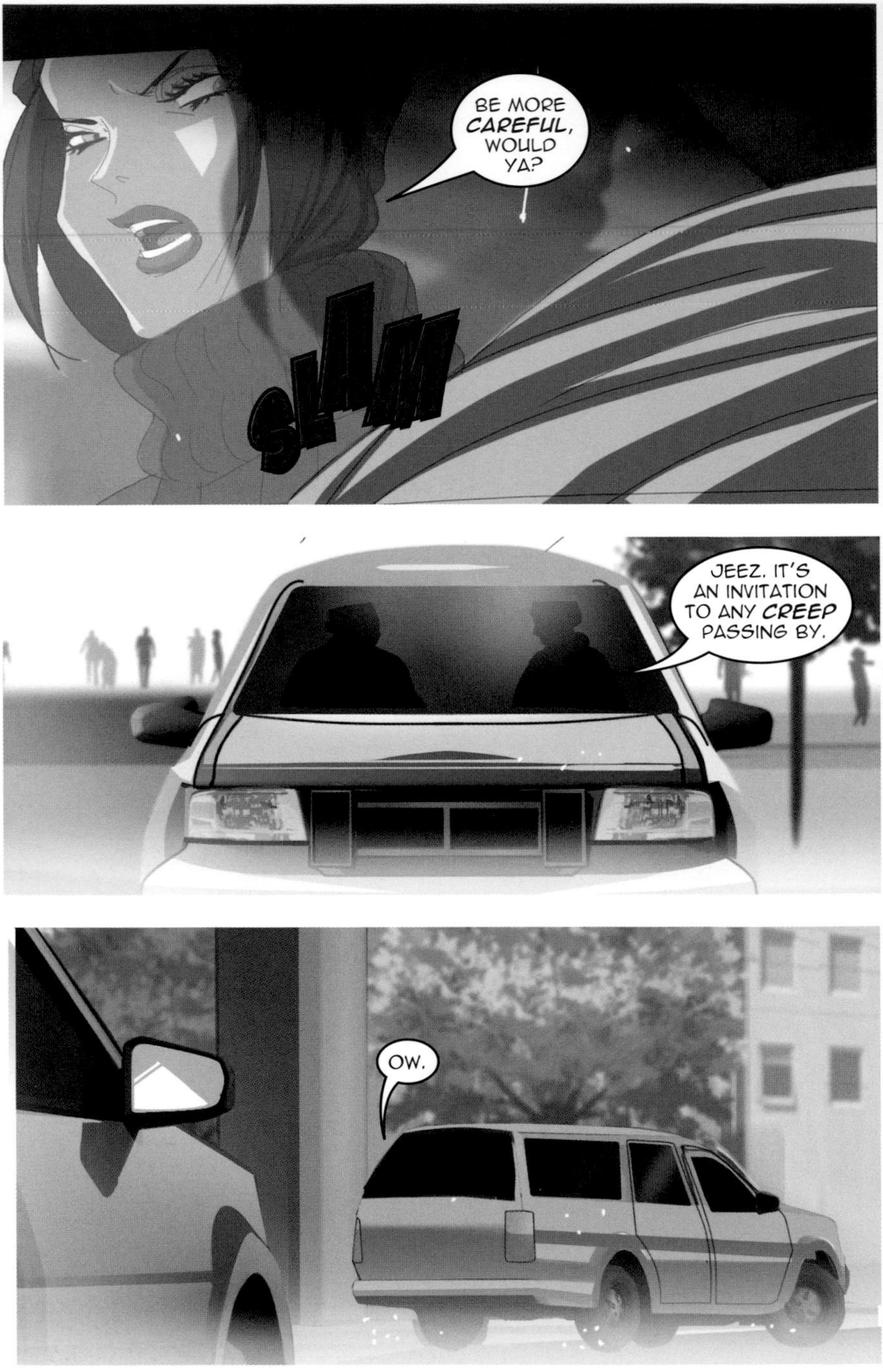
BE MORE CAREFUL, WOULD YA?
SLAM
JEEZ. IT'S AN INVITATION TO ANY CREEP PASSING BY.
OW.

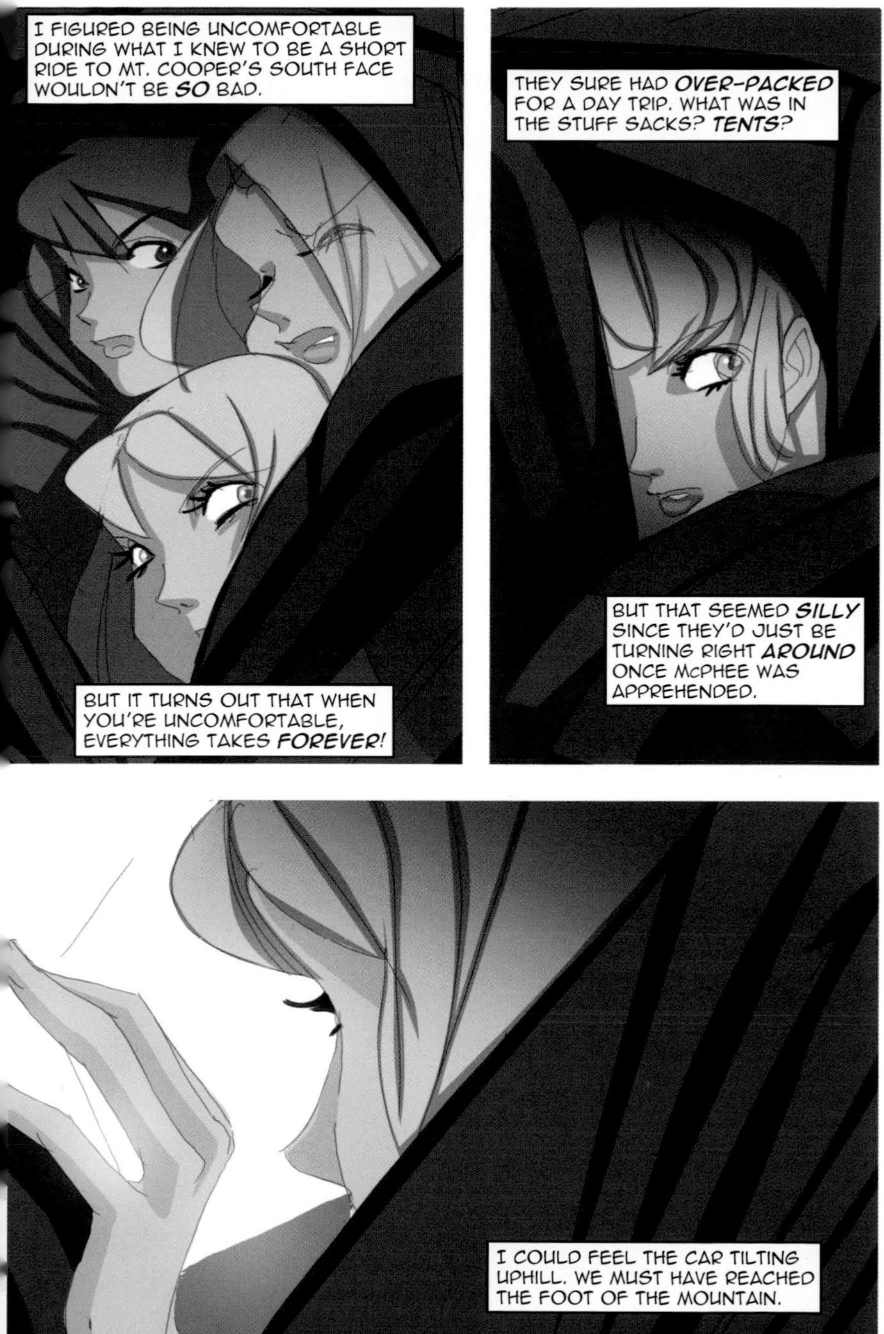
I FIGURED BEING UNCOMFORTABLE DURING WHAT I KNEW TO BE A SHORT RIDE TO MT. COOPER'S SOUTH FACE WOULDN'T BE *SO* BAD.
BUT IT TURNS OUT THAT WHEN YOU'RE UNCOMFORTABLE, EVERYTHING TAKES *FOREVER*!
THEY SURE HAD *OVER-PACKED* FOR A DAY TRIP. WHAT WAS IN THE STUFF SACKS? *TENTS*?
BUT THAT SEEMED *SILLY* SINCE THEY'D JUST BE TURNING RIGHT *AROUND* ONCE McPHEE WAS APPREHENDED.
I COULD FEEL THE CAR TILTING UPHILL. WE MUST HAVE REACHED THE FOOT OF THE MOUNTAIN.

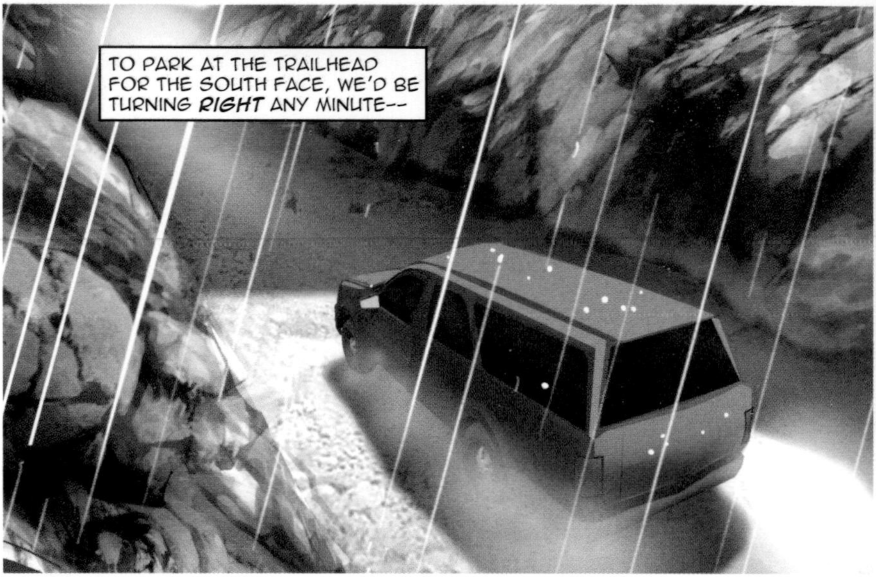
TO PARK AT THE TRAILHEAD FOR THE SOUTH FACE, WE'D BE TURNING ***RIGHT*** ANY MINUTE--

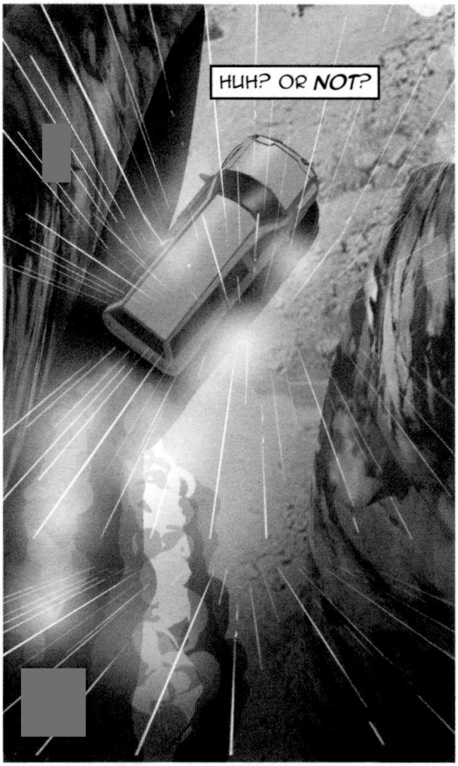
HUH? OR ***NOT***?

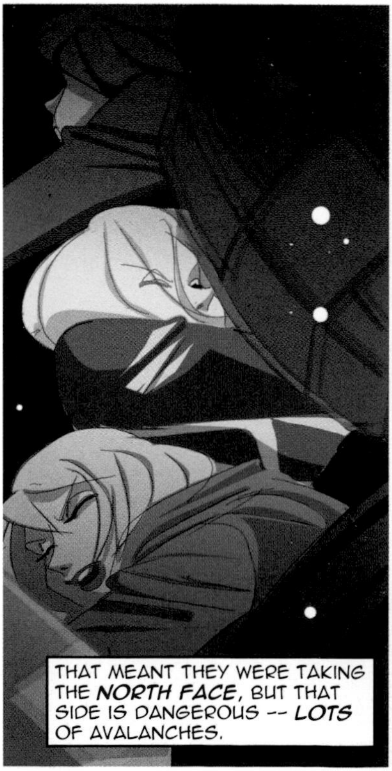
THAT MEANT THEY WERE TAKING THE ***NORTH FACE***, BUT THAT SIDE IS DANGEROUS -- ***LOTS*** OF AVALANCHES.

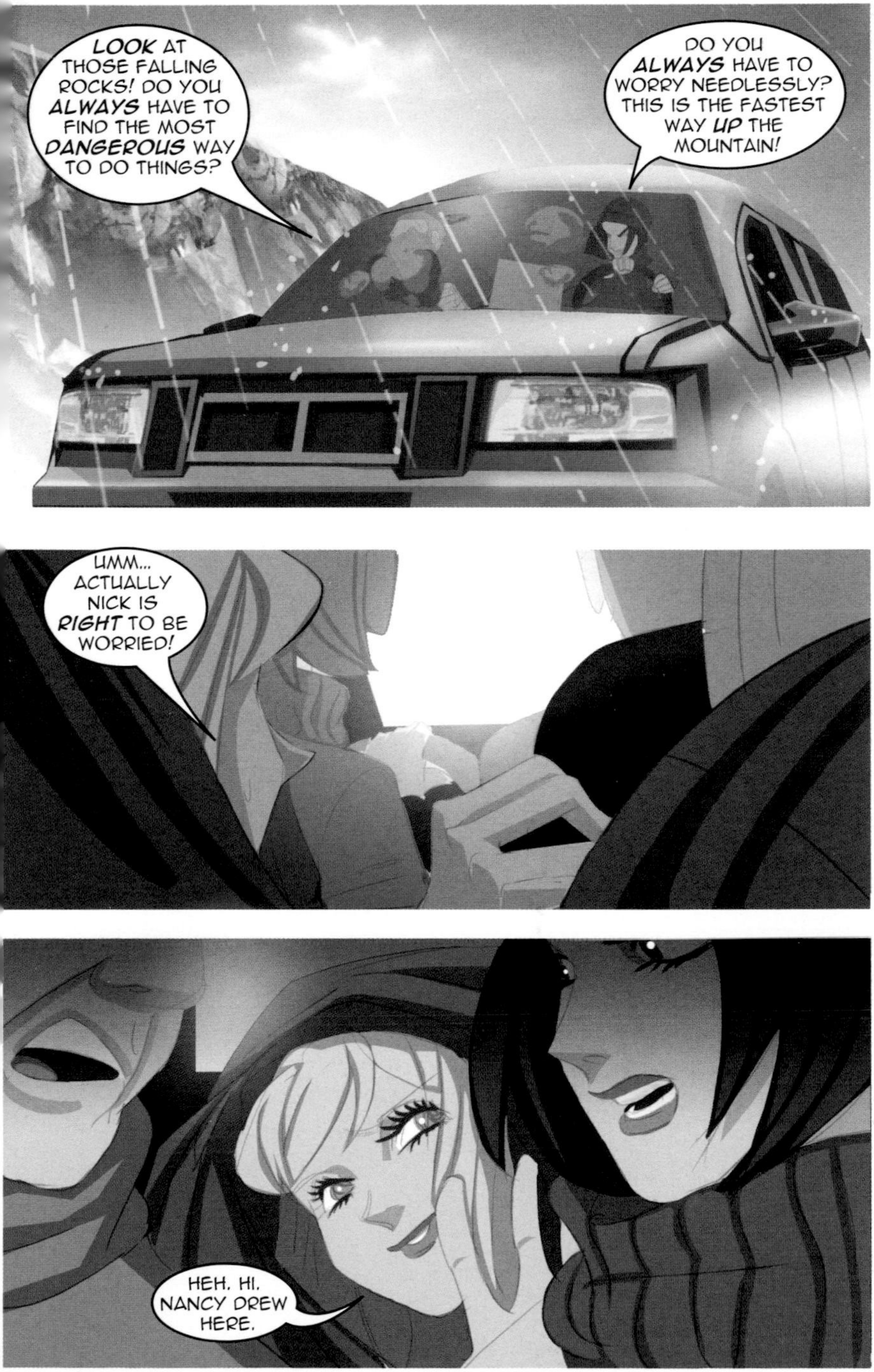
LOOK AT THOSE FALLING ROCKS! DO YOU ALWAYS HAVE TO FIND THE MOST DANGEROUS WAY TO DO THINGS?
DO YOU ALWAYS HAVE TO WORRY NEEDLESSLY? THIS IS THE FASTEST WAY UP THE MOUNTAIN!
UMM... ACTUALLY NICK IS RIGHT TO BE WORRIED!
HEH. HI. NANCY DREW HERE.

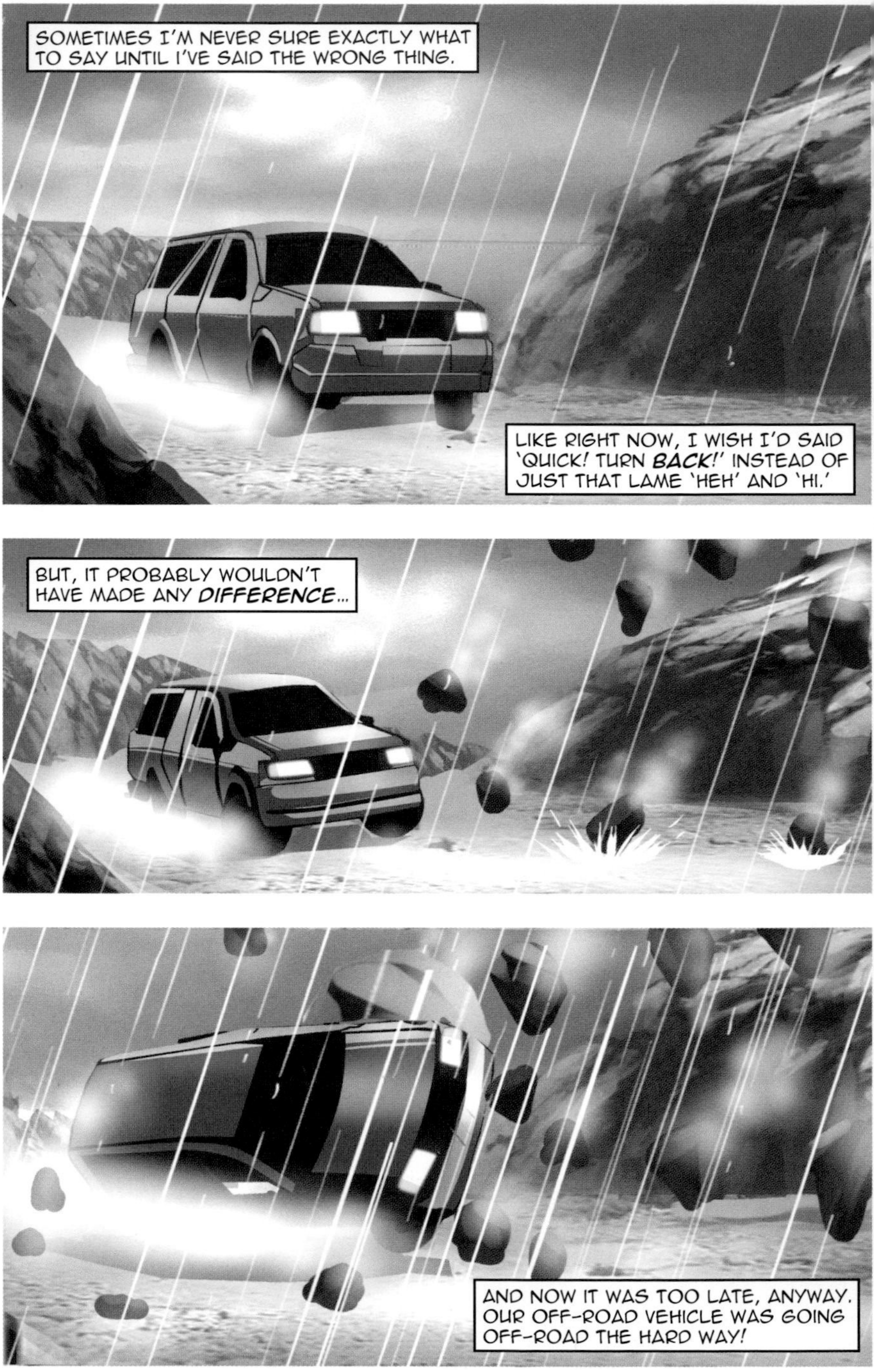
SOMETIMES I'M NEVER SURE EXACTLY WHAT TO SAY UNTIL I'VE SAID THE WRONG THING.
LIKE RIGHT NOW, I WISH I'D SAID 'QUICK! TURN BACK!' INSTEAD OF JUST THAT LAME 'HEH' AND 'HI.'
BUT, IT PROBABLY WOULDN'T HAVE MADE ANY DIFFERENCE...
AND NOW IT WAS TOO LATE, ANYWAY. OUR OFF-ROAD VEHICLE WAS GOING OFF-ROAD THE HARD WAY!

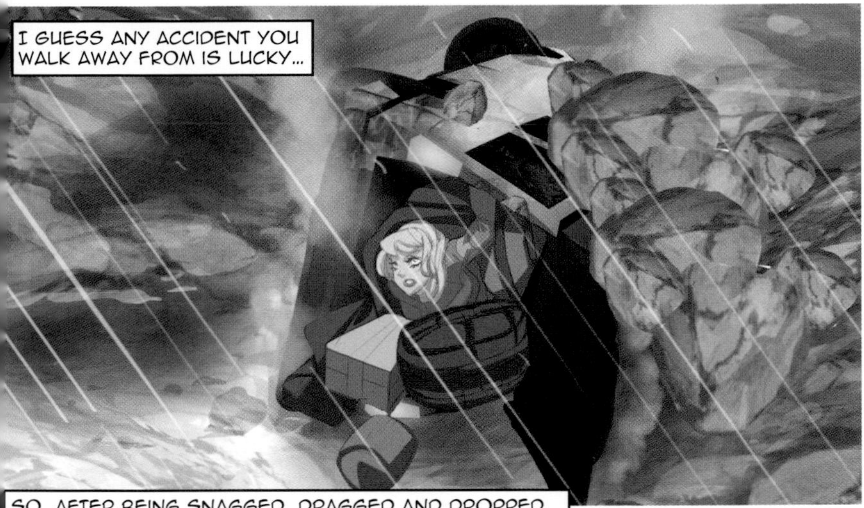
I GUESS ANY ACCIDENT YOU WALK AWAY FROM IS LUCKY...

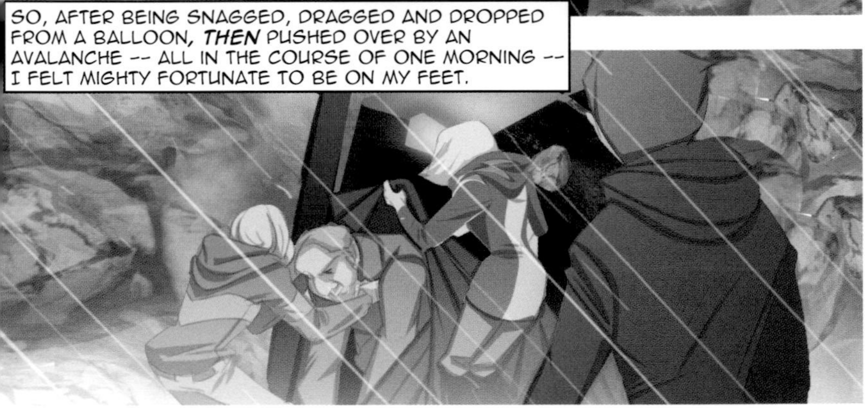
SO, AFTER BEING SNAGGED, DRAGGED AND DROPPED FROM A BALLOON, THEN PUSHED OVER BY AN AVALANCHE -- ALL IN THE COURSE OF ONE MORNING -- I FELT MIGHTY FORTUNATE TO BE ON MY FEET.

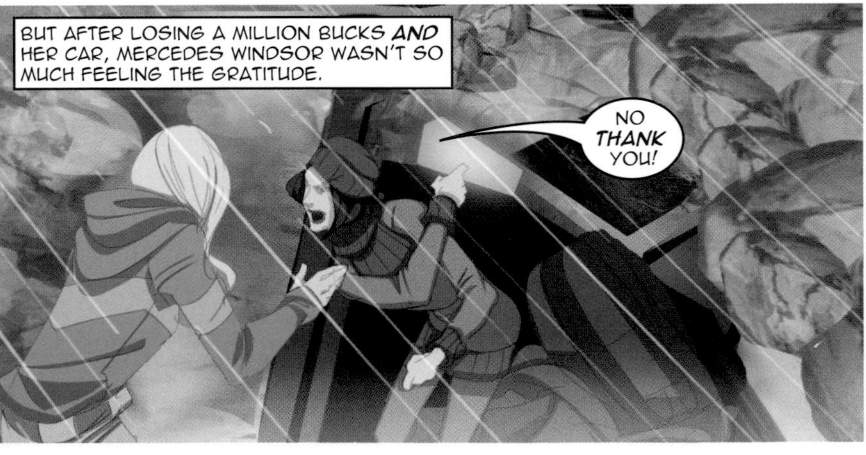
BUT AFTER LOSING A MILLION BUCKS AND HER CAR, MERCEDES WINDSOR WASN'T SO MUCH FEELING THE GRATITUDE.
NO THANK YOU!

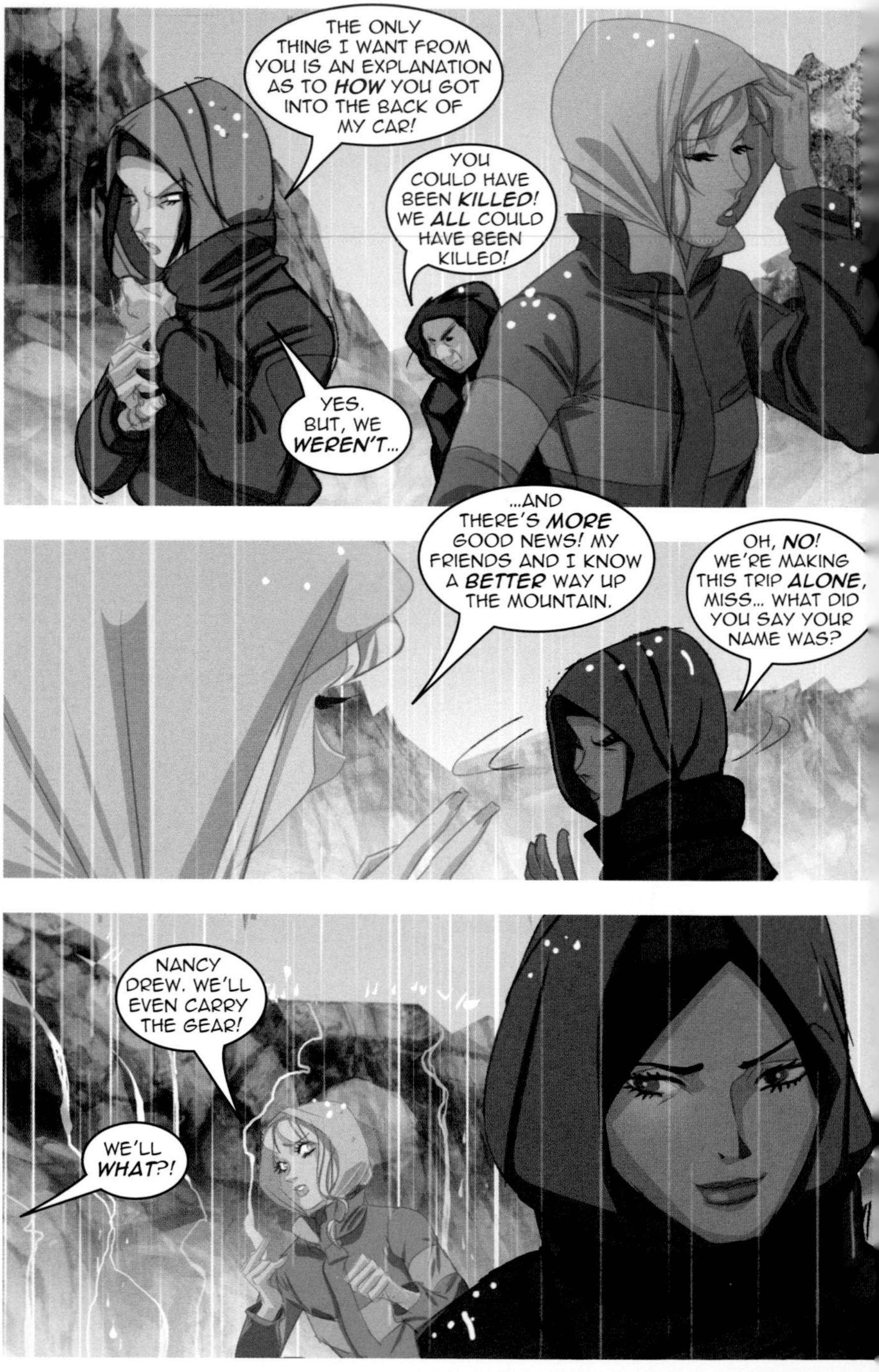
THE ONLY THING I WANT FROM YOU IS AN EXPLANATION AS TO HOW YOU GOT INTO THE BACK OF MY CAR!
YOU COULD HAVE BEEN KILLED! WE ALL COULD HAVE BEEN KILLED!
YES. BUT, WE WEREN'T...
...AND THERE'S MORE GOOD NEWS! MY FRIENDS AND I KNOW A BETTER WAY UP THE MOUNTAIN.
OH, NO! WE'RE MAKING THIS TRIP ALONE, MISS... WHAT DID YOU SAY YOUR NAME WAS?
NANCY DREW. WE'LL EVEN CARRY THE GEAR!
WE'LL WHAT?!

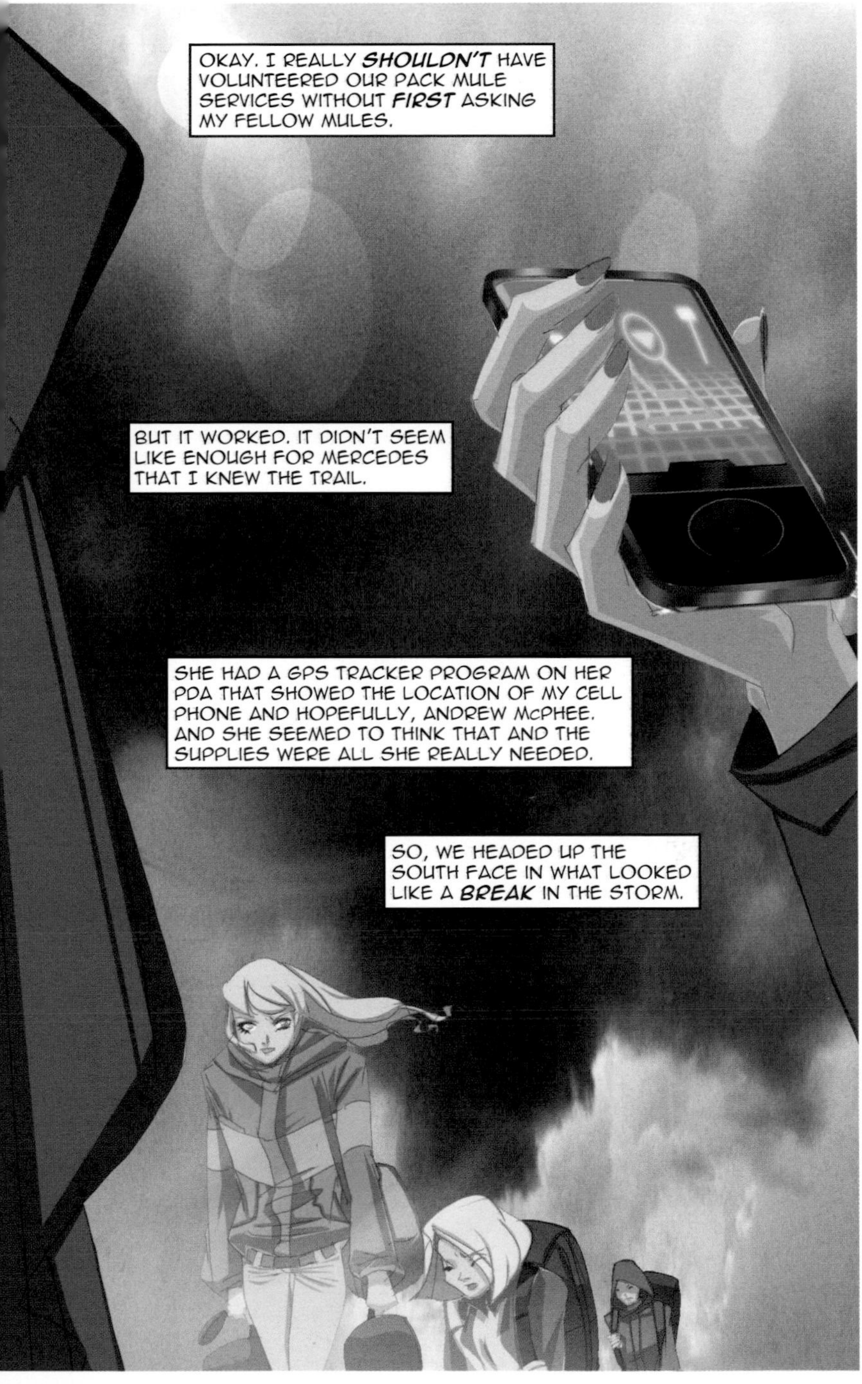
OKAY. I REALLY SHOULDN'T HAVE VOLUNTEERED OUR PACK MULE SERVICES WITHOUT FIRST ASKING MY FELLOW MULES.
BUT IT WORKED. IT DIDN'T SEEM LIKE ENOUGH FOR MERCEDES THAT I KNEW THE TRAIL.
SHE HAD A GPS TRACKER PROGRAM ON HER PDA THAT SHOWED THE LOCATION OF MY CELL PHONE AND HOPEFULLY, ANDREW McPHEE. AND SHE SEEMED TO THINK THAT AND THE SUPPLIES WERE ALL SHE REALLY NEEDED.
SO, WE HEADED UP THE SOUTH FACE IN WHAT LOOKED LIKE A BREAK IN THE STORM.

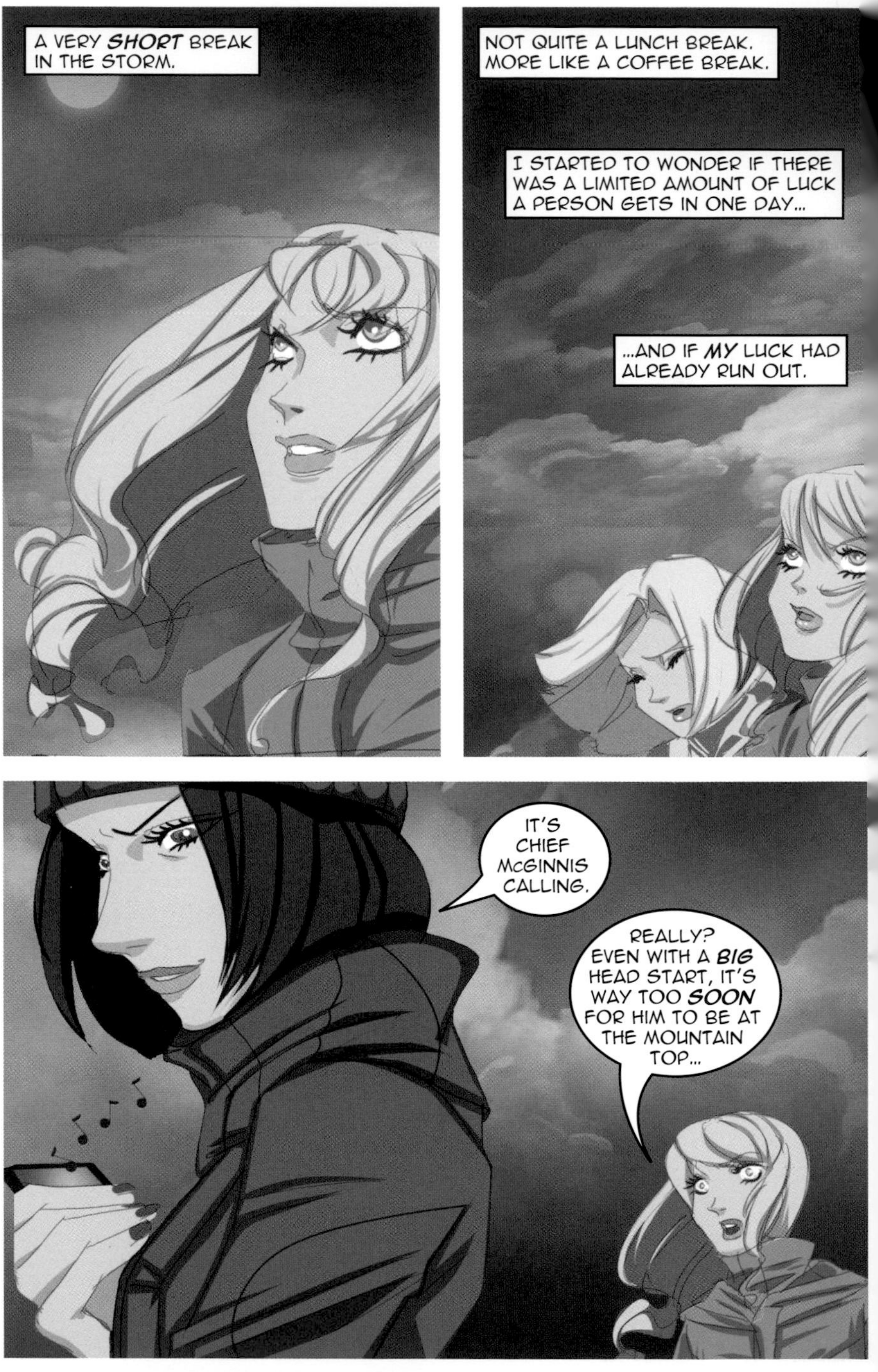

A VERY SHORT BREAK IN THE STORM.
NOT QUITE A LUNCH BREAK. MORE LIKE A COFFEE BREAK.
I STARTED TO WONDER IF THERE WAS A LIMITED AMOUNT OF LUCK A PERSON GETS IN ONE DAY...
...AND IF MY LUCK HAD ALREADY RUN OUT.
IT'S CHIEF McGINNIS CALLING.
REALLY? EVEN WITH A BIG HEAD START, IT'S WAY TOO SOON FOR HIM TO BE AT THE MOUNTAIN TOP...

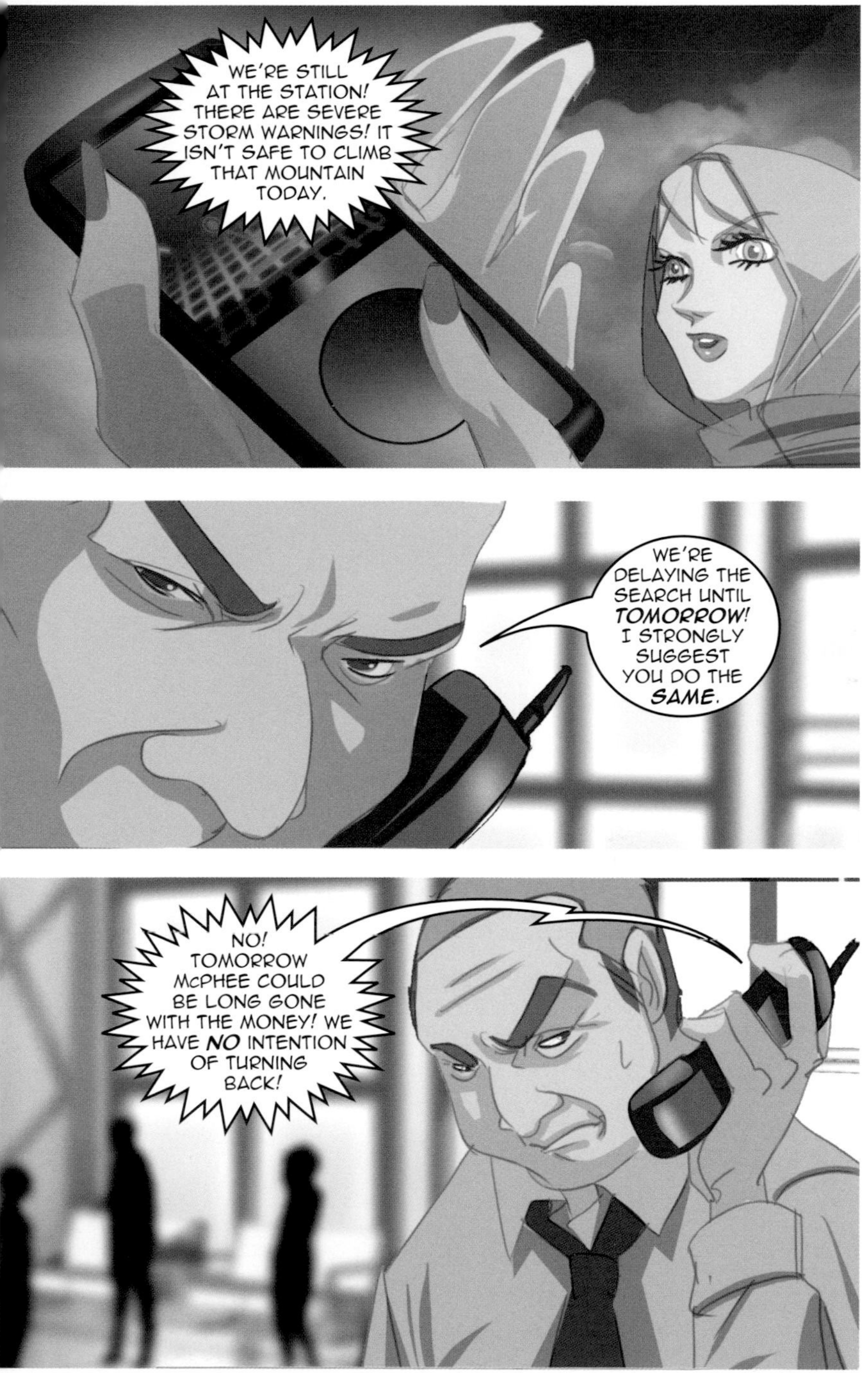

WE'RE STILL AT THE STATION! THERE ARE SEVERE STORM WARNINGS! IT ISN'T SAFE TO CLIMB THAT MOUNTAIN TODAY.
WE'RE DELAYING THE SEARCH UNTIL TOMORROW! I STRONGLY SUGGEST YOU DO THE SAME.
NO! TOMORROW McPHEE COULD BE LONG GONE WITH THE MONEY! WE HAVE NO INTENTION OF TURNING BACK!

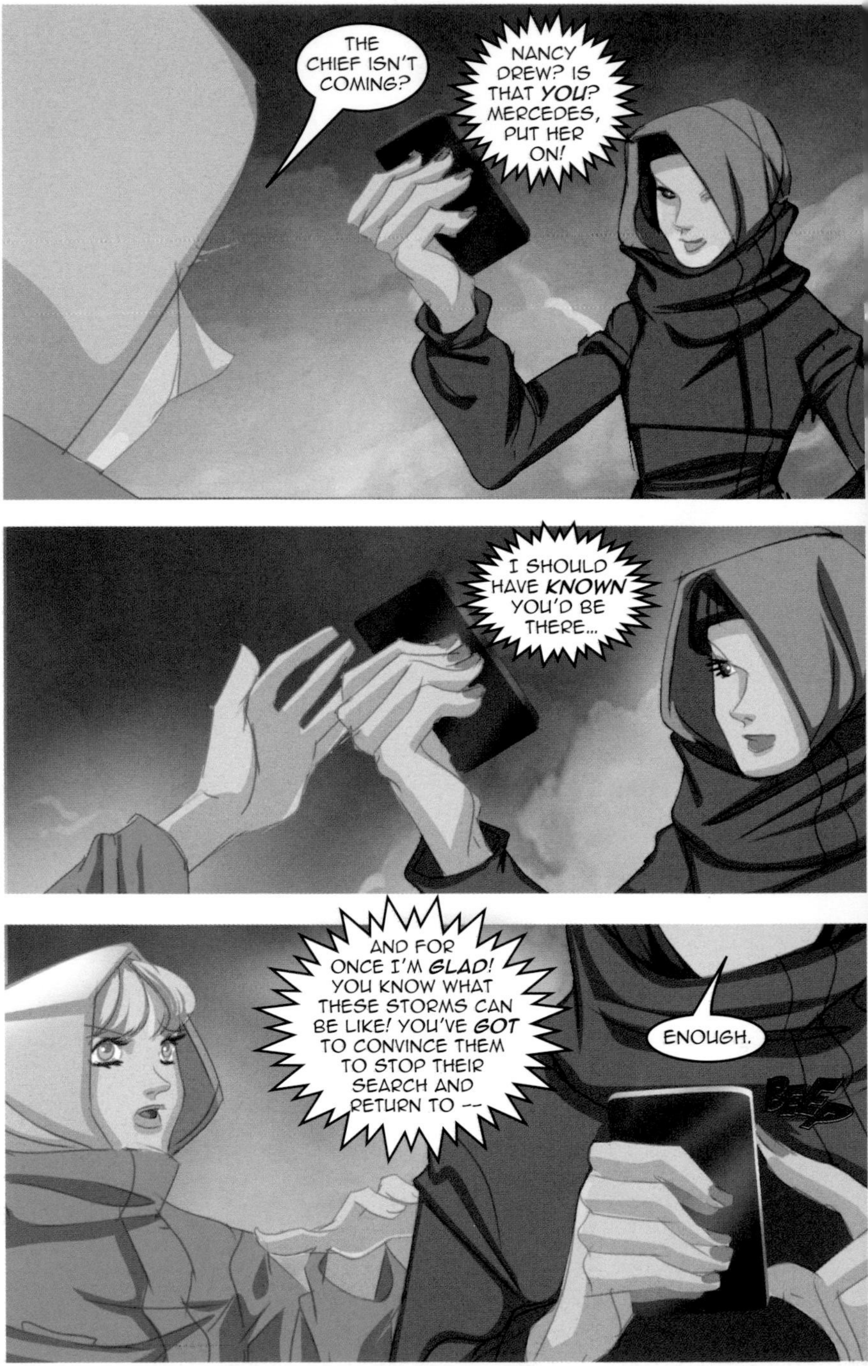
THE CHIEF ISN'T COMING?
NANCY DREW? IS THAT YOU? MERCEDES, PUT HER ON!
I SHOULD HAVE KNOWN YOU'D BE THERE...
AND FOR ONCE I'M GLAD! YOU KNOW WHAT THESE STORMS CAN BE LIKE! YOU'VE GOT TO CONVINCE THEM TO STOP THEIR SEARCH AND RETURN TO --
ENOUGH.

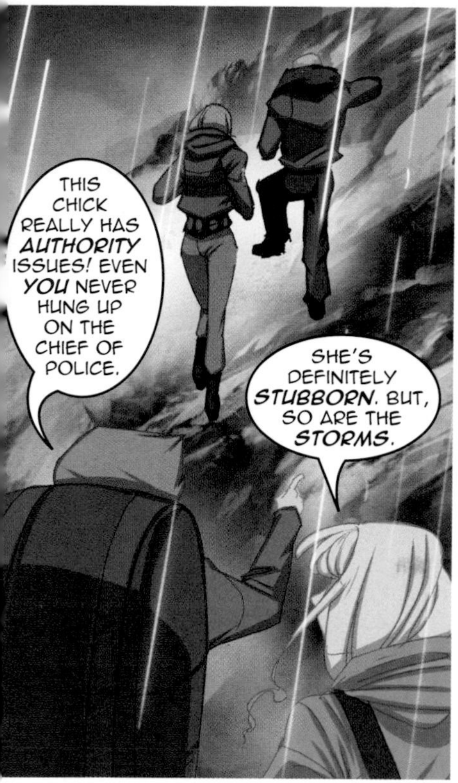
THIS CHICK REALLY HAS AUTHORITY ISSUES! EVEN YOU NEVER HUNG UP ON THE CHIEF OF POLICE.
SHE'S DEFINITELY STUBBORN. BUT, SO ARE THE STORMS.

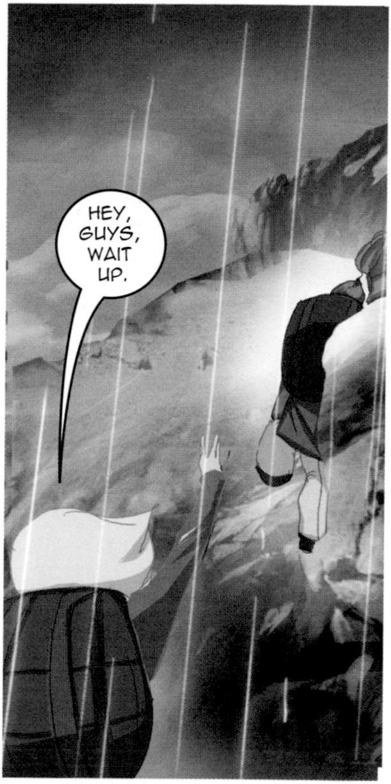
HEY, GUYS, WAIT UP.

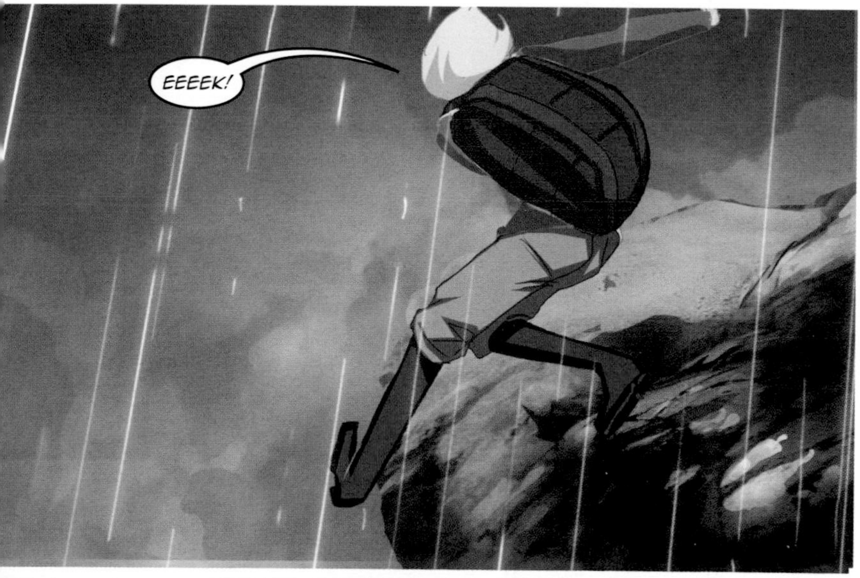
EEEEK!

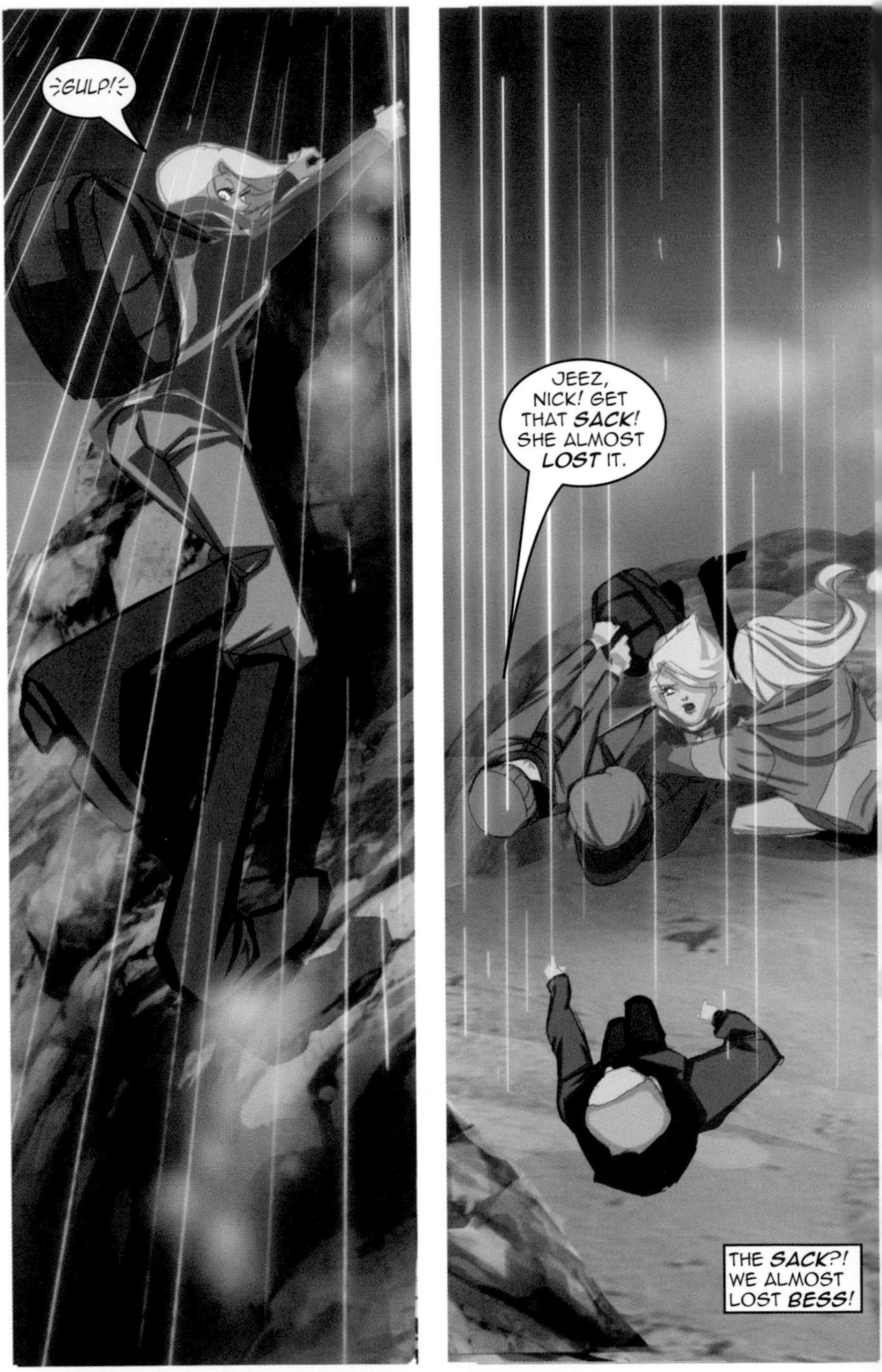
GULP!
JEEZ, NICK! GET THAT SACK! SHE ALMOST LOST IT.
THE SACK?! WE ALMOST LOST BESS!

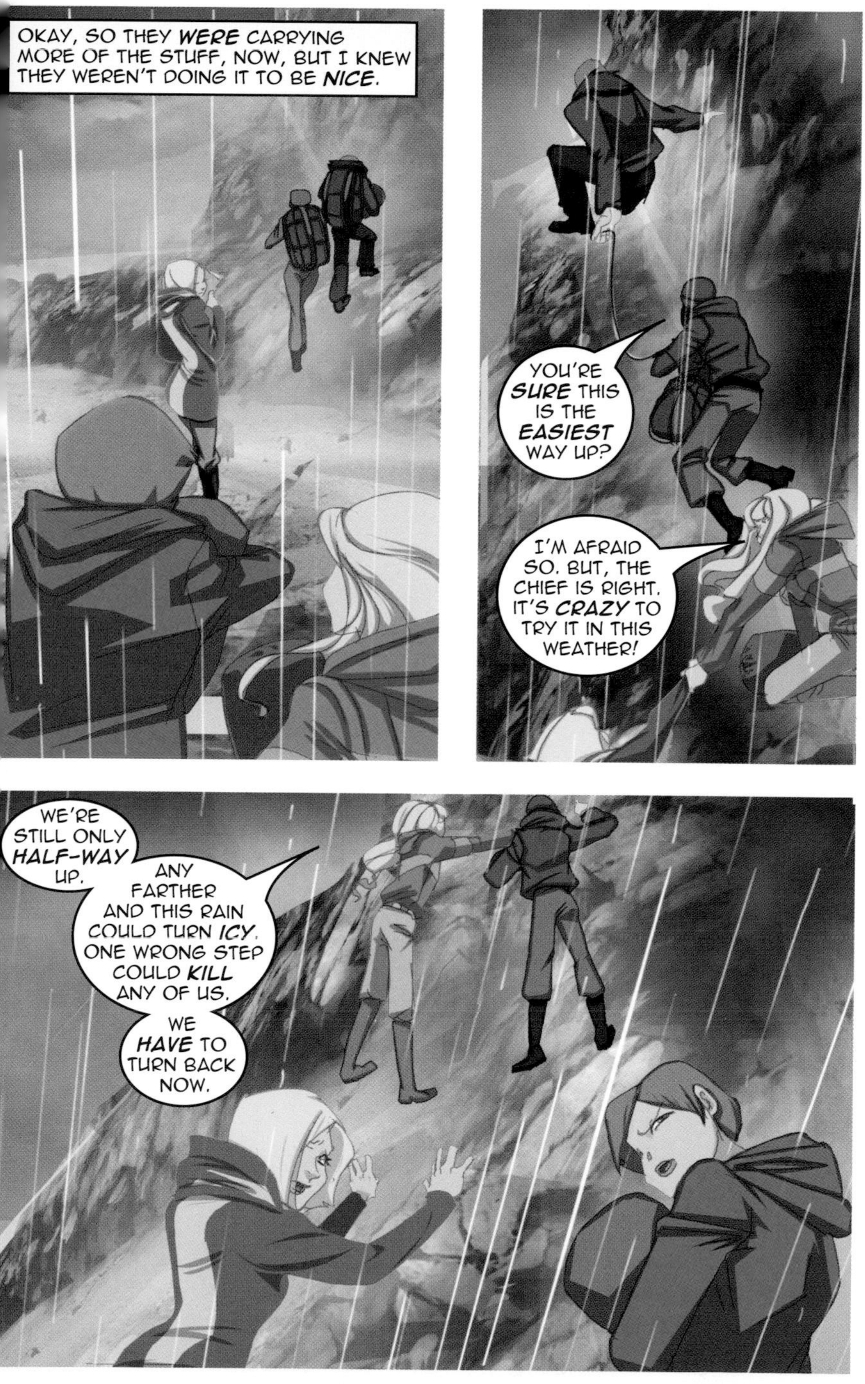
OKAY, SO THEY WERE CARRYING MORE OF THE STUFF, NOW, BUT I KNEW THEY WEREN'T DOING IT TO BE NICE.
YOU'RE SURE THIS IS THE EASIEST WAY UP?
I'M AFRAID SO. BUT, THE CHIEF IS RIGHT. IT'S CRAZY TO TRY IT IN THIS WEATHER!
WE'RE STILL ONLY HALF-WAY UP.
ANY FARTHER AND THIS RAIN COULD TURN ICY. ONE WRONG STEP COULD KILL ANY OF US.
WE HAVE TO TURN BACK NOW.

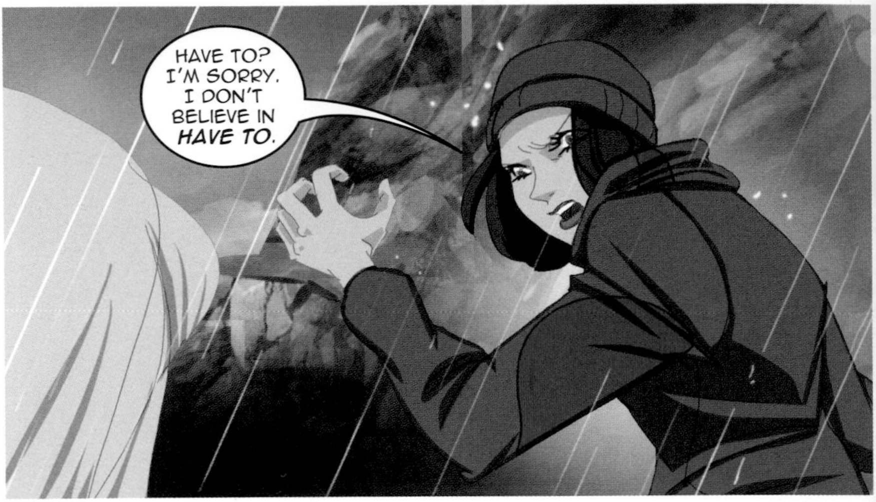
HAVE TO? I'M SORRY. I DON'T BELIEVE IN *HAVE TO*.

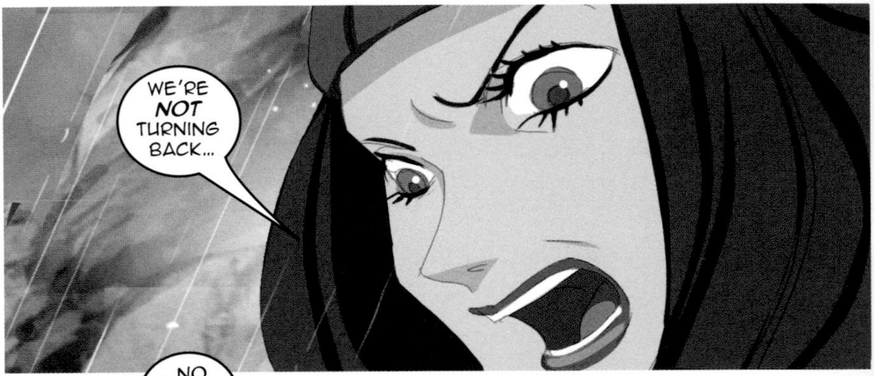
WE'RE *NOT* TURNING BACK...

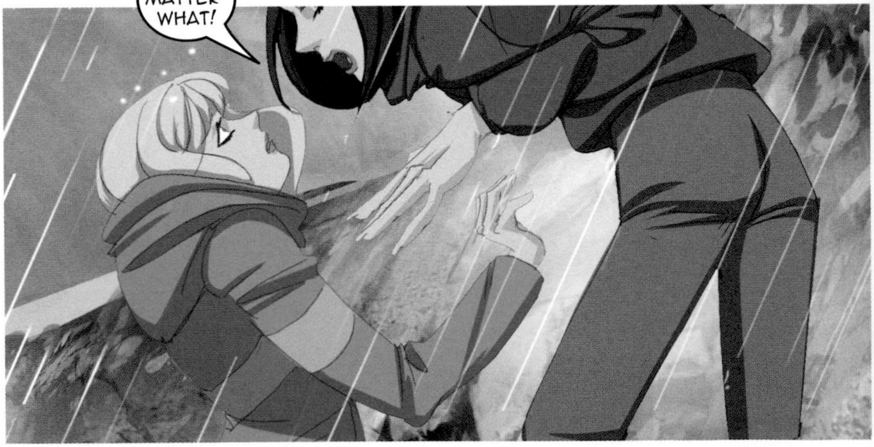
...NO MATTER WHAT!

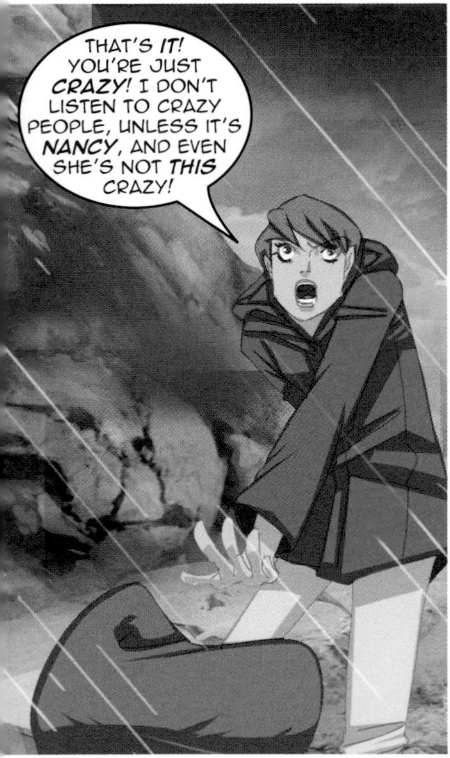
THAT'S IT! YOU'RE JUST CRAZY! I DON'T LISTEN TO CRAZY PEOPLE, UNLESS IT'S NANCY, AND EVEN SHE'S NOT THIS CRAZY!

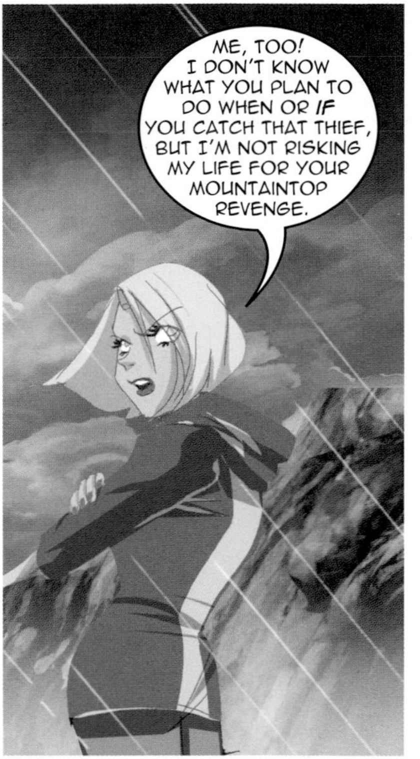
ME, TOO! I DON'T KNOW WHAT YOU PLAN TO DO WHEN OR IF YOU CATCH THAT THIEF, BUT I'M NOT RISKING MY LIFE FOR YOUR MOUNTAINTOP REVENGE.

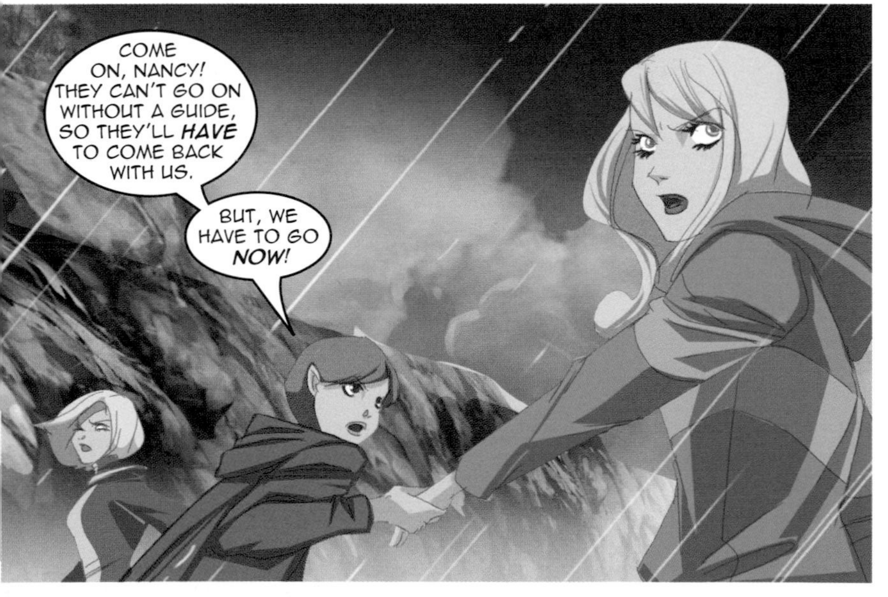
COME ON, NANCY! THEY CAN'T GO ON WITHOUT A GUIDE, SO THEY'LL HAVE TO COME BACK WITH US.
BUT, WE HAVE TO GO NOW!

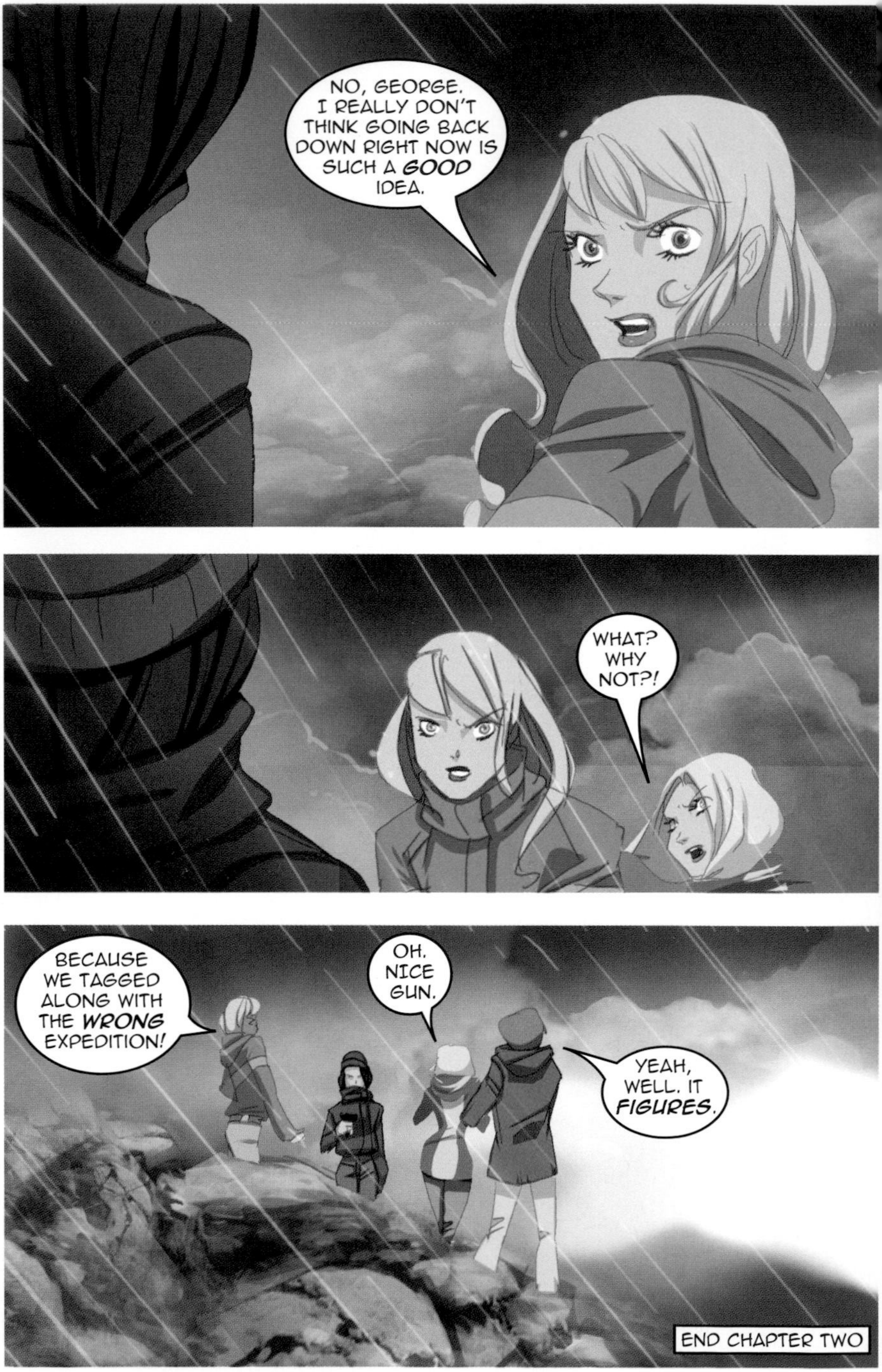

NO, GEORGE. I REALLY DON'T THINK GOING BACK DOWN RIGHT NOW IS SUCH A *GOOD* IDEA.
WHAT? WHY NOT?!
BECAUSE WE TAGGED ALONG WITH THE *WRONG* EXPEDITION!
OH. NICE GUN.
YEAH, WELL. IT *FIGURES*.
END CHAPTER TWO

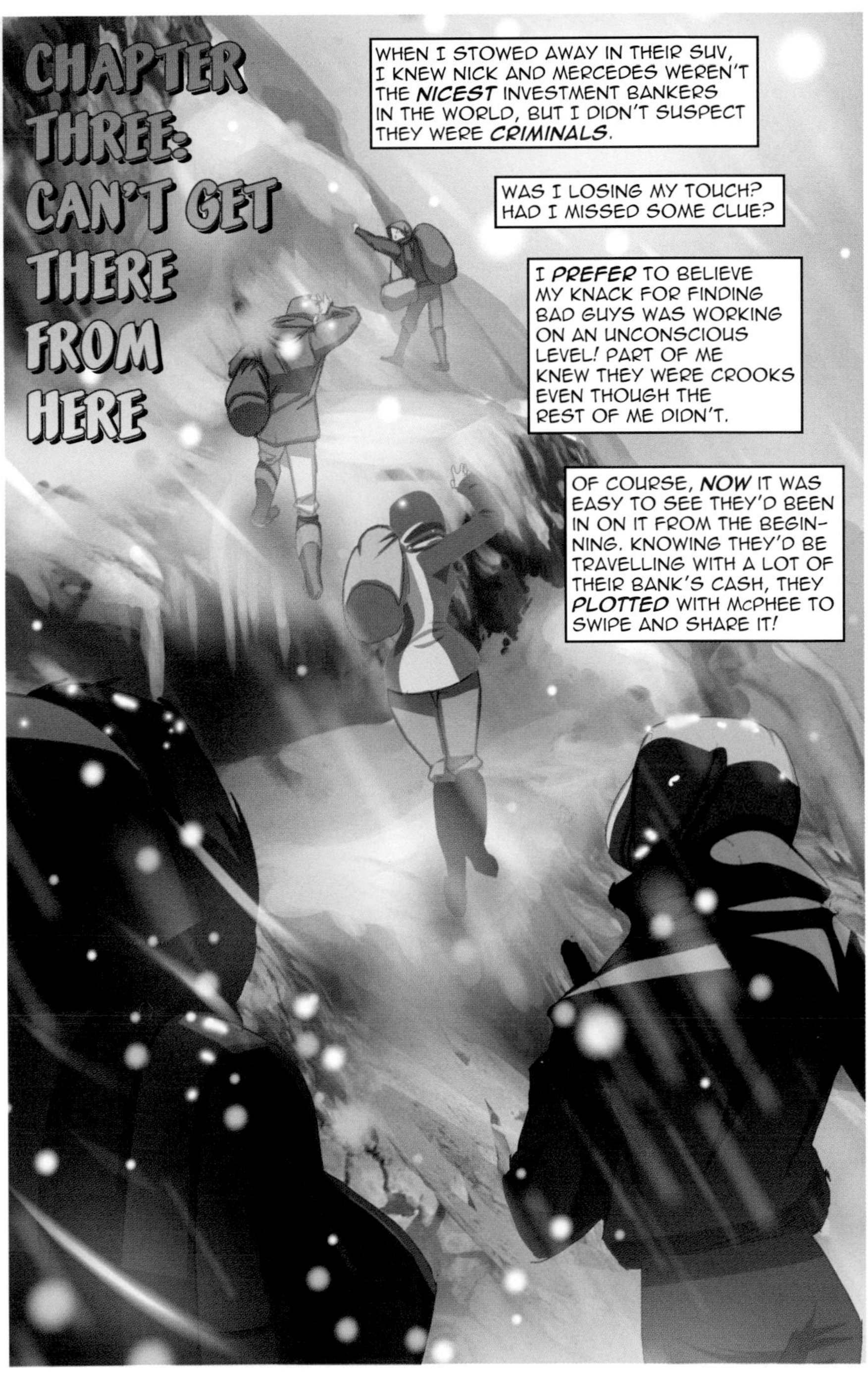
CHAPTER THREE: CAN'T GET THERE FROM HERE
WHEN I STOWED AWAY IN THEIR SUV, I KNEW NICK AND MERCEDES WEREN'T THE NICEST INVESTMENT BANKERS IN THE WORLD, BUT I DIDN'T SUSPECT THEY WERE CRIMINALS.
WAS I LOSING MY TOUCH? HAD I MISSED SOME CLUE?
I PREFER TO BELIEVE MY KNACK FOR FINDING BAD GUYS WAS WORKING ON AN UNCONSCIOUS LEVEL! PART OF ME KNEW THEY WERE CROOKS EVEN THOUGH THE REST OF ME DIDN'T.
OF COURSE, NOW IT WAS EASY TO SEE THEY'D BEEN IN ON IT FROM THE BEGINNING. KNOWING THEY'D BE TRAVELLING WITH A LOT OF THEIR BANK'S CASH, THEY PLOTTED WITH McPHEE TO SWIPE AND SHARE IT!

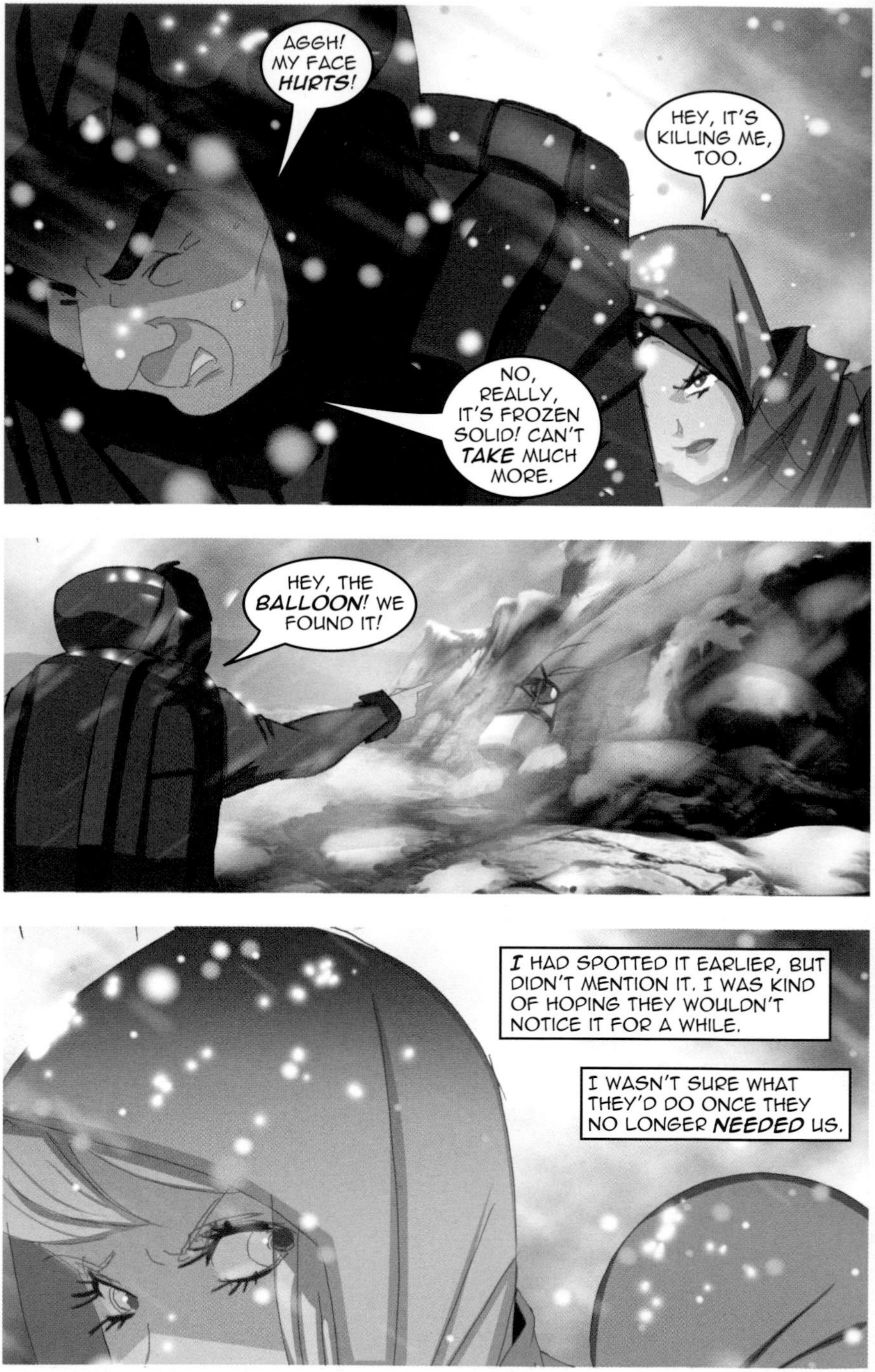
AGGH! MY FACE HURTS!
HEY, IT'S KILLING ME, TOO.
NO, REALLY, IT'S FROZEN SOLID! CAN'T TAKE MUCH MORE.
HEY, THE BALLOON! WE FOUND IT!
I HAD SPOTTED IT EARLIER, BUT DIDN'T MENTION IT. I WAS KIND OF HOPING THEY WOULDN'T NOTICE IT FOR A WHILE.
I WASN'T SURE WHAT THEY'D DO ONCE THEY NO LONGER NEEDED US.

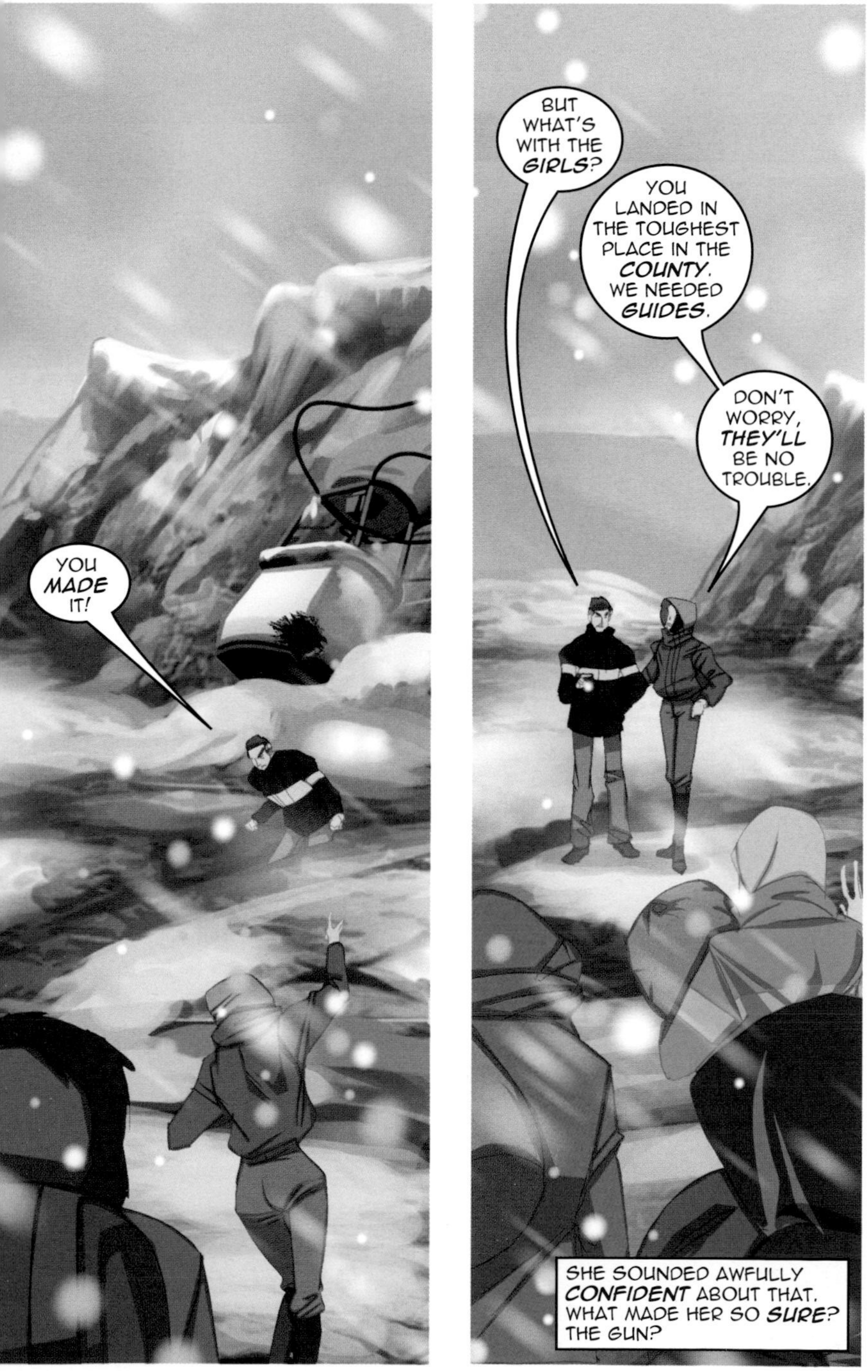
YOU MADE IT!
BUT WHAT'S WITH THE GIRLS?
YOU LANDED IN THE TOUGHEST PLACE IN THE COUNTY. WE NEEDED GUIDES.
DON'T WORRY, THEY'LL BE NO TROUBLE.
SHE SOUNDED AWFULLY CONFIDENT ABOUT THAT. WHAT MADE HER SO SURE? THE GUN?

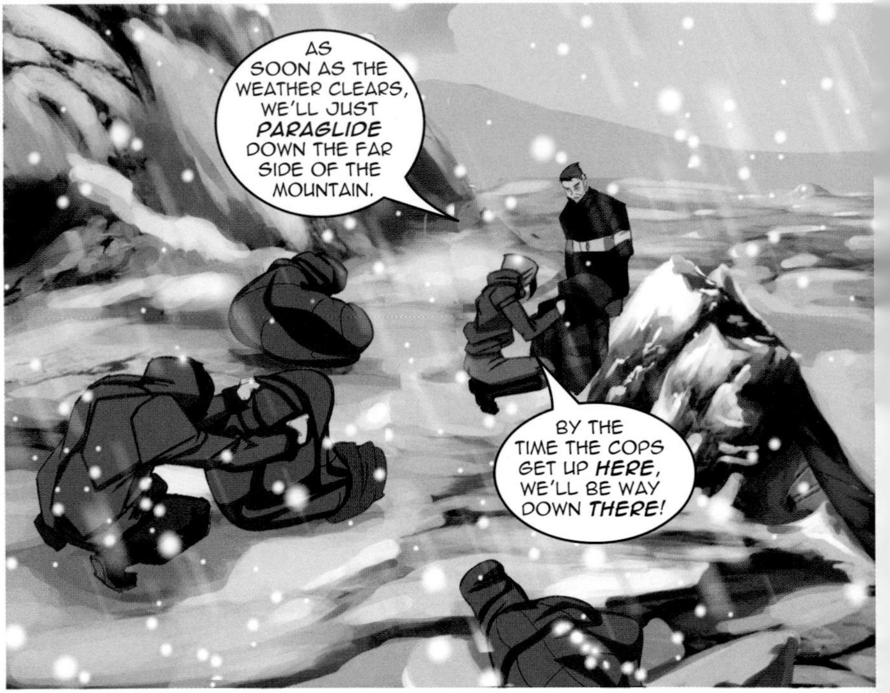
AS SOON AS THE WEATHER CLEARS, WE'LL JUST PARAGLIDE DOWN THE FAR SIDE OF THE MOUNTAIN.
BY THE TIME THE COPS GET UP HERE, WE'LL BE WAY DOWN THERE!

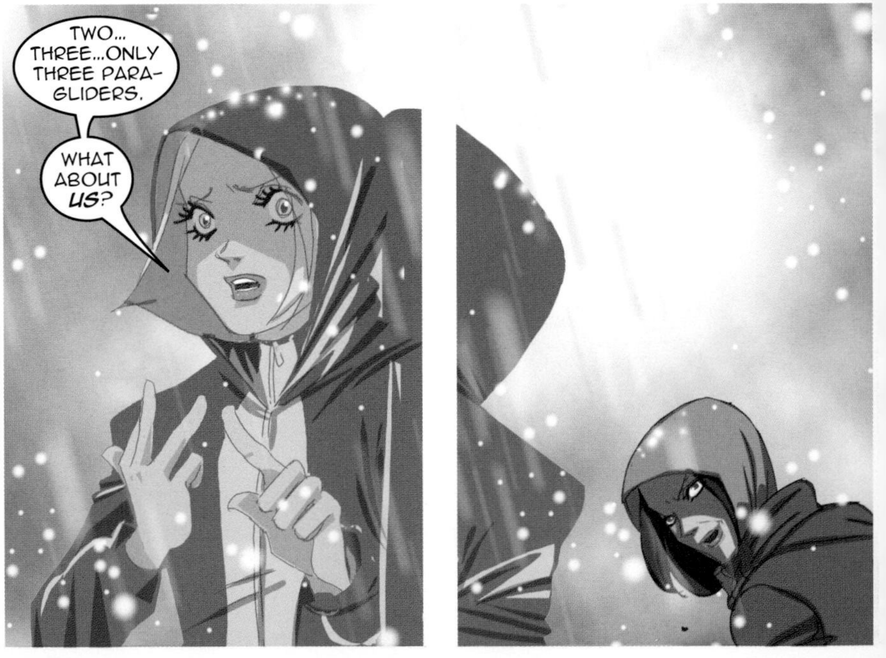
TWO... THREE...ONLY THREE PARA-GLIDERS.
WHAT ABOUT US?

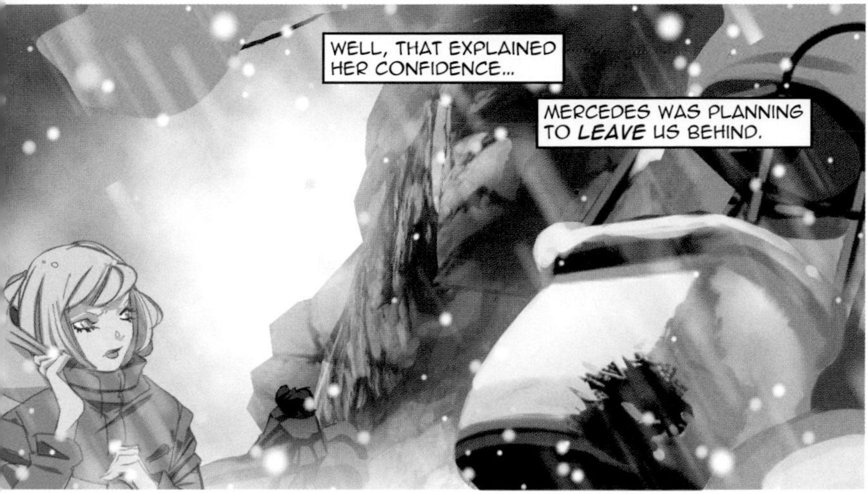
WELL, THAT EXPLAINED HER CONFIDENCE...
MERCEDES WAS PLANNING TO *LEAVE* US BEHIND.

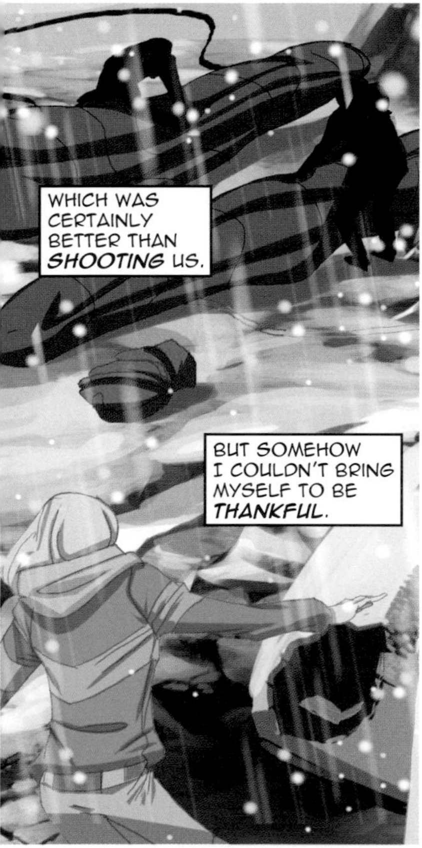
WHICH WAS CERTAINLY BETTER THAN *SHOOTING* US.
BUT SOMEHOW I COULDN'T BRING MYSELF TO BE *THANKFUL*.

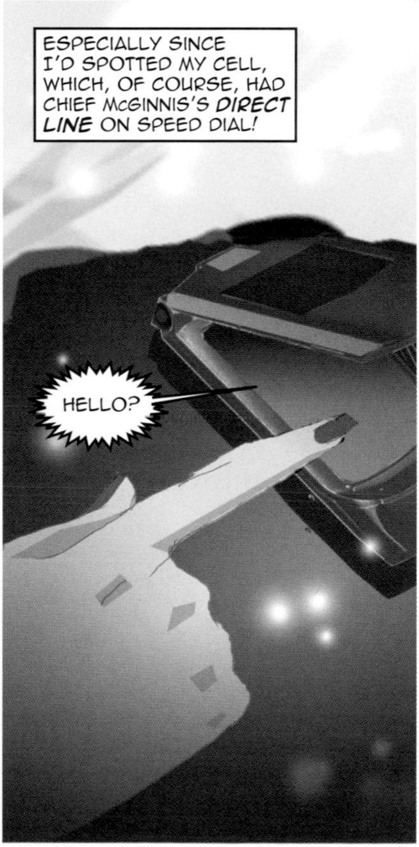
ESPECIALLY SINCE I'D SPOTTED MY CELL, WHICH, OF COURSE, HAD CHIEF McGINNIS'S *DIRECT LINE* ON SPEED DIAL!
HELLO?

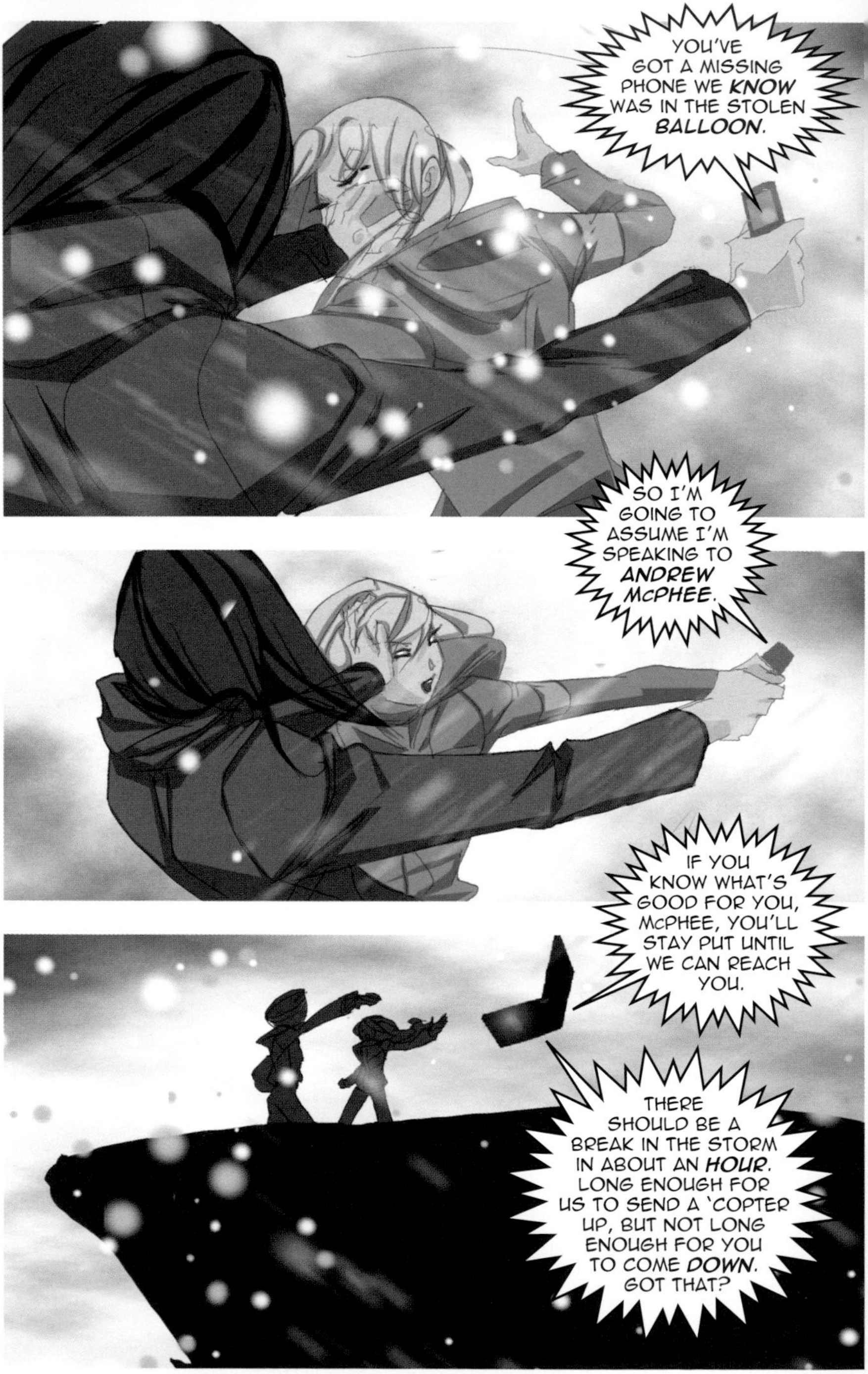
YOU'VE GOT A MISSING PHONE WE KNOW WAS IN THE STOLEN BALLOON.
SO I'M GOING TO ASSUME I'M SPEAKING TO ANDREW McPHEE.
IF YOU KNOW WHAT'S GOOD FOR YOU, McPHEE, YOU'LL STAY PUT UNTIL WE CAN REACH YOU.
THERE SHOULD BE A BREAK IN THE STORM IN ABOUT AN HOUR. LONG ENOUGH FOR US TO SEND A 'COPTER UP, BUT NOT LONG ENOUGH FOR YOU TO COME DOWN. GOT THAT?

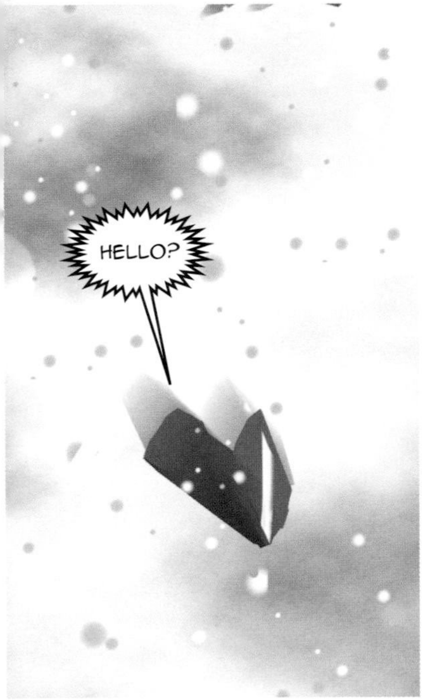
HELLO?

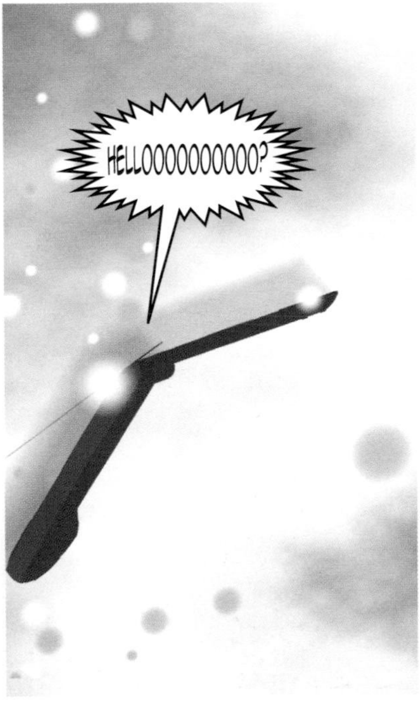
HELLOOOOOOOOOO?

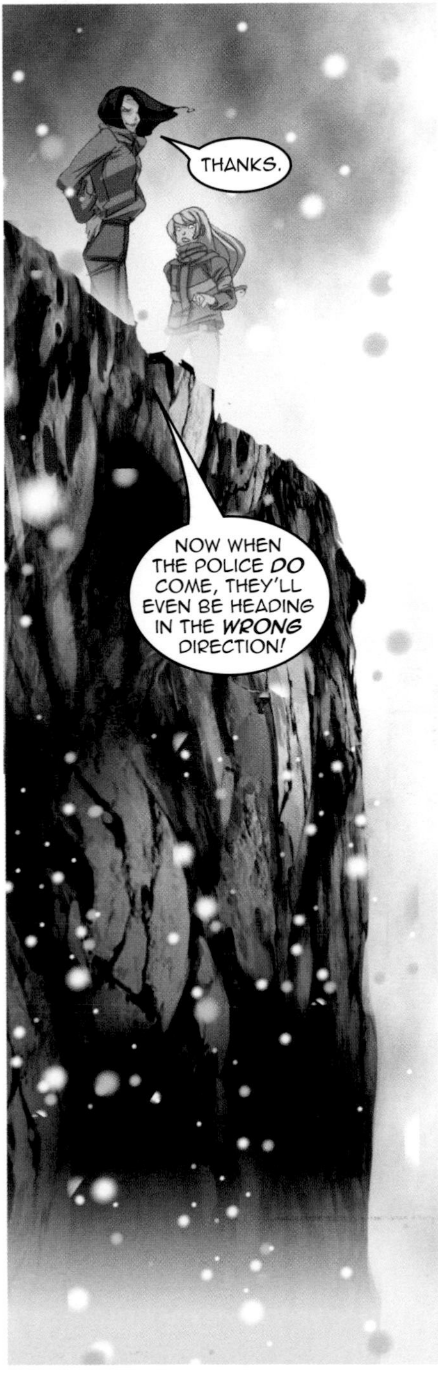
THANKS.
NOW WHEN THE POLICE DO COME, THEY'LL EVEN BE HEADING IN THE WRONG DIRECTION!

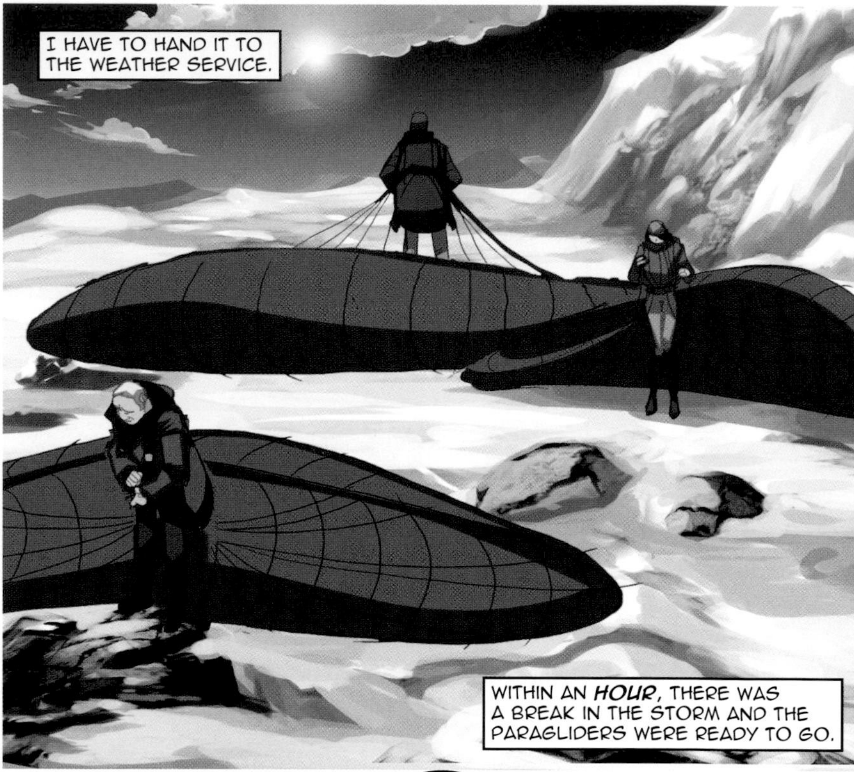
I HAVE TO HAND IT TO THE WEATHER SERVICE.
WITHIN AN ***HOUR***, THERE WAS A BREAK IN THE STORM AND THE PARAGLIDERS WERE READY TO GO.

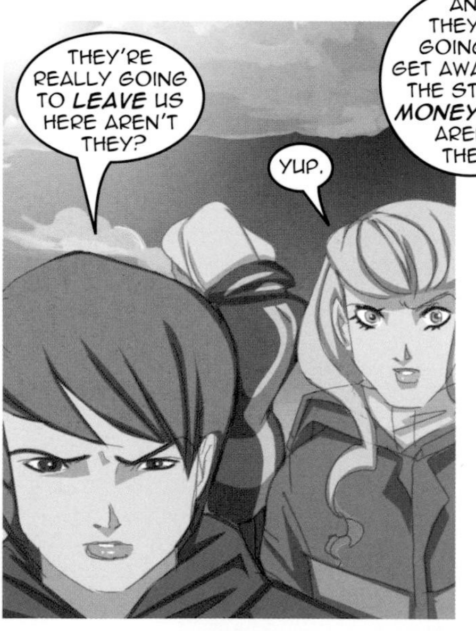
THEY'RE REALLY GOING TO ***LEAVE*** US HERE AREN'T THEY?
YUP.

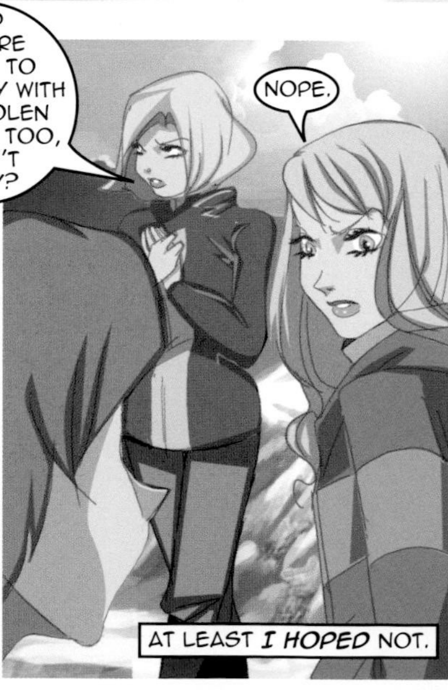
AND THEY'RE GOING TO GET AWAY WITH THE STOLEN ***MONEY***, TOO, AREN'T THEY?
NOPE.
AT LEAST ***I HOPED*** NOT.

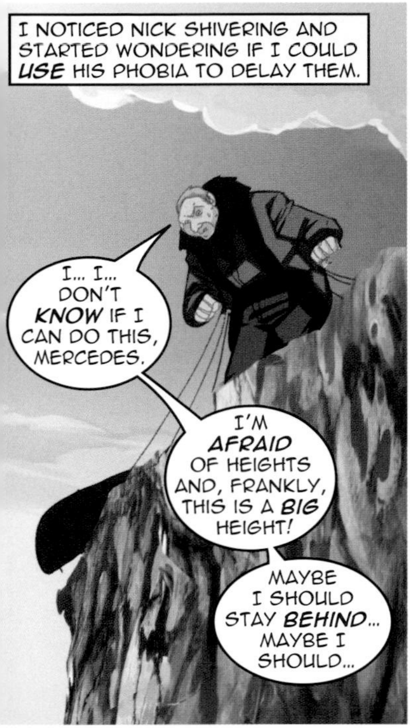
I NOTICED NICK SHIVERING AND STARTED WONDERING IF I COULD *USE* HIS PHOBIA TO DELAY THEM.
I... I... DON'T *KNOW* IF I CAN DO THIS, MERCEDES.
I'M *AFRAID* OF HEIGHTS AND, FRANKLY, THIS IS A *BIG* HEIGHT!
MAYBE I SHOULD STAY *BEHIND*... MAYBE I SHOULD...

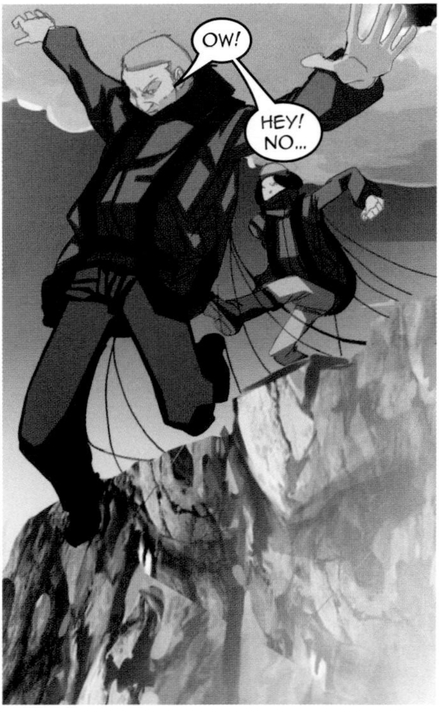
OW!
HEY! NO...

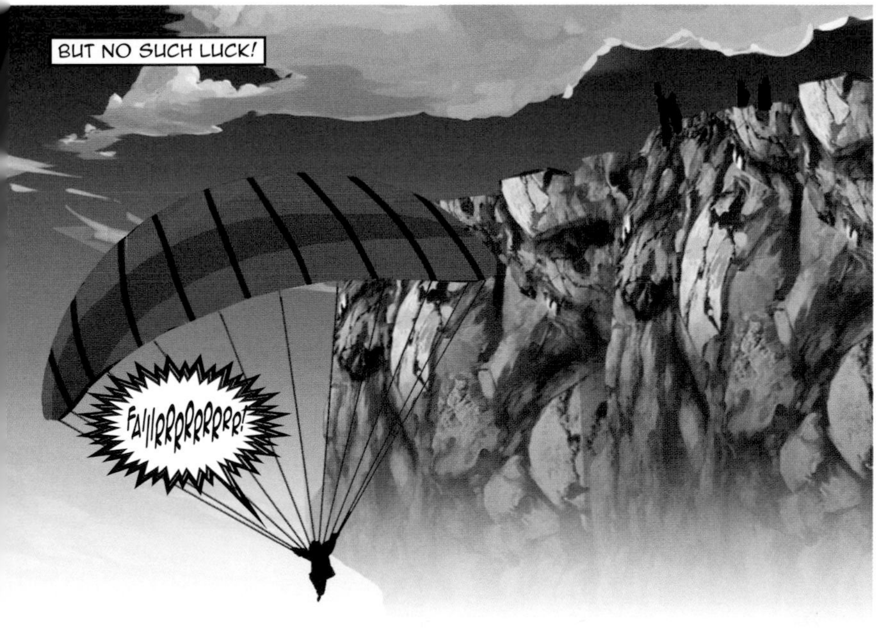
BUT NO SUCH LUCK!
FAIIIRRRRRRRR!

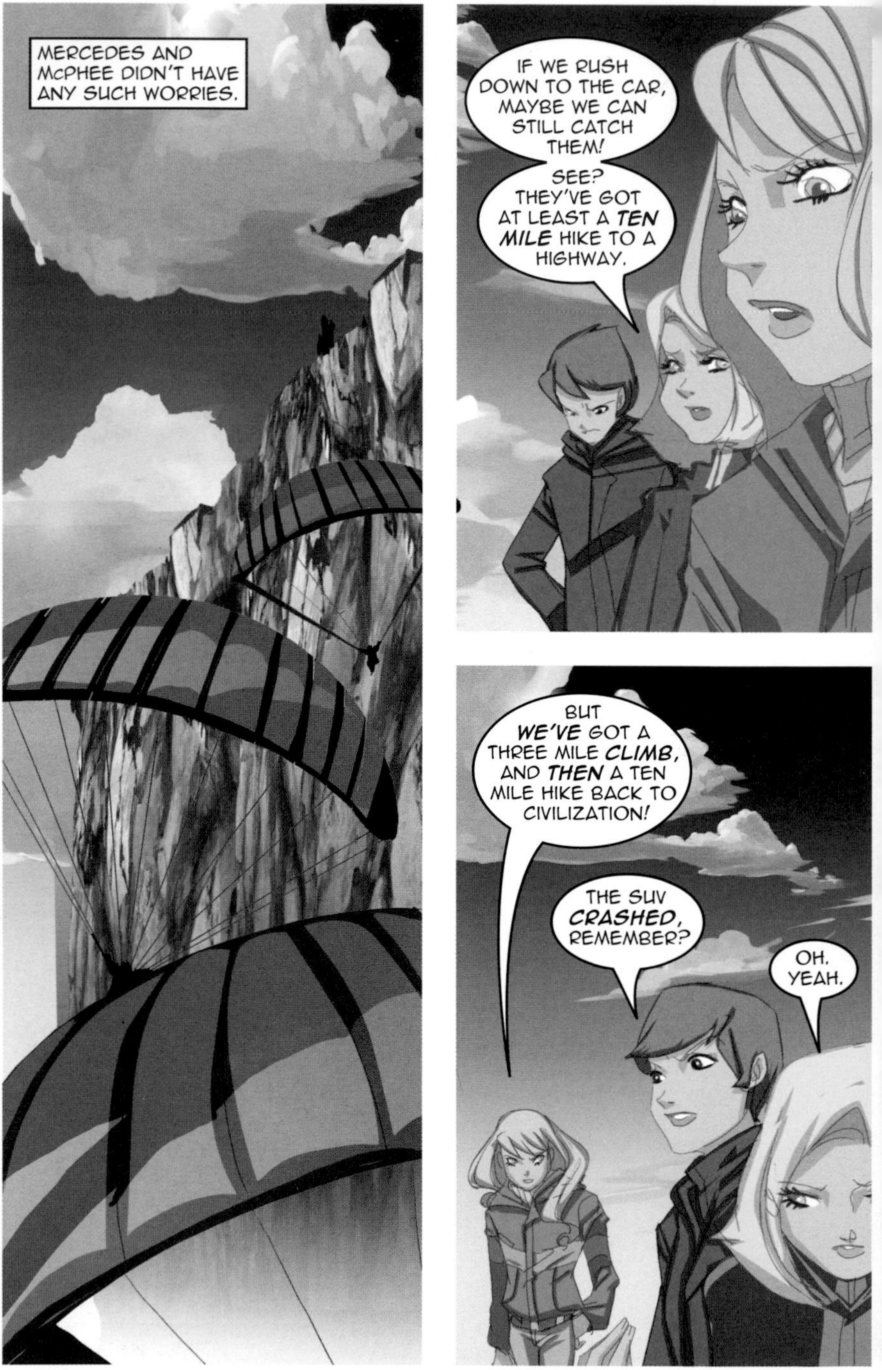
MERCEDES AND McPHEE DIDN'T HAVE ANY SUCH WORRIES.
IF WE RUSH DOWN TO THE CAR, MAYBE WE CAN STILL CATCH THEM!
SEE? THEY'VE GOT AT LEAST A TEN MILE HIKE TO A HIGHWAY.
BUT WE'VE GOT A THREE MILE CLIMB, AND THEN A TEN MILE HIKE BACK TO CIVILIZATION!
THE SUV CRASHED, REMEMBER?
OH. YEAH.

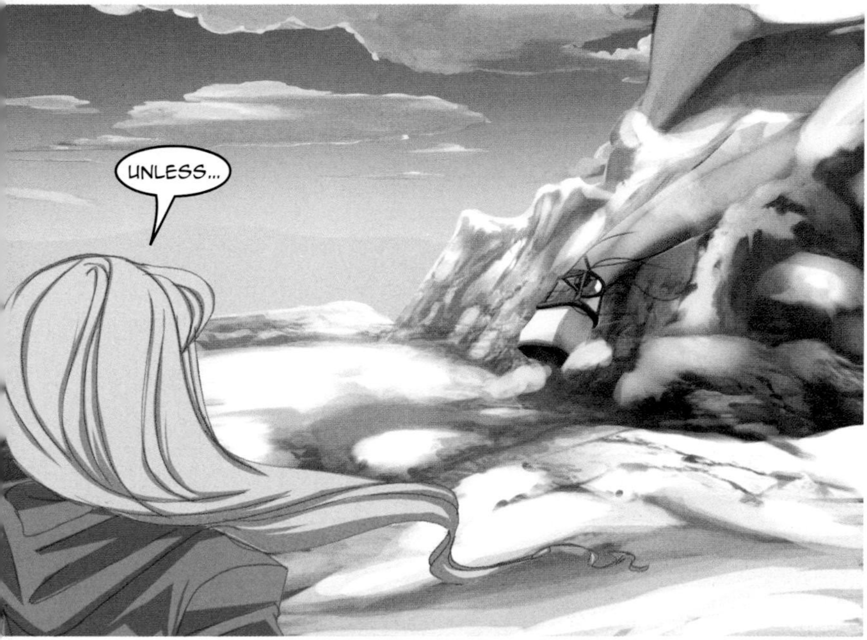
UNLESS...

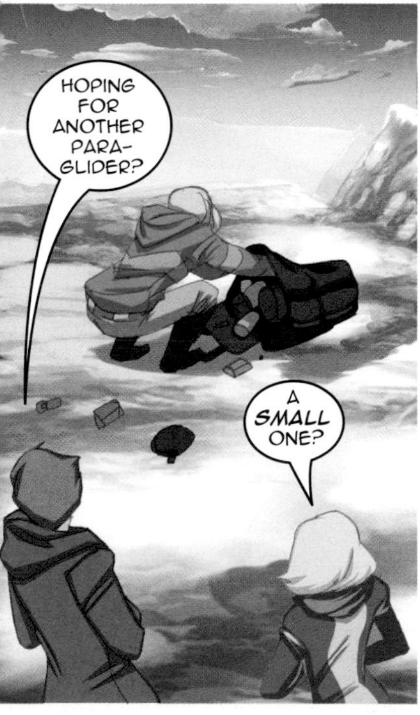
HOPING FOR ANOTHER PARA-GLIDER?
A SMALL ONE?

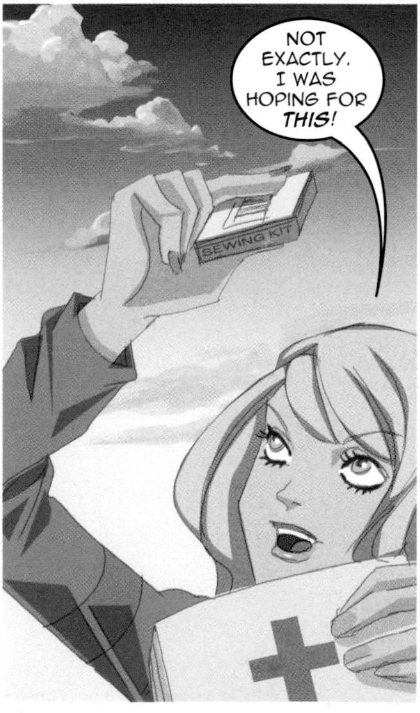
NOT EXACTLY. I WAS HOPING FOR THIS!
SEWING KIT

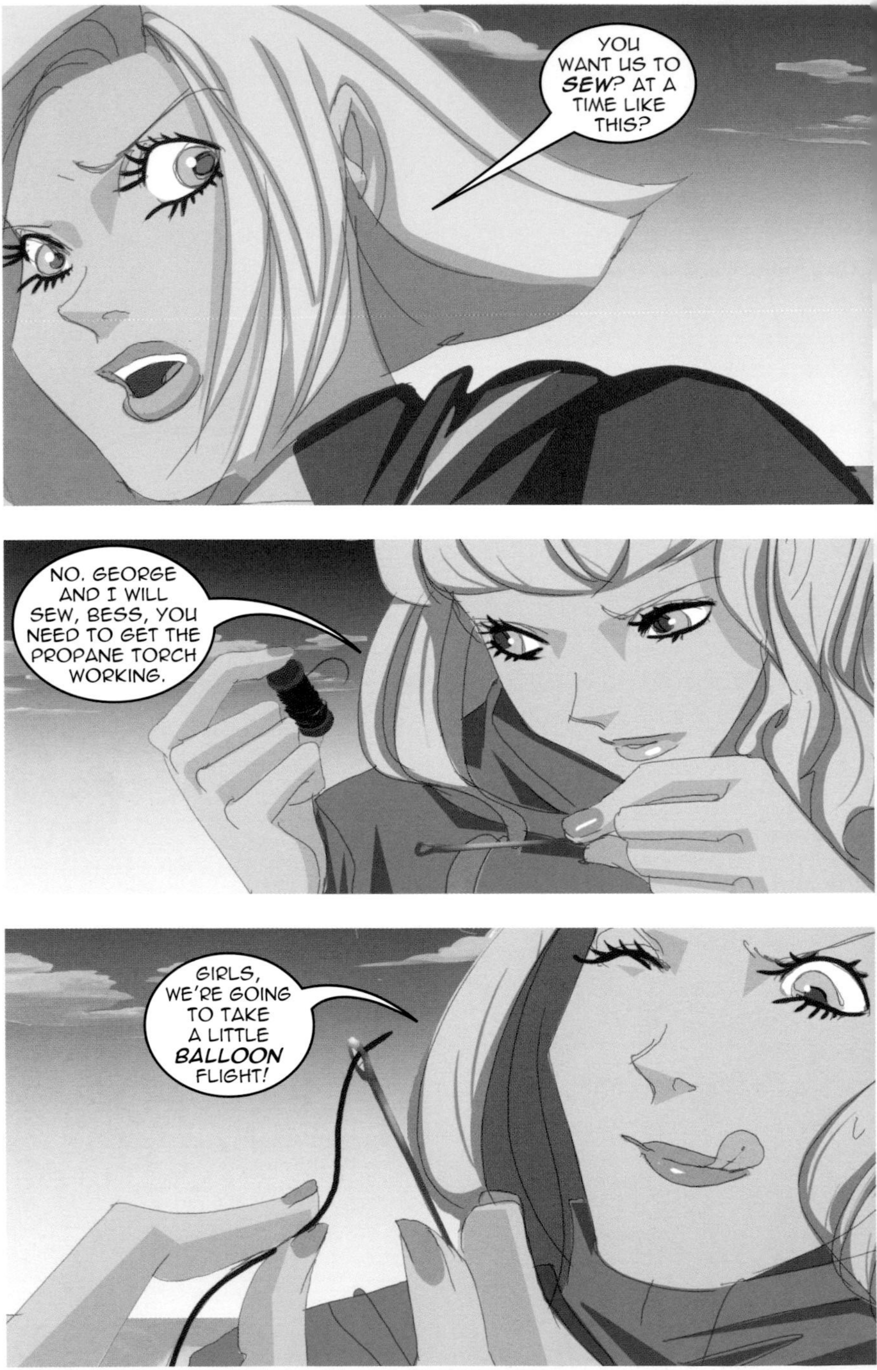
YOU WANT US TO SEW? AT A TIME LIKE THIS?
NO. GEORGE AND I WILL SEW, BESS, YOU NEED TO GET THE PROPANE TORCH WORKING.
GIRLS, WE'RE GOING TO TAKE A LITTLE BALLOON FLIGHT!

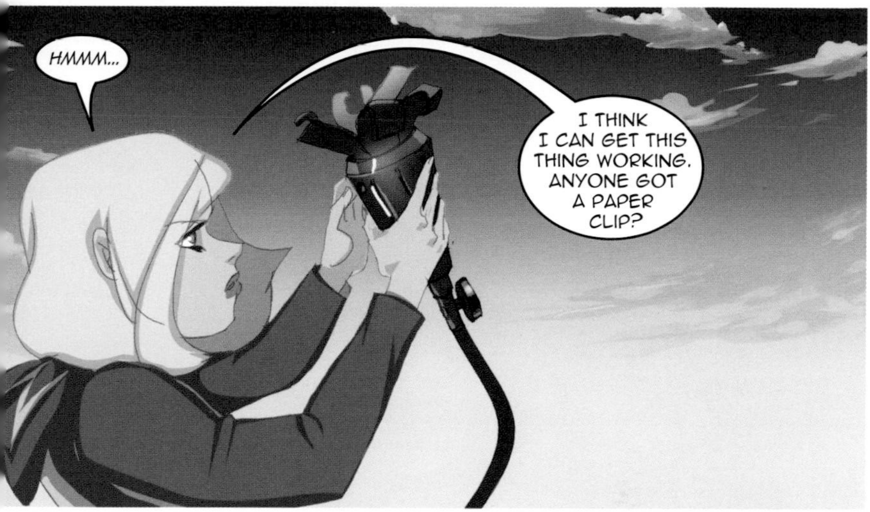
HMMM...
I THINK I CAN GET THIS THING WORKING. ANYONE GOT A PAPER CLIP?

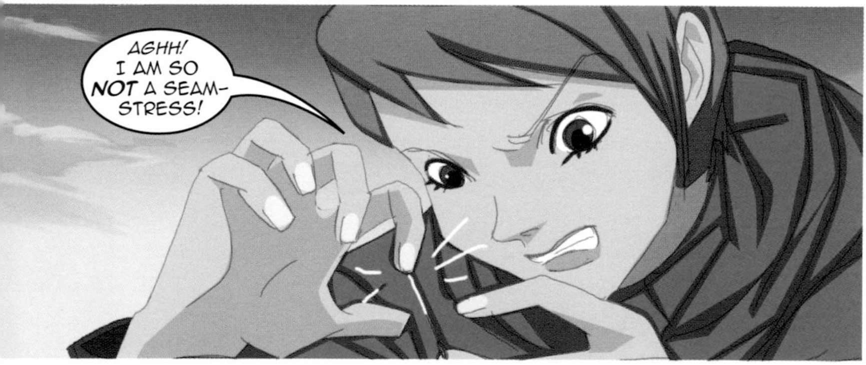
AGHH! I AM SO **NOT** A SEAMSTRESS!

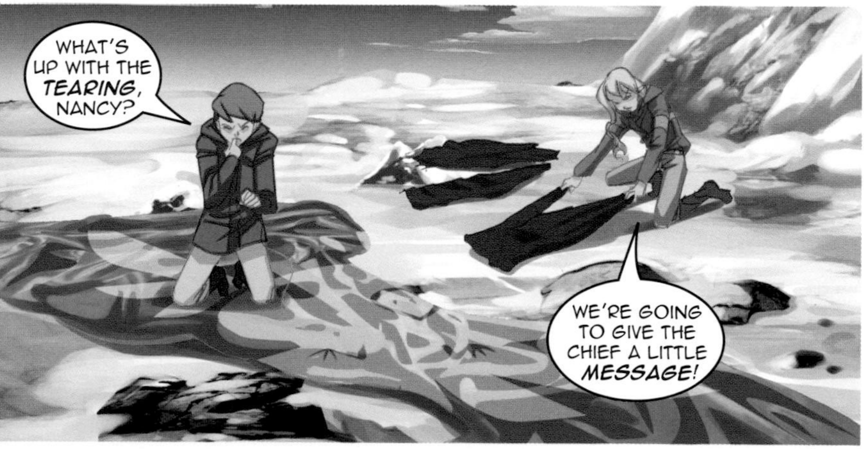
WHAT'S UP WITH THE ***TEARING***, NANCY?
WE'RE GOING TO GIVE THE CHIEF A LITTLE ***MESSAGE***!

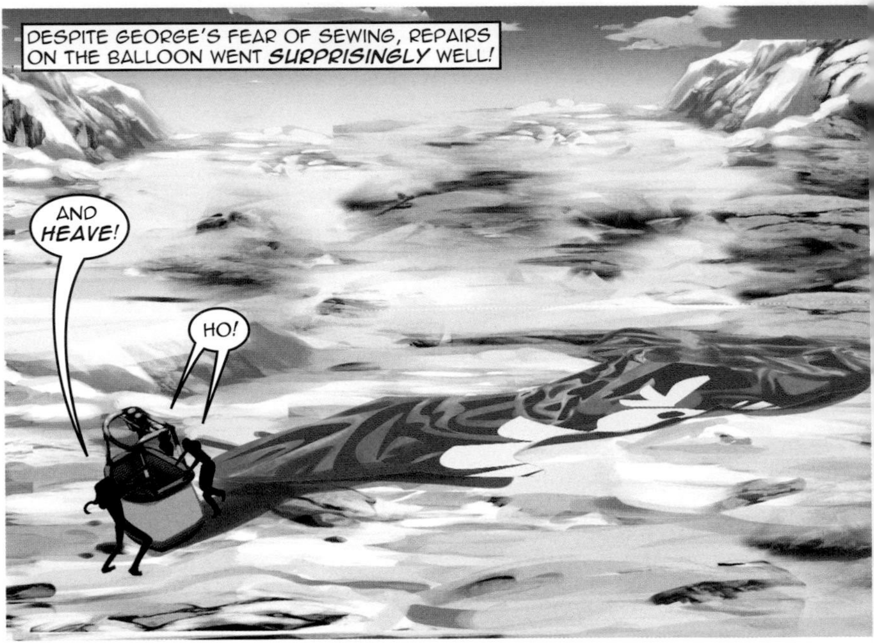
DESPITE GEORGE'S FEAR OF SEWING, REPAIRS ON THE BALLOON WENT SURPRISINGLY WELL!
AND HEAVE!
HO!

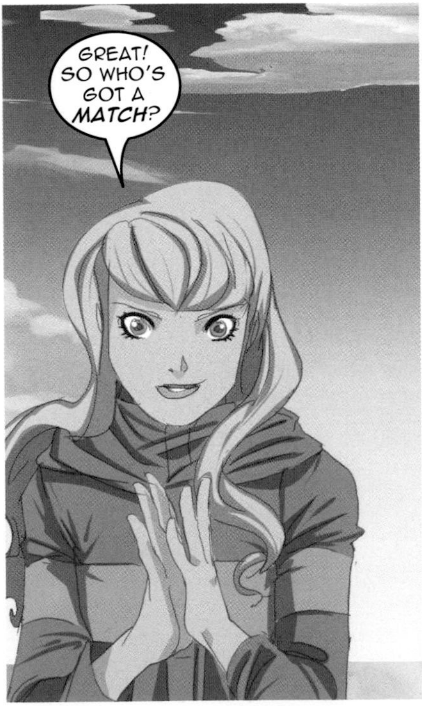
GREAT! SO WHO'S GOT A MATCH?

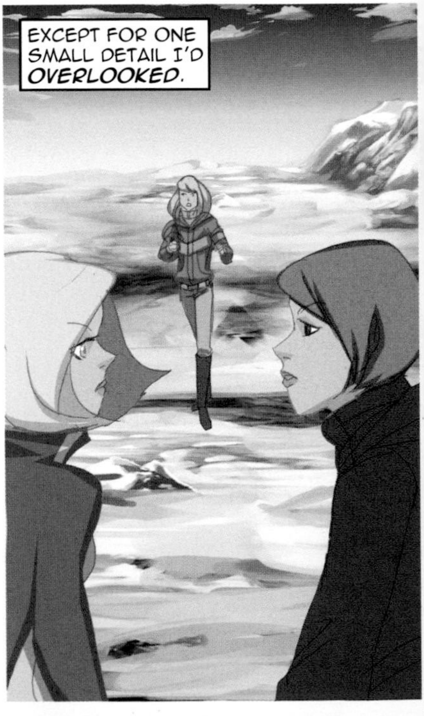
EXCEPT FOR ONE SMALL DETAIL I'D OVERLOOKED.

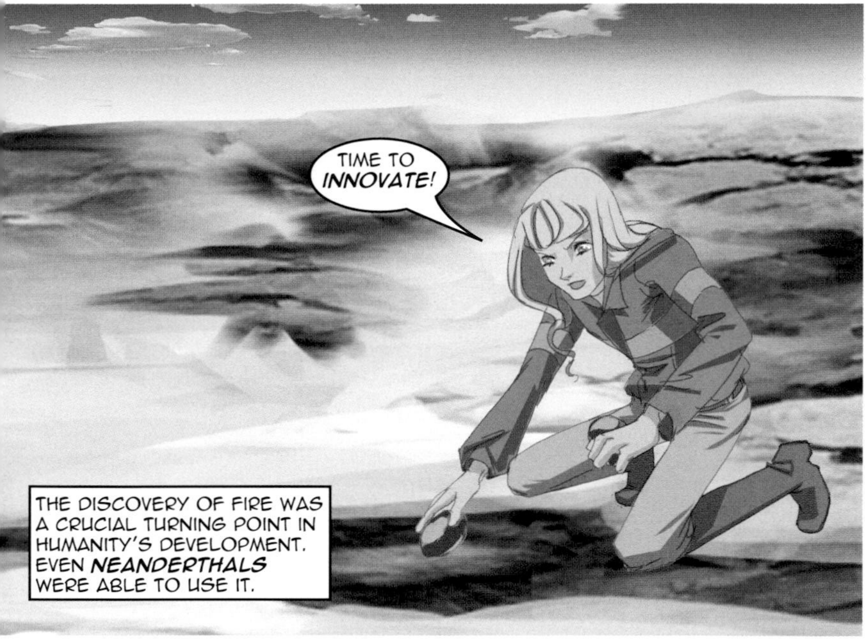
TIME TO *INNOVATE*!
THE DISCOVERY OF FIRE WAS A CRUCIAL TURNING POINT IN HUMANITY'S DEVELOPMENT. EVEN ***NEANDERTHALS*** WERE ABLE TO USE IT.

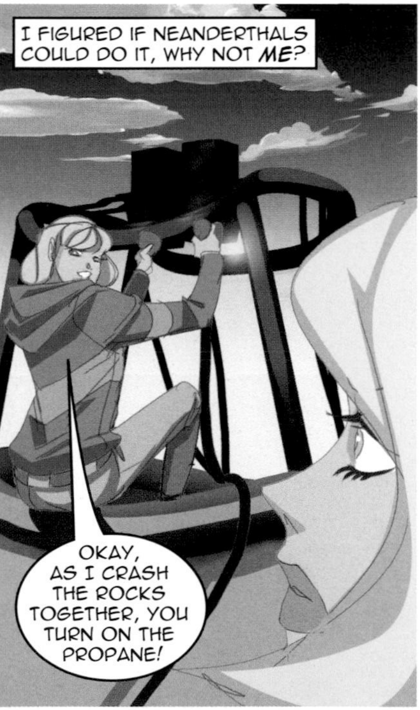
I FIGURED IF NEANDERTHALS COULD DO IT, WHY NOT ***ME***?
OKAY, AS I CRASH THE ROCKS TOGETHER, YOU TURN ON THE PROPANE!

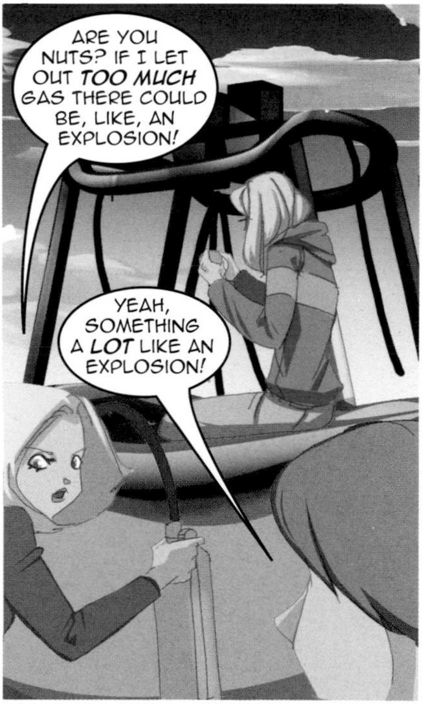
ARE YOU NUTS? IF I LET OUT ***TOO MUCH*** GAS THERE COULD BE, LIKE, AN EXPLOSION!
YEAH, SOMETHING A ***LOT*** LIKE AN EXPLOSION!

WISH ME LUCK, THEN!
GOOD LUCK! ULP!
IF I WORKED FAST, THERE WOULDN'T BE ENOUGH PROPANE TO CAUSE A PROBLEM.
I HOPED.
ALL I NEEDED WAS ONE LITTLE SPARK!

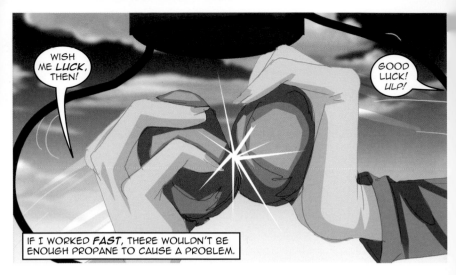

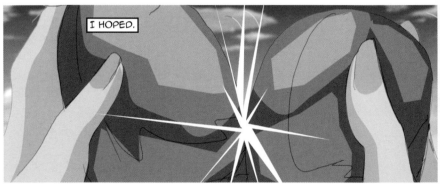

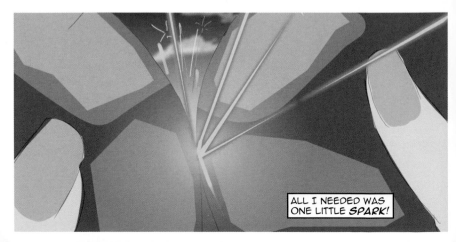

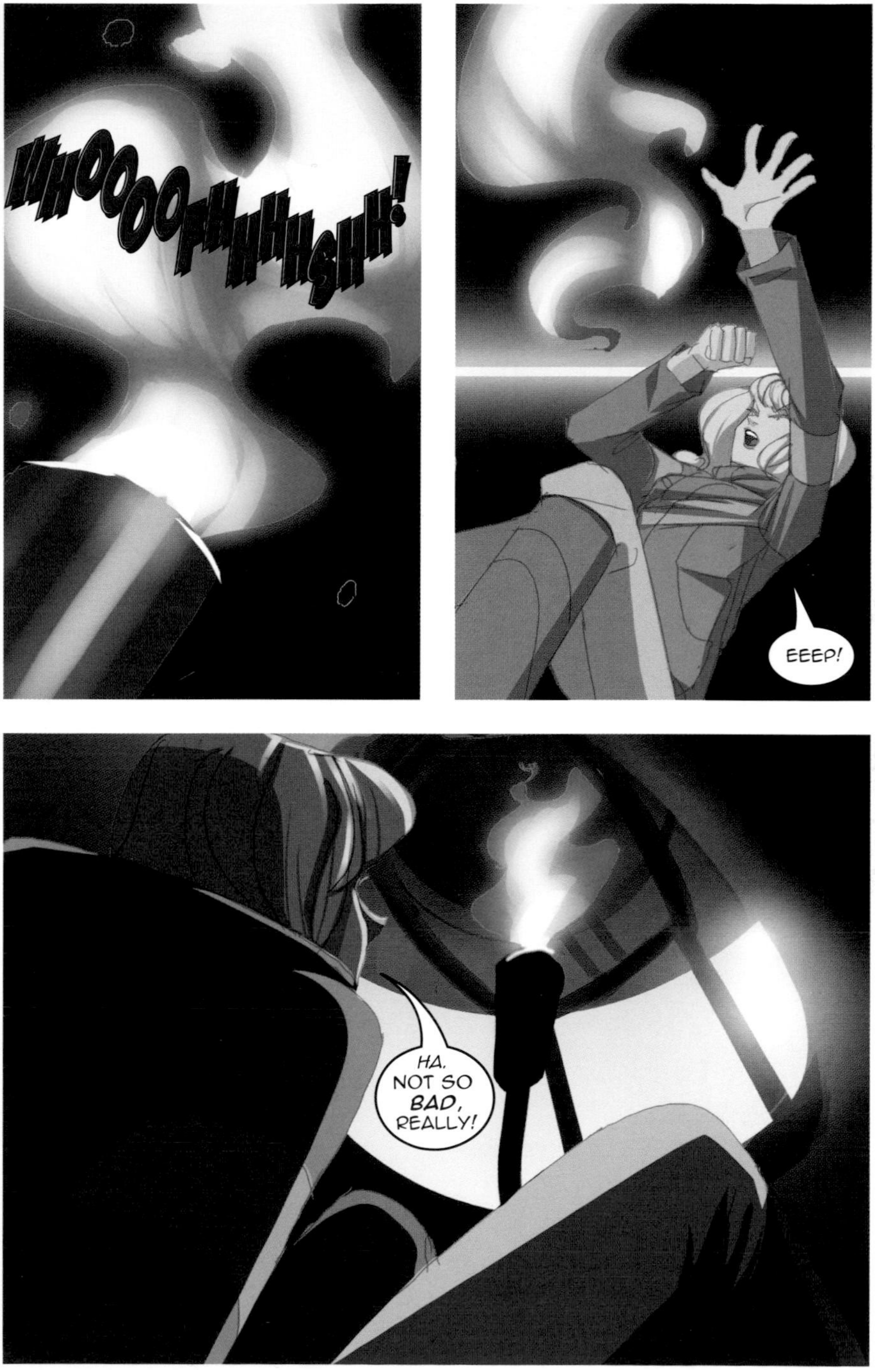
WHOOOOPHHHHSHH!
EEEP!
HA, NOT SO BAD, REALLY!

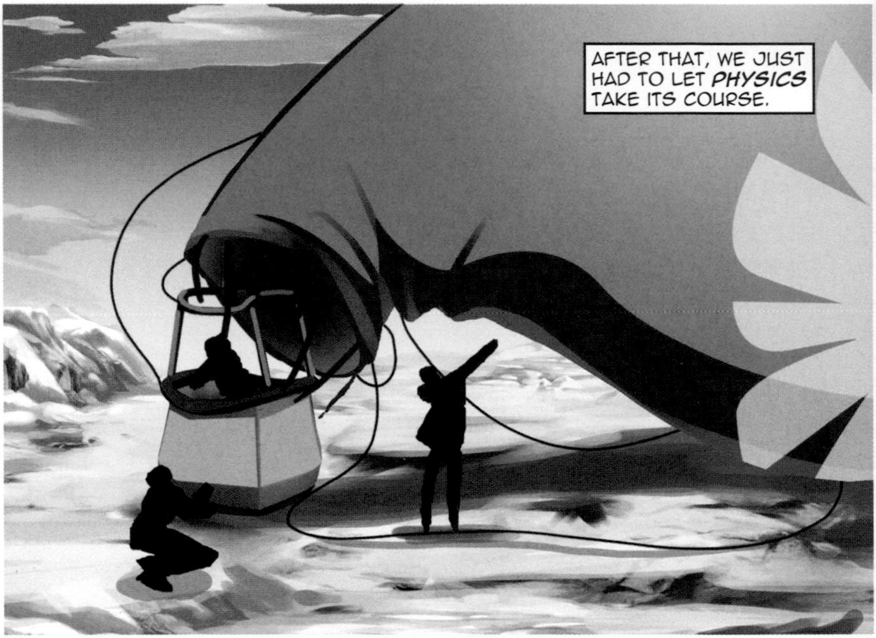
AFTER THAT, WE JUST HAD TO LET *PHYSICS* TAKE ITS COURSE.

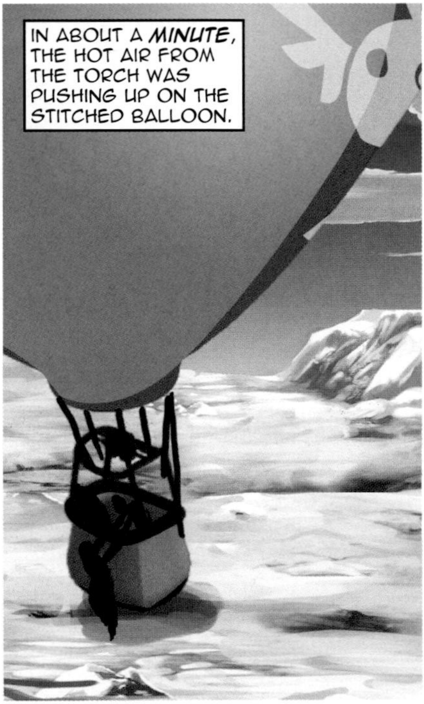
IN ABOUT A *MINUTE*, THE HOT AIR FROM THE TORCH WAS PUSHING UP ON THE STITCHED BALLOON.

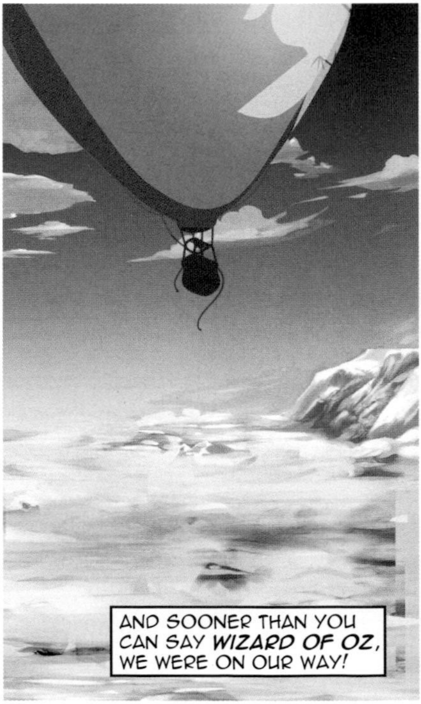
AND SOONER THAN YOU CAN SAY *WIZARD OF OZ*, WE WERE ON OUR WAY!

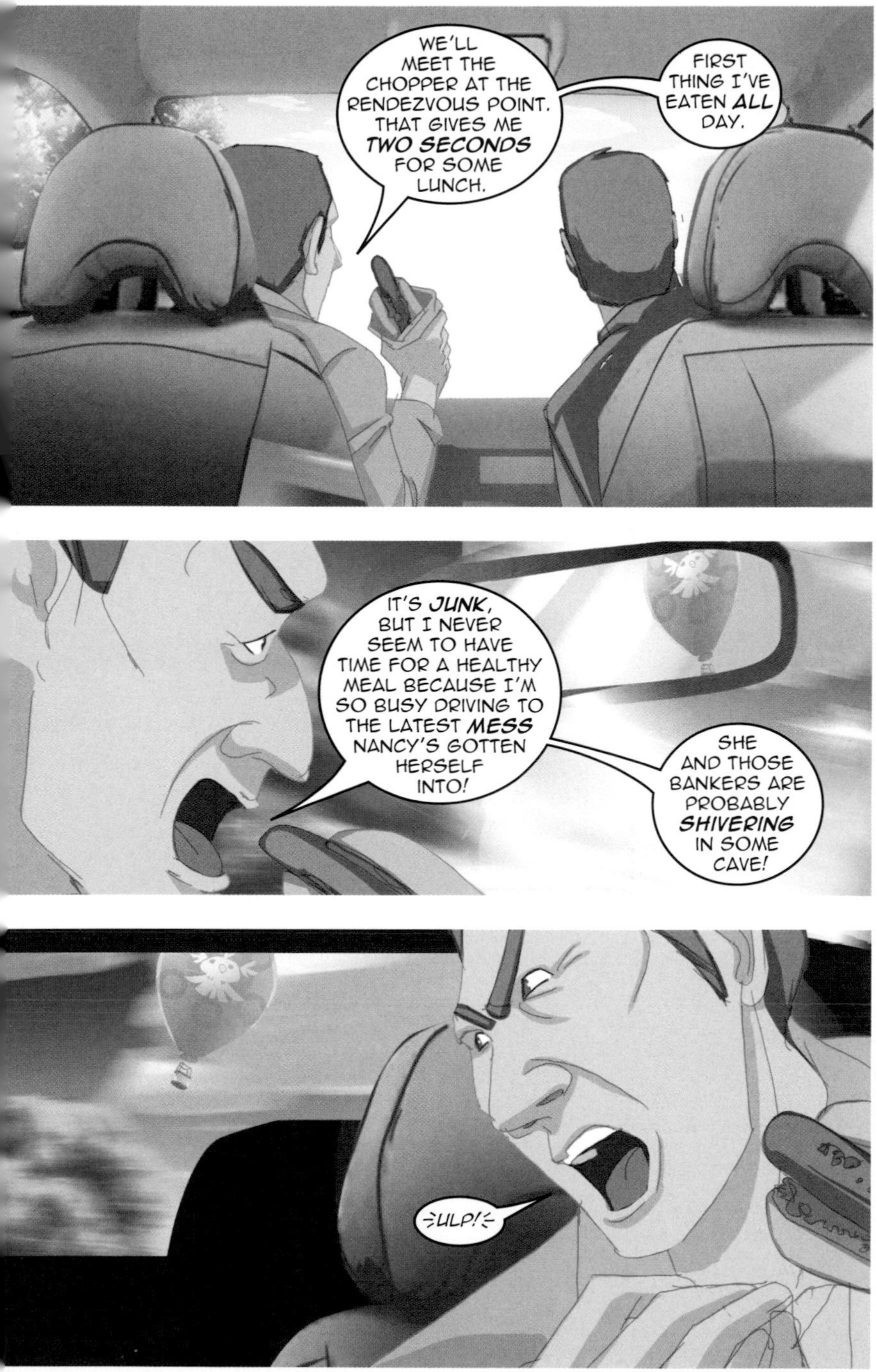
WE'LL MEET THE CHOPPER AT THE RENDEZVOUS POINT. THAT GIVES ME **TWO SECONDS** FOR SOME LUNCH.
FIRST THING I'VE EATEN **ALL** DAY.
IT'S **JUNK**, BUT I NEVER SEEM TO HAVE TIME FOR A HEALTHY MEAL BECAUSE I'M SO BUSY DRIVING TO THE LATEST **MESS** NANCY'S GOTTEN HERSELF INTO!
SHE AND THOSE BANKERS ARE PROBABLY **SHIVERING** IN SOME CAVE!
ULP!

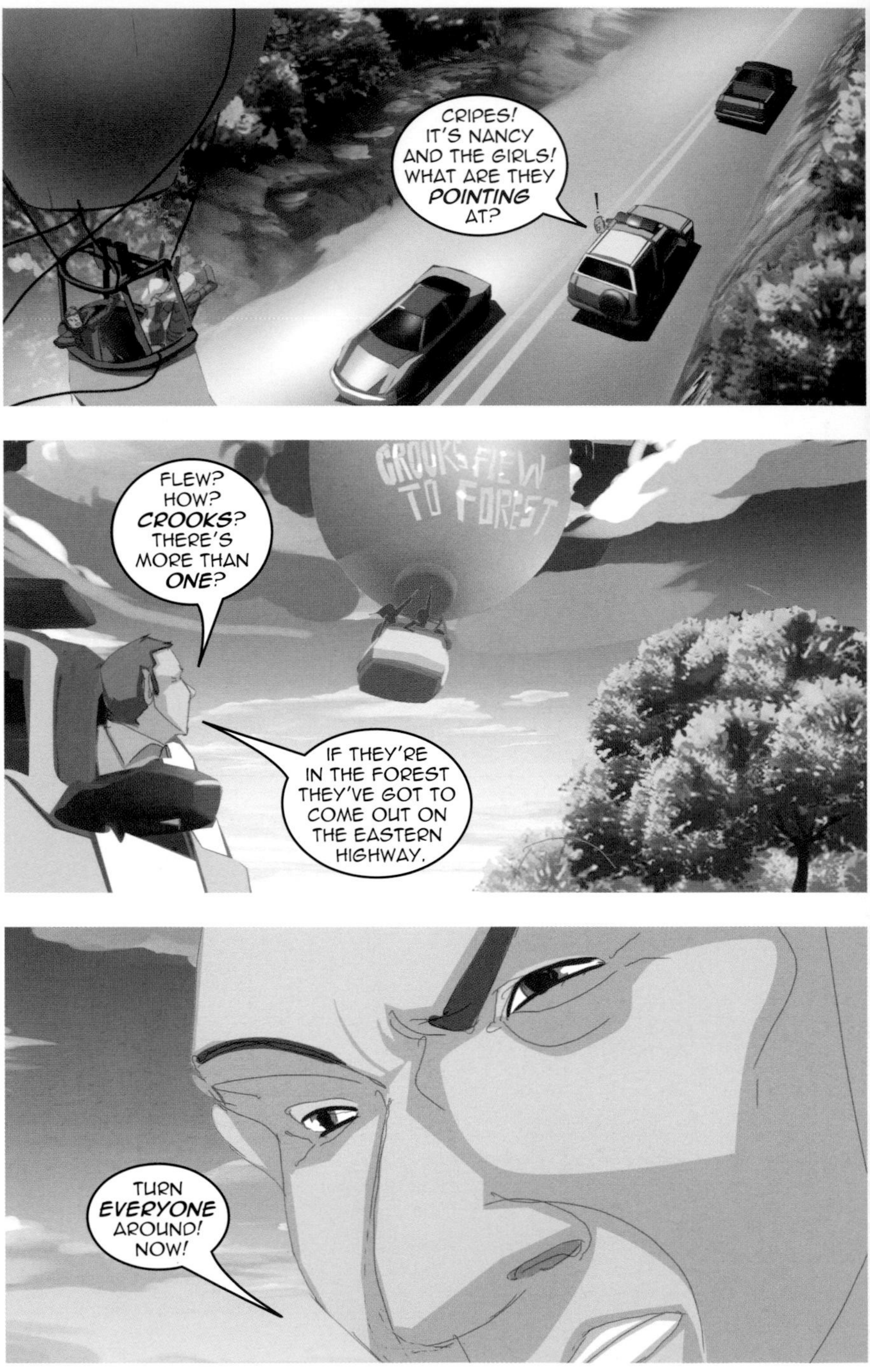
CRIPES! IT'S NANCY AND THE GIRLS! WHAT ARE THEY *POINTING* AT?
!
CROOKS FLEW TO FOREST
FLEW? HOW? *CROOKS*? THERE'S MORE THAN *ONE*?
IF THEY'RE IN THE FOREST THEY'VE GOT TO COME OUT ON THE EASTERN HIGHWAY.
TURN *EVERYONE* AROUND! NOW!

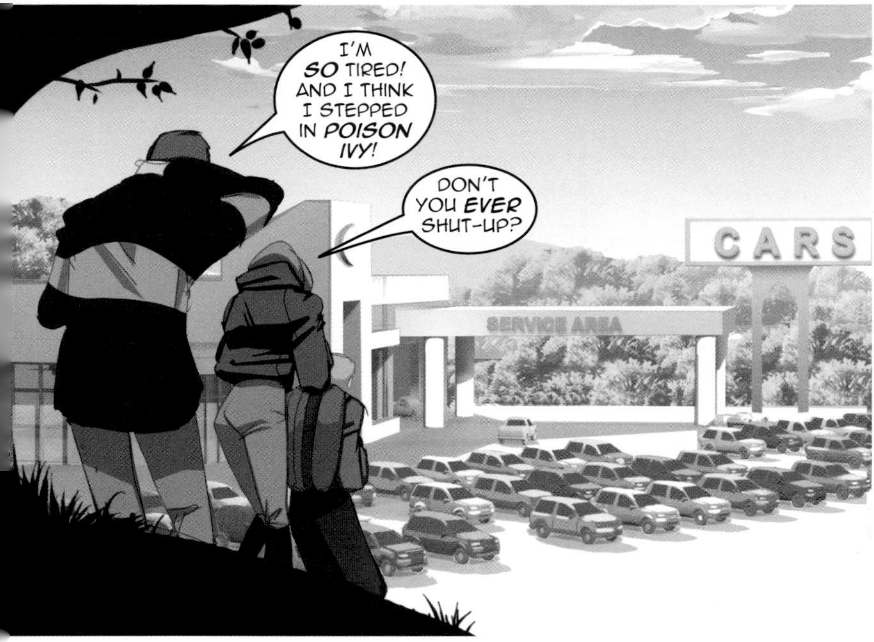
I'M *SO* TIRED! AND I THINK I STEPPED IN *POISON IVY*!
DON'T YOU *EVER* SHUT-UP?
CARS
SERVICE AREA

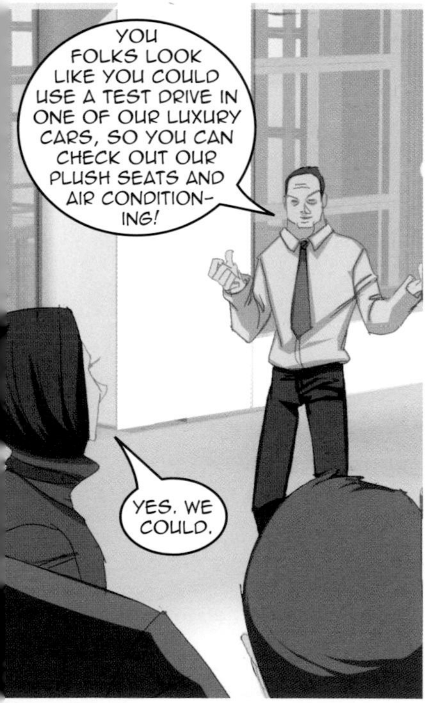
YOU FOLKS LOOK LIKE YOU COULD USE A TEST DRIVE IN ONE OF OUR LUXURY CARS, SO YOU CAN CHECK OUT OUR PLUSH SEATS AND AIR CONDITION-ING!
YES. WE COULD.

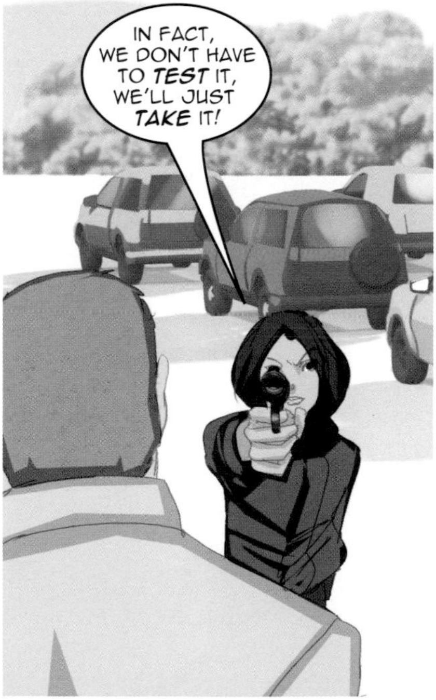
IN FACT, WE DON'T HAVE TO *TEST* IT, WE'LL JUST *TAKE* IT!

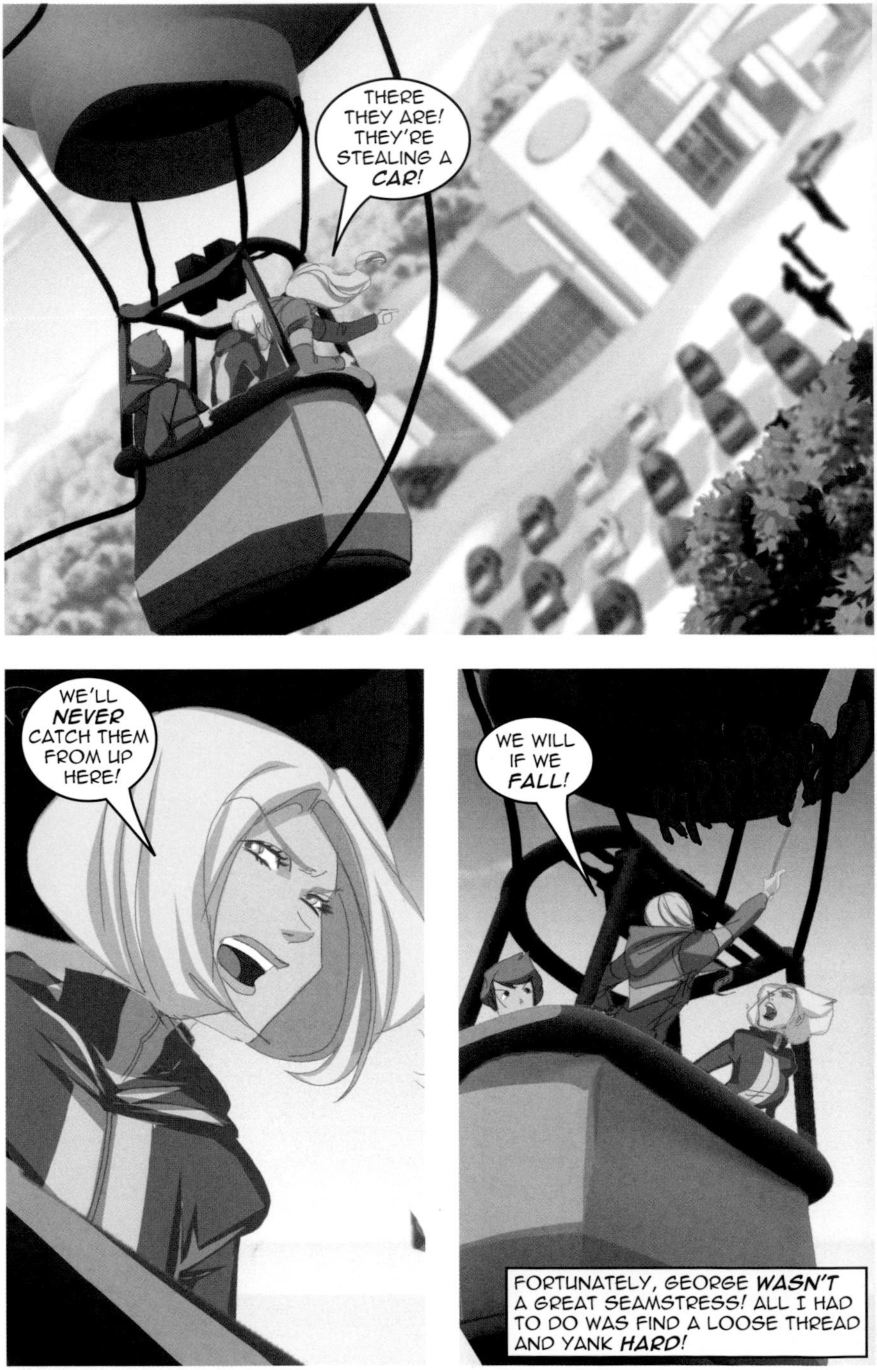
THERE THEY ARE! THEY'RE STEALING A CAR!
WE'LL NEVER CATCH THEM FROM UP HERE!
WE WILL IF WE FALL!
FORTUNATELY, GEORGE WASN'T A GREAT SEAMSTRESS! ALL I HAD TO DO WAS FIND A LOOSE THREAD AND YANK HARD!

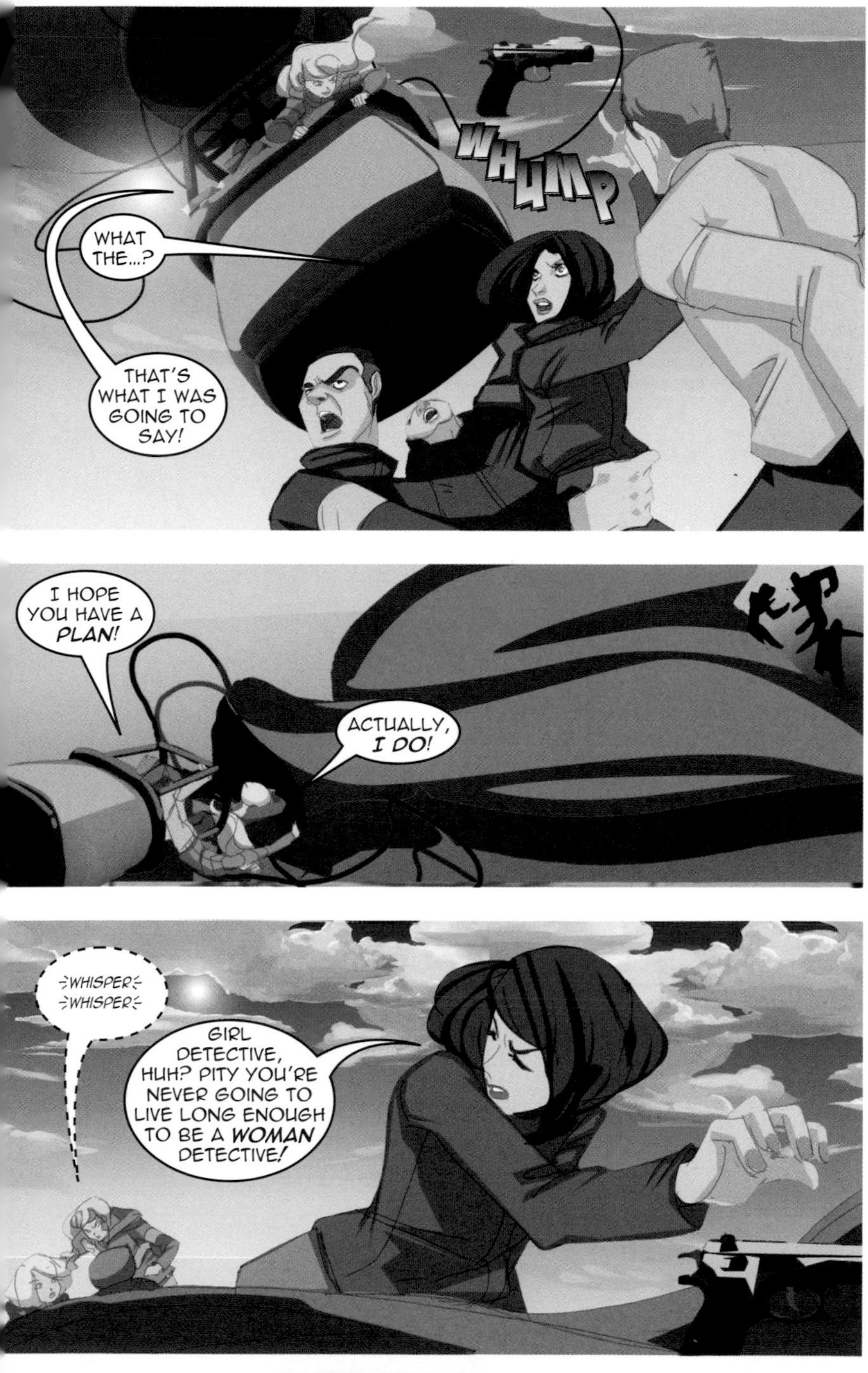
WHUMP
WHAT THE...?
THAT'S WHAT I WAS GOING TO SAY!
I HOPE YOU HAVE A *PLAN*!
ACTUALLY, *I DO*!
WHISPER WHISPER
GIRL DETECTIVE, HUH? PITY YOU'RE NEVER GOING TO LIVE LONG ENOUGH TO BE A *WOMAN* DETECTIVE!

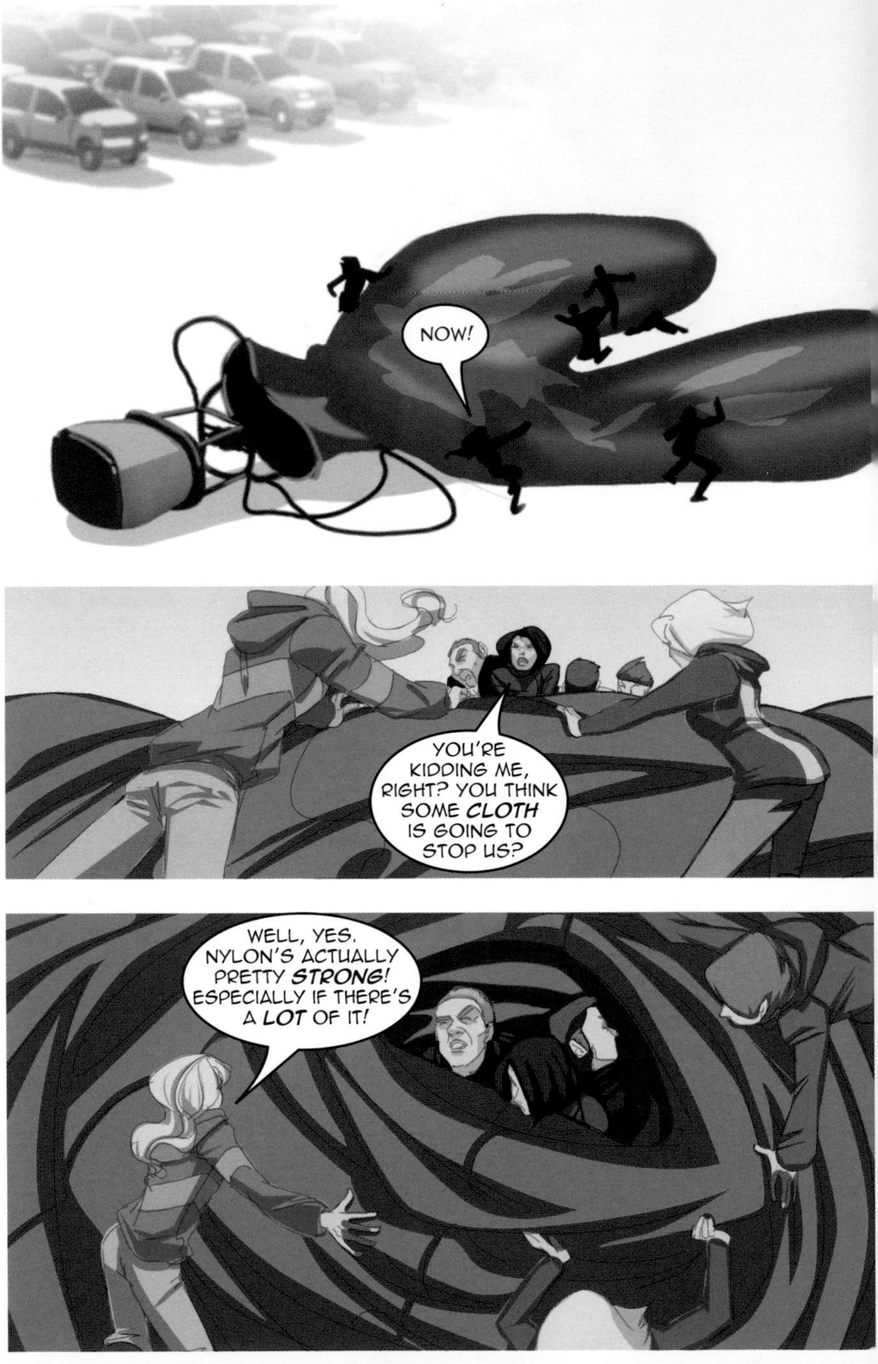
NOW!
YOU'RE KIDDING ME, RIGHT? YOU THINK SOME CLOTH IS GOING TO STOP US?
WELL, YES. NYLON'S ACTUALLY PRETTY STRONG! ESPECIALLY IF THERE'S A LOT OF IT!

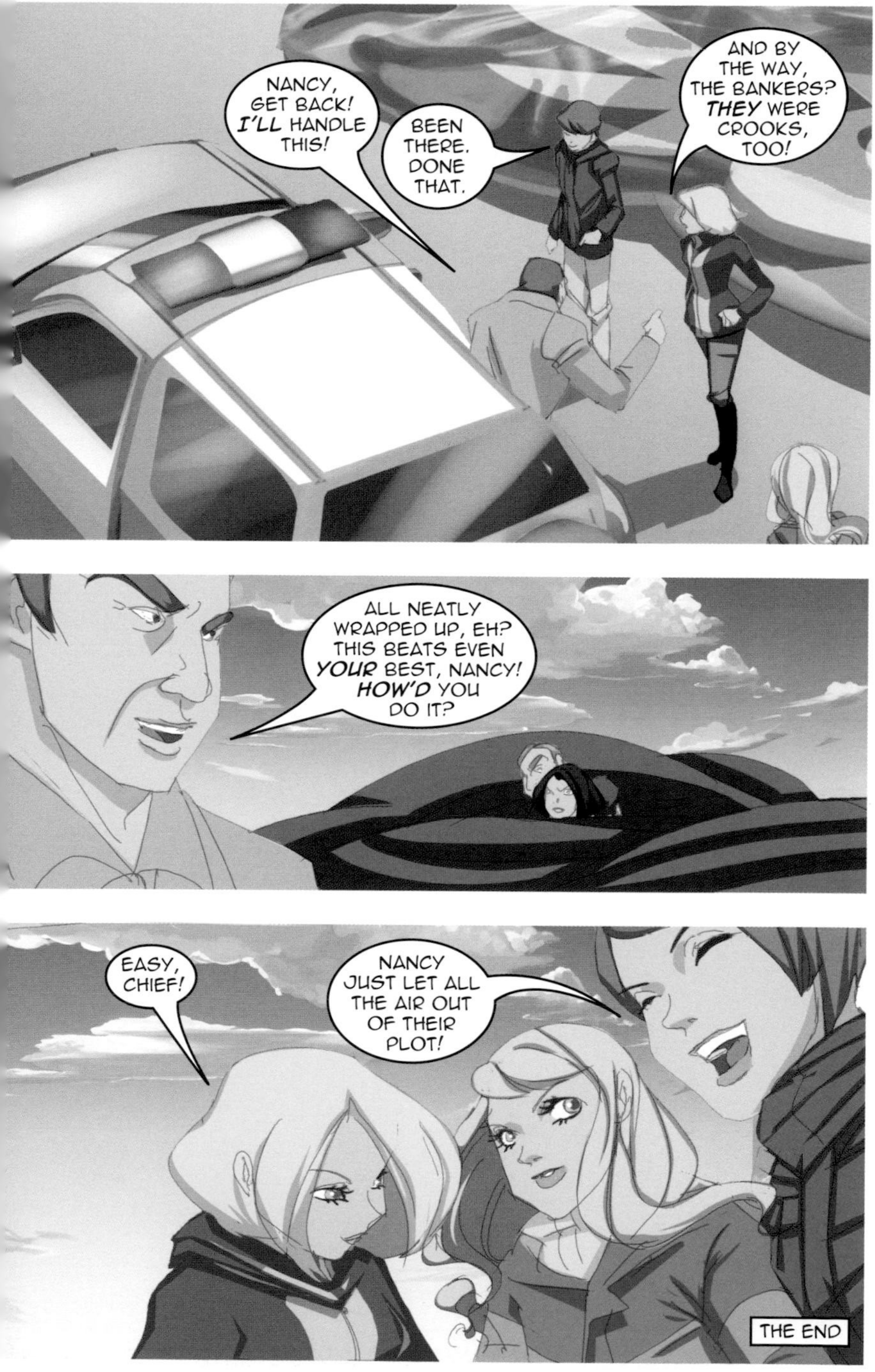
NANCY, GET BACK! I'LL HANDLE THIS!
BEEN THERE. DONE THAT.
AND BY THE WAY, THE BANKERS? THEY WERE CROOKS, TOO!
ALL NEATLY WRAPPED UP, EH? THIS BEATS EVEN YOUR BEST, NANCY! HOW'D YOU DO IT?
EASY, CHIEF!
NANCY JUST LET ALL THE AIR OUT OF THEIR PLOT!
THE END

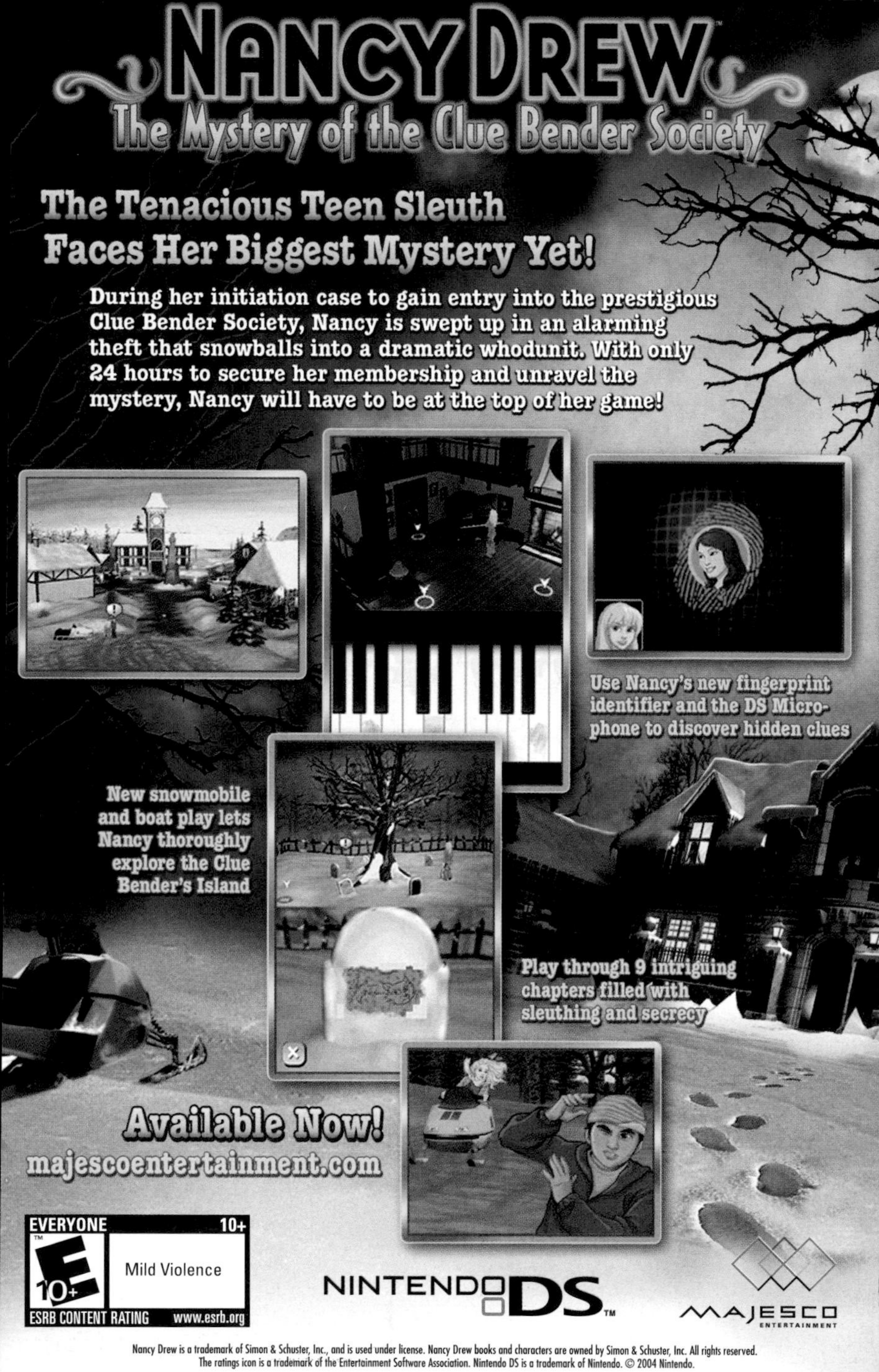
NANCY DREW
The Mystery of the Clue Bender Society
The Tenacious Teen Sleuth
Faces Her Biggest Mystery Yet!
During her initiation case to gain entry into the prestigious Clue Bender Society, Nancy is swept up in an alarming theft that snowballs into a dramatic whodunit. With only 24 hours to secure her membership and unravel the mystery, Nancy will have to be at the top of her game!
Use Nancy's new fingerprint identifier and the DS Microphone to discover hidden clues
New snowmobile and boat play lets Nancy thoroughly explore the Clue Bender's Island
Play through 9 intriguing chapters filled with sleuthing and secrecy
Available Now!
majescoentertainment.com
EVERYONE 10+
E 10+
Mild Violence
ESRB CONTENT RATING www.esrb.org
NINTENDO DS
MAJESCO ENTERTAINMENT

SPECIAL PREVIEW OF NANCY DREW GRAPHIC NOVEL #17 –
"NIGHT OF THE LIVING CHATCHKE"

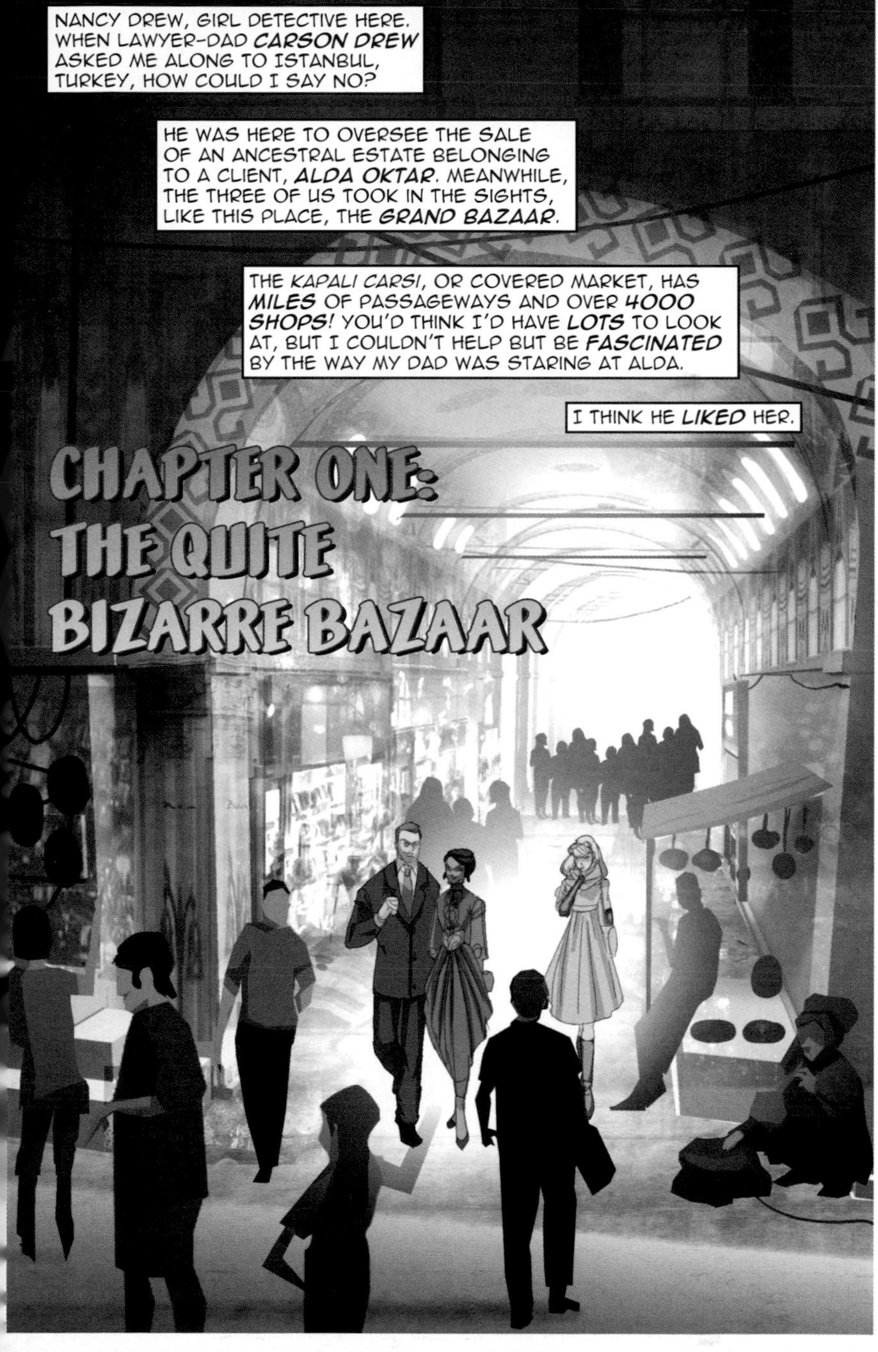
NANCY DREW, GIRL DETECTIVE HERE. WHEN LAWYER-DAD CARSON DREW ASKED ME ALONG TO ISTANBUL, TURKEY, HOW COULD I SAY NO?
HE WAS HERE TO OVERSEE THE SALE OF AN ANCESTRAL ESTATE BELONGING TO A CLIENT, ALDA OKTAR. MEANWHILE, THE THREE OF US TOOK IN THE SIGHTS, LIKE THIS PLACE, THE GRAND BAZAAR.
THE KAPALI CARSI, OR COVERED MARKET, HAS MILES OF PASSAGEWAYS AND OVER 4000 SHOPS! YOU'D THINK I'D HAVE LOTS TO LOOK AT, BUT I COULDN'T HELP BUT BE FASCINATED BY THE WAY MY DAD WAS STARING AT ALDA.
I THINK HE LIKED HER.
CHAPTER ONE: THE QUITE BIZARRE BAZAAR

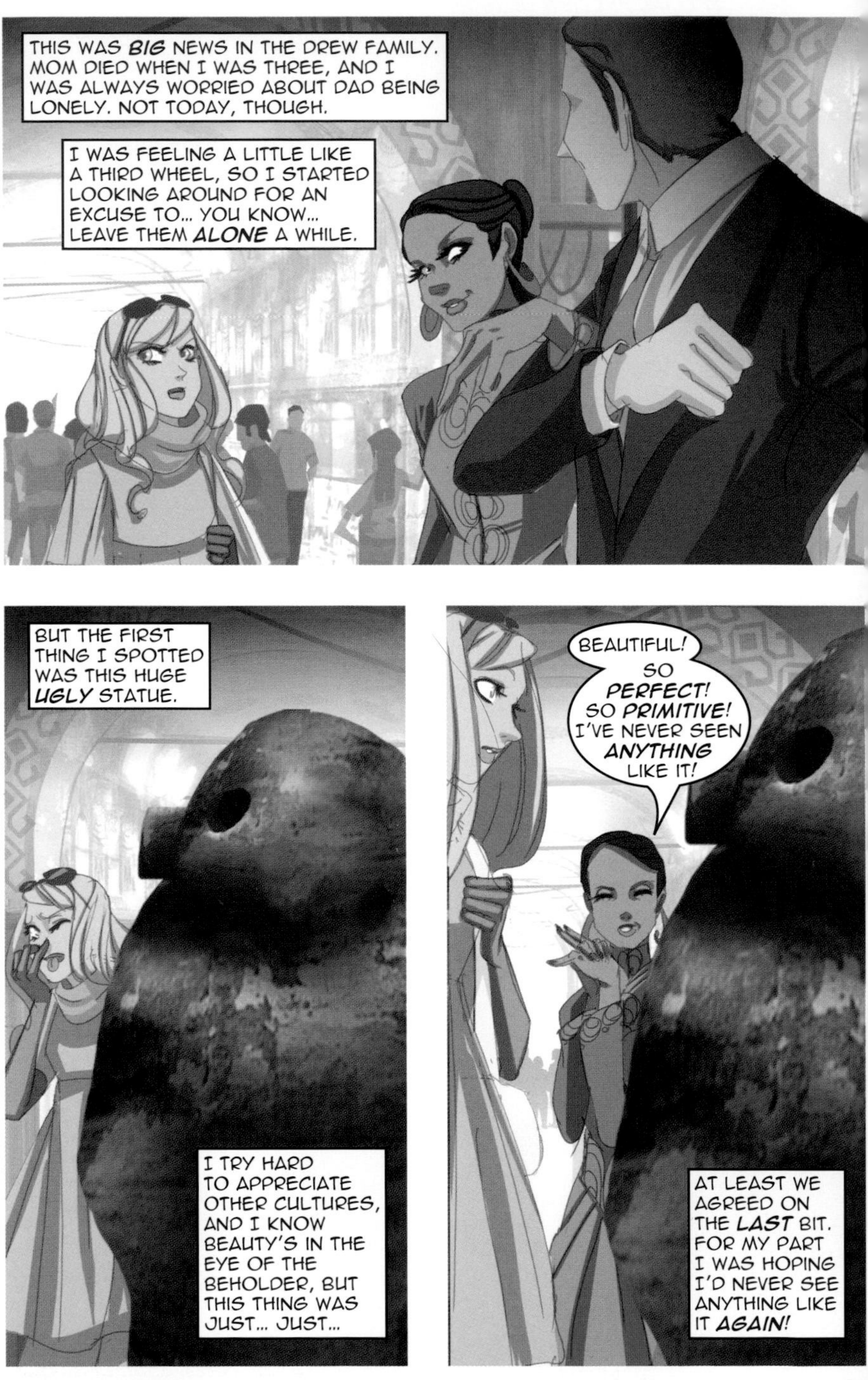
THIS WAS BIG NEWS IN THE DREW FAMILY. MOM DIED WHEN I WAS THREE, AND I WAS ALWAYS WORRIED ABOUT DAD BEING LONELY. NOT TODAY, THOUGH.
I WAS FEELING A LITTLE LIKE A THIRD WHEEL, SO I STARTED LOOKING AROUND FOR AN EXCUSE TO... YOU KNOW... LEAVE THEM ALONE A WHILE.
BUT THE FIRST THING I SPOTTED WAS THIS HUGE UGLY STATUE.
I TRY HARD TO APPRECIATE OTHER CULTURES, AND I KNOW BEAUTY'S IN THE EYE OF THE BEHOLDER, BUT THIS THING WAS JUST... JUST...
BEAUTIFUL! SO PERFECT! SO PRIMITIVE! I'VE NEVER SEEN ANYTHING LIKE IT!
AT LEAST WE AGREED ON THE LAST BIT. FOR MY PART I WAS HOPING I'D NEVER SEE ANYTHING LIKE IT AGAIN!

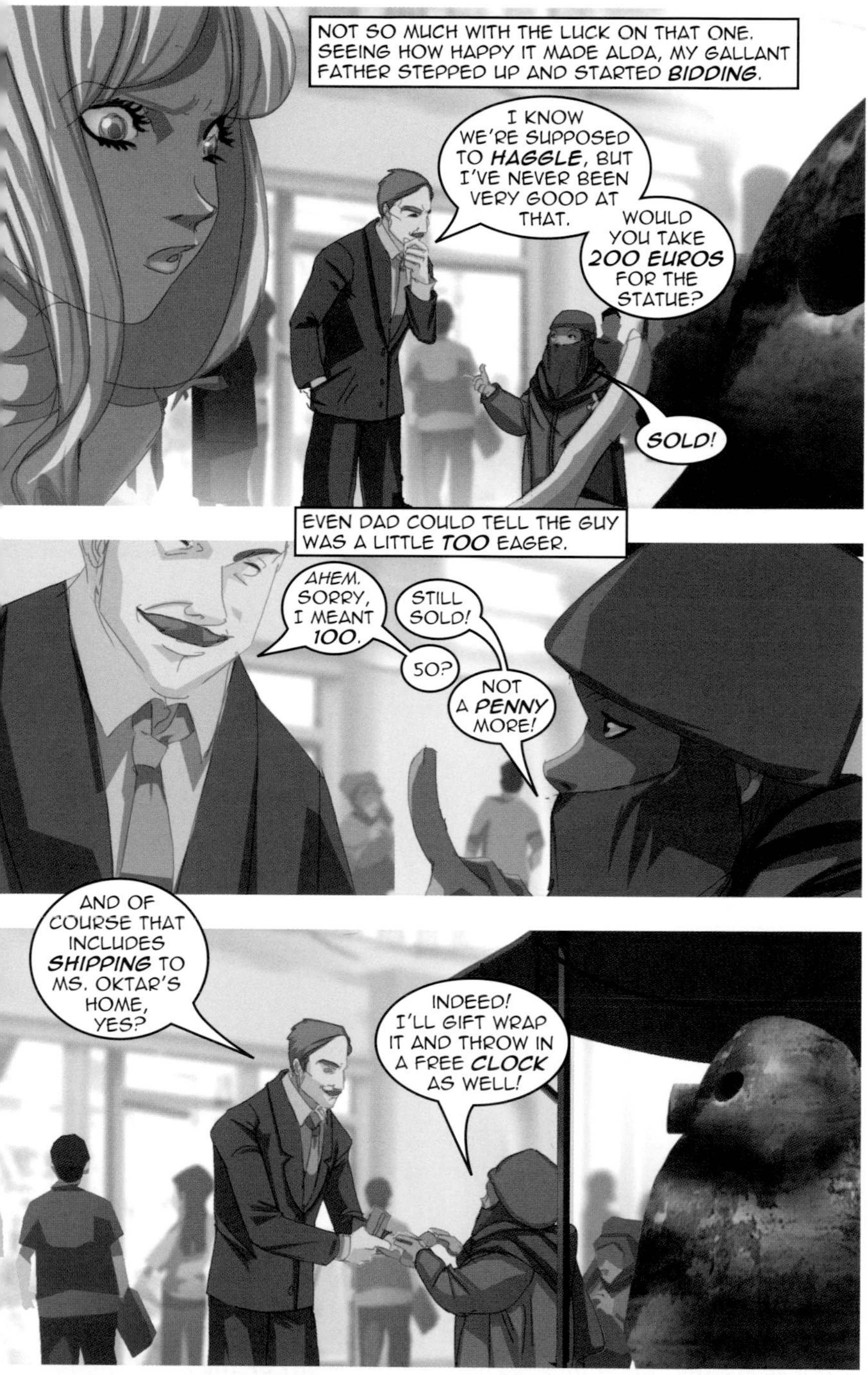
NOT SO MUCH WITH THE LUCK ON THAT ONE. SEEING HOW HAPPY IT MADE ALDA, MY GALLANT FATHER STEPPED UP AND STARTED *BIDDING*.
I KNOW WE'RE SUPPOSED TO *HAGGLE*, BUT I'VE NEVER BEEN VERY GOOD AT THAT.
WOULD YOU TAKE *200 EUROS* FOR THE STATUE?
SOLD!
EVEN DAD COULD TELL THE GUY WAS A LITTLE *TOO* EAGER.
AHEM. SORRY, I MEANT *100*.
STILL SOLD!
50?
NOT A *PENNY* MORE!
AND OF COURSE THAT INCLUDES *SHIPPING* TO MS. OKTAR'S HOME, YES?
INDEED! I'LL GIFT WRAP IT AND THROW IN A FREE *CLOCK* AS WELL!

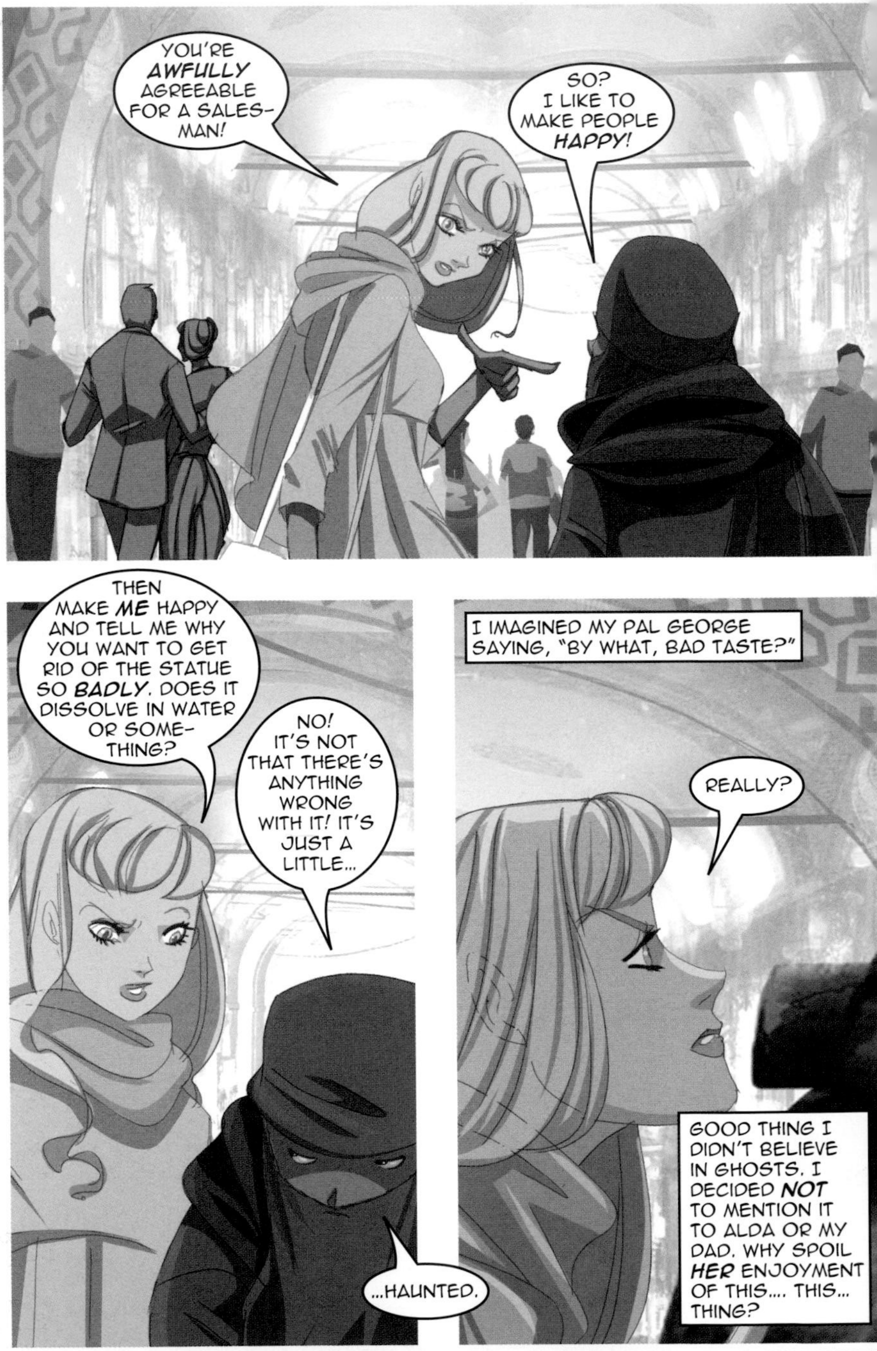
YOU'RE *AWFULLY* AGREEABLE FOR A SALES-MAN!
SO? I LIKE TO MAKE PEOPLE *HAPPY*!
THEN MAKE *ME* HAPPY AND TELL ME WHY YOU WANT TO GET RID OF THE STATUE SO *BADLY*. DOES IT DISSOLVE IN WATER OR SOME-THING?
NO! IT'S NOT THAT THERE'S ANYTHING WRONG WITH IT! IT'S JUST A LITTLE...
...HAUNTED.
I IMAGINED MY PAL GEORGE SAYING, "BY WHAT, BAD TASTE?"
REALLY?
GOOD THING I DIDN'T BELIEVE IN GHOSTS. I DECIDED *NOT* TO MENTION IT TO ALDA OR MY DAD. WHY SPOIL *HER* ENJOYMENT OF THIS.... THIS... THING?

DON'T MISS NANCY DREW GRAPHIC NOVEL #17 – "NIGHT OF THE LIVING CHATCHKE"

THE HARDY BOYS

A NEW GRAPHIC NOVEL EVERY 3 MONTHS!

#11 "Abracadeath"
ISBN - 978-1-59707-080-5
#12 "Dude Ranch O' Death"
ISBN - 978-1-59707-088-1
#13 "The Deadliest Stunt"
ISBN - 978-1-59707-102-4
#14 "Haley Danielle's Top Eight!"
ISBN – 978-159707-113-0
NEW! #15 "Live Free, Die Hardy!"
ISBN – 978-159707-123-9
Also available – Hardy Boys #1-10
All: Pocket sized, 96-112 pp., full-color, $7.95
Also available in hardcover! $12.95

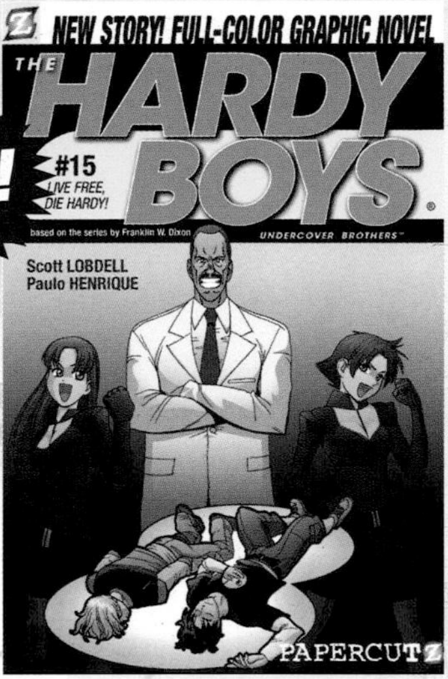
NEW!
NEW STORY! FULL-COLOR GRAPHIC NOVEL
THE HARDY BOYS
#15
LIVE FREE, DIE HARDY!
based on the series by Franklin W. Dixon
UNDERCOVER BROTHERS
Scott LOBDELL
Paulo HENRIQUE
PAPERCUTZ

THE HARDY BOYS
Graphic Novels #1-4 Box Set
ISBN – 978-1-59707-040-9
THE HARDY BOYS
Graphic Novels #5-8 Box Set
ISBN – 978-1-59707-075-1
THE HARDY BOYS
Graphic Novels #9-12 Box Set
ISBN-978-1-59707-125-3
All: Full-color, $29.95

CLASSICS *Illustrated*

Featuring Stories by the World's Greatest Authors

#1 "Great Expectations"
ISBN 978-159707-097-3
#2 "The Invisible Man"
ISBN 978-159707-106-2
NEW! #3 "Through the Looking Glass"
ISBN 978-159707-115-4
All: 6 1/2 x 9, 56 pp., full-color, $9.95

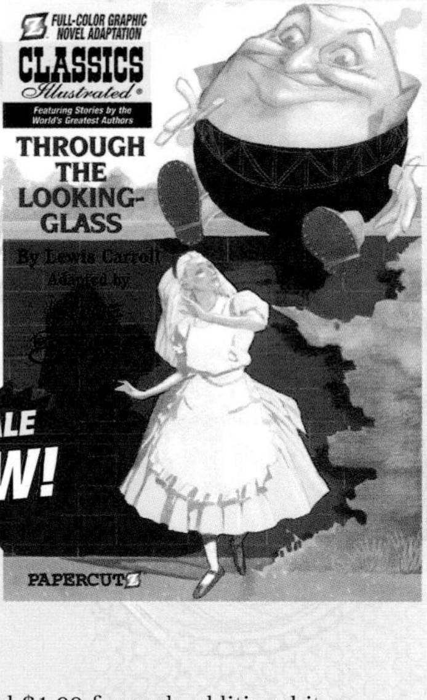
ON SALE NOW!
FULL-COLOR GRAPHIC NOVEL ADAPTATION
CLASSICS Illustrated
Featuring Stories by the World's Greatest Authors
THROUGH THE LOOKING-GLASS
By Lewis Carroll
PAPERCUTZ

Please add $4.00 postage and handling. Add $1.00 for each additional item.
Make check payable to NBM publishing.
Send To:
Papercutz, 40 Exchange Place, Suite 1308,
New York, New York 10005, 1-800-886-1223
www.papercutz.com

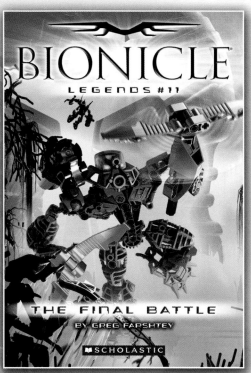

WATCH OUT FOR PAPERCUTZ™

Hey, Papercutz people, it's me your ol pal, Papercutz Editor-in-Chief Jim Salicrup, or as my stepdaughter calls me "Jimmy-Pooh-Head," here with an extra-special treat for Nancy Drew fans – a special preview of Nancy Drew #33 "Secret Identity."

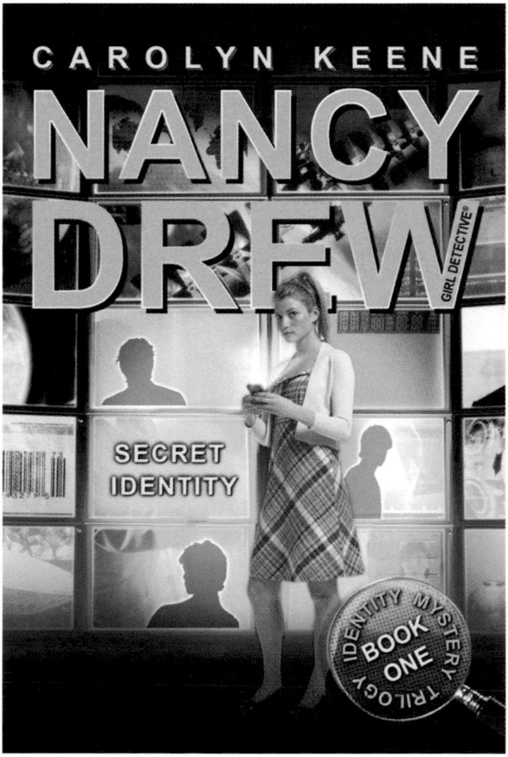
CAROLYN KEENE
NANCY DREW
GIRL DETECTIVE®
SECRET IDENTITY
IDENTITY MYSTERY TRILOGY
BOOK ONE

As you all know, in addition to her all-new graphic novels from Papercutz, Nancy appears every month in all-new novels, and by special arrangement with our good friends at Simon & Schuster we're able to offer this special preview of the latest and greatest Nancy Drew mystery. But I warn you, after you read this special preview, you'll want to read the rest of the book! I'm mean, how can you possibly resist?

Happy Sleuthing,

Jim

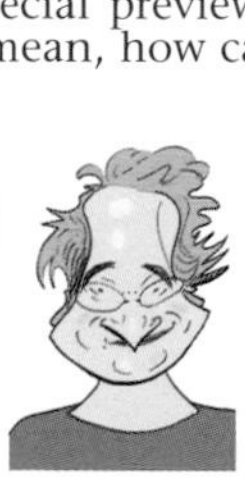

Caricature of Jim drawn by Steve Brodner at the MoCCA Art Fest

PROLOGUE

Thank goodness her friend picked up the phone on the first ring. "Hey there."

She felt like she might explode from excitement. "Oh . . . my . . gosh. You will not believe what is happening to me right now."

Her friend sounded wary. "What?"

"Well, I've been playing BetterLife ever since I got home."

"Duh. That's practically all you do these days."

She couldn't help smiling. That wasn't far from the truth. But the virtual-reality site had become *the* place to be over the last couple months; she probably socialized more online than she did in real life. "Stop. So Sassy Girl Forty-eight is at the mall, and guess who started flirting with me there?"

"Santa Claus."

She sighed. "No. Come on, be serious."

There was a pause of a few seconds. "I don't know. Why don't you tell me?"

"Jake!" she squealed and paused, waiting for the news to sink in. "Jake. Jake Seltzer! Isn't that amazing?"

There was another pause. "But he'd have a different username and look, right? I mean, it's a game, not real life. How did you know it was him?"

She sighed again. "Dude, his character in the game looks just like him. He has the blue streak in his hair, and the nose ring. His name is Guitar Lover Fifteen, and you know how Jake likes music. It has to be him!"

"Wow." Her friend seemed to mull over this information for a few seconds. "The guy you have a crush on is flirting with you online? Do you think he knows who you really are?"

"I think he does. He's said a few things about seeing me in real life, or wanting to flirt with me in real life but being too shy." She smiled to herself. Her heart was beating double-time; that's how excited Jake made her. On-screen, his character was smiling at her adoringly. Other virtual characters walked through the mall all around them, but it was like they were the only two people in the world.

Suddenly there was a loud beep, and she glanced at the dialogue box, where a new message from GuitarLvr15 to Sassygirl48 had appeared.

"SECRET IDENTITY"

I LIKE UR BLOND HAIR. U R SO PRETTY, U MUST HAVE GUYS FALLING ALL OVER U.

She squealed. "Oh gosh! You won't believe what he just said." She read the message off to her friend, smiling bigger with each word.

"Wow! Is he talking about you or your avatar?"

She turned to the screen. Her avatar, which she'd spent a week designing, looked as much like her as she'd been able to get: long blond hair, brown eyes, petite. She wore the trendiest clothes she could find; when the outfits available on the site looked too boring, she'd designed her own. All in all, the character was her virtual mini-me. But still . . . "I think he's talking about me. He knows who I am, and he's trying to flirt! We're totally meant to be!"

Her friend let out a breath. "This is almost too good to be true! You should write back, 'You're the only guy I care about.'"

The girl giggled, shaking her head. "Ha! I should, really. Do you think?"

"Totally. I'm being serious."

She gulped. Clicking on the dialogue box, she typed:

U R THE ONLY BOY I CARE ABOUT.

She paused, her mouse hovering over the Send button. Was it time to let Jake know about her crush? She'd hesitated all this time because she didn't want to get hurt. But now it seemed clearer than clear that Jake liked her just as much as she liked him.

Quickly, before she could think better of it, she clicked back into the box and added:

IT'S BEEN THAT WAY FOR A LONG TIME.

She clicked send. "Omigod. You won't believe what I just sent." She read the message back to her friend.

"'Omigosh' is right! Well, now he'll know you like him."

She gulped. "Really like him. But does he like me?"

Beep. She felt her stomach clench as she turned back to the computer for his answer. A new comment had appeared in the dialogue box. She almost felt too nervous to read it, but it drew her eyes like a magnet.

I CARE ABOUT U 2. I'VE JUST BEEN 2 SHY TO TELL U IN REAL LIFE.

She gasped.

"What's up?"

"He wrote back." She read his message to her friend, feeling like she might float away. Was this really happening? The guy of her dreams, liking her too?

Beep. Another comment popped up on her screen.

MAYBE WE SHOULD GET TOGETHER IN REAL LIFE SOMETIME.

"Oh wow." She thought her heart might beat out of her chest. "He just wrote more! He wants to get together sometime. In real life."

"Gosh." Her friend didn't sound as excited as she was, but that was to be expected. "That's great, Shannon. I mean, that's really exciting! Are you going to meet him?"

"Duh." She smiled. *Dozens of girls would jump at the chance to date Jake Seltzer,* she thought as she clicked in the dialogue box to respond. *Well, now they'll all be jealous of me.*

Jake's avatar was still smiling at her, waiting for a response. She made her character nod as she quickly typed, that sounds great. Just tell me where and when. . . .

GuitarLvr15's smile widened. Even in the game, his eyes were bright blue, and they seemed to twinkle extragorgeously as he took Sassygirl48's hand and squeezed it. Her computer beeped again and another message came through.

I KNOW WHO U ARE. I'LL E-MAIL U. WE CAN MAKE PLANS THEN.

"Oh." She couldn't help gasping to her friend, squeezing the phone to her ear. "Oh, he's going to e-mail me! This is so perfect. . . ."

Her friend sounded rushed. "That's great, Shannon. I have to go, though—my mom just called us down for dinner."

"Oh, okay." She felt a little disappointed. She'd wanted to discuss this whole thing until it finally seemed real to her. Still, she couldn't complain. She couldn't stop staring at her computer screen, even though GuitarLvr15 was walking away. "Do you think he'll e-mail me right now? Or will it take a few hours . . . ?"

"I don't know. . . . It sounded like he was going to do it right away."

Shannon smiled. "Okay. I'll tell you what he writes to me."

"Totally. Bye."

"Bye."

She let out a satisfied sigh. It was all so perfect: The guy she'd always known was meant for her actually liked her back. She'd always daydreamed about ending up with Jake, and now it was actually happening.

A little chime sounded as a window popped up on her screen: you have new mail. Her heart quickening, she brought up her account and quickly logged in. *Where should we go on our first date?* she wondered. *Dinner would be great, but what's a romantic restaurant . . . ?*

As the e-mail came up, she scanned the first few lines and felt her heart jump into her throat.

SASSYGIRL48,

DON'T GET YOUR HOPES UP. EVEN IN CYBERSPACE, I WOULD NEVER BE CAUGHT DEAD WITH A STUCK-UP WASTE OF SPACE LIKE YOU.

YOU DESERVE TO BE ALONE IN THIS GAME, IN REAL LIFE, ALWAYS. YOU DESERVE TO SUFFER LIKE YOU'VE MADE OTHERS SUFFER.

HOME SWEET MYSTERY

Is this the sort of romantic dinner you had in mind?" I couldn't help but smile as my boyfriend Ned took my hand and whispered to me as we moved into his dining room for dinner. We'd been apart for a week, since I'd been on a supercomplicated case that had brought me to New York, and had planned to make tonight our official "catch-up date" at our favorite Italian restaurant. But this afternoon Ned had called with a change in plans: there'd been a mix-up with faculty housing at the university, so he volunteered to host a visiting professor from Iran and his family at the Nickerson home. They wanted to have a small dinner to welcome them, and tonight was the only night that worked for everyone.

I leaned in close to him. "Romance, shromance. A piece of your mother's apple pie will make up for anything we missed."

Ned chuckled and squeezed my hand. "Maybe so. But we'll have to plan a make-up date."

"Agreed." I squeezed back and smiled.

The truth was, it still felt nice to be back in River Heights and doing all the normal things I like to do that don't involve cab chases or setting things on fire. My most recent case had turned into something bigger and crazier than I ever could have anticipated, and I was enjoying being "Normal Nancy" again, instead of "Action Hero Nancy." Being back in Ned's house felt wonderful. And the Nickersons' new house-guests, Professor Mirza al-Fulani and his daughter, Arij, who was twelve, plus his son, Ibrahim, who was sixteen, just couldn't be nicer.

"So, Nancy," Ibrahim began with a smile as we sat down at the dining room table, "have your travels for investigations ever taken you out of the country? Have you been to the Middle East at all?"

I smiled. The al-Fulanis were from Iran, and I was enjoying Ibrahim's upbeat attempts to understand American culture. "I'm afraid not, Ibrahim. I don't get the chance to travel all that much, even within the United States. But I would love to visit the Middle East someday. There's so much history there."

Professor al-Fulani smiled at me. "This is true, Nancy. It is still sometimes strange for my children and I to wrap our heads around American history, because your country is so new. So much has changed in only two hundred years, whereas in our part of the world, there are thousands of years of history."

Ibrahim piped up excitedly. "Will we study American history at the high school, Nancy?"

I nodded. "Actually, you will, Ibrahim. It's a required class for juniors."

"Excellent." Ibrahim dug into his salad with a grin, glancing at his sister. "I want to learn as much as I can about this country while we are here. I am so eager to meet my classmates."

Arij smiled and nodded, glancing at Ned and me. "Maybe you could look at the outfit I plan to wear tomorrow, Nancy," she said shyly. "I want to fit in well, and make friends quickly."

I laughed. "I don't know if I'm the best person to give fashion advice, but I'd be happy to offer my opinion!"

Ned squeezed my arm. "Don't sell yourself short, Nance," he cautioned. "After all, you are the reigning Miss Pretty Face River Heights!"

I rolled my eyes at him. While that was true, I wasn't exactly aching to talk about my short and ill-fated career as a pageant queen, which had been part of the case I'd been investigating in New York City. Still, he was smiling. I knew he found my totally out-of-character pageant win amusing.

"SECRET IDENTITY"

"Nancy," Ibrahim said, "I am curious about how you solve cases. You have told us a little about your unusual hobby, and I must ask: Do you wear disguises? Do you ever have to lie to people to get the information you need?"

I squirmed in my seat. Ibrahim's face was warm and open, and I knew his questions were coming from an honest curiosity. Still, I liked to keep my trade secrets and didn't exactly want to confess to bending the truth in the service of, well, the truth in front of Ned's father and a bunch of people I'd just met.

"Let's just say I do what the case requires," I replied, reaching for the bread basket. "Every case is different. More bread, anybody?"

Mrs. Nickerson chuckled.

"Ibrahim and Arij," Ned cut in smoothly, "have you ever been to an American high school before, or will tomorrow be your first time?"

"Oh, no," Ibrahim replied, shaking his head. "We have attended school in America before. My father travels often for work, you know, and we have traveled with him for months at a time."

Professor al-Fulani nodded. "My children lived with me while I taught at a university in Wisconsin, and also briefly in Florida. Unfortunately both placements were only for a few months, so they weren't able to settle in as much as they would have liked."

Arij nodded, pushing her salad around on her plate. "Sometimes it's hard to make friends," she admitted, a note of sadness creeping into her voice. "People hear my accent or they see my hijab and they think . . . They think I am something that I am not."

Silence bloomed around the table. I nodded sympathetically, imagining how difficult it must be for Arij and Ibrahim to fit in.

"I don't think that will be the case here, Arij," Ned said in a warm voice. "At least, I hope not. We're a university town, and used to diversity."

Mr. Nickerson cleared his throat. "You have any trouble, Arij or Ibrahim, and you let me know," he added. "Ned and I will do everything we can to make your stay here as pleasant as possible."

Arij smiled. She looked a little relieved. "I can't wait to meet everyone," she said quietly.

"Ibrahim and Arij seem very nice," I remarked to Ned a couple hours later as we stood on his porch to say our good nights. "I think they'll enjoy living here, don't you? I think they'll have a good experience at the high school."

Ned nodded. "I hope so," he admitted. "They're definitely a couple of great kids—so friendly and curious. I think as long as their classmates give them a chance, they'll have plenty of friends."

I nodded. The night was growing darker, and crickets chirped in the distance. I took a deep breath. River Heights, I thought happily. Home.

"So . . . ," Ned began, reaching out to squeeze my hand.

"So," I repeated, looking up at him with a smile. "Dinner? Later this week? Just the two of us?"

Ned grinned and nodded. "I'll call you," he said, leaning over to give me a peck on the cheek. "I'm so glad you're back, safe and sound."

"Me too," I said honestly, squeezing his hand again. "Thank your mom for dinner. It was delicious."

Stepping down onto the driveway, I pulled out the keys to my hybrid car and felt a wave of exhaustion wash over me. I imagined my nice warm bed at home, beckoning me. Without a case or anything urgent on the agenda, I could sleep in a bit tomorrow, too. I sighed, carefully driving through the streets that led me home. What a relief to be back among the people I loved, and with a little downtime.

At home, I parked the car in our driveway and yawned as I walked around to the back door. I felt like I had tunnel vision—all I could see was the route to my bedroom, where I'd soon be off to dreamland. Which is why I didn't notice that the kitchen light was on. And three people were sitting at the kitchen table, watching me curiously.

"Nancy?"

A familiar voice pulled me out of my tunnel vision, and I turned to find an unusual sight: my friend Bess; her twelve-year-old sister, Maggie; and our housekeeper and unofficial member of the family, Hannah, were munching on oatmeal-raisin cookies.

"Bess?" I asked, walking in. What on Earth?

Bess stood, placing her hand on Maggie's shoulder. "We were waiting for you to come home," she said. "Hope you're not too tired, Nance. Because I think we've got a case for you."

Thus conludes our special preview. Don't miss Nancy Drew #33 "Secret Identity."

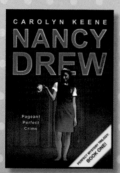
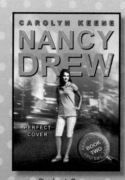
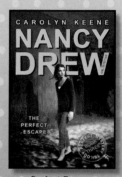

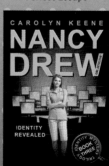